THE COLOURS BETWIXT

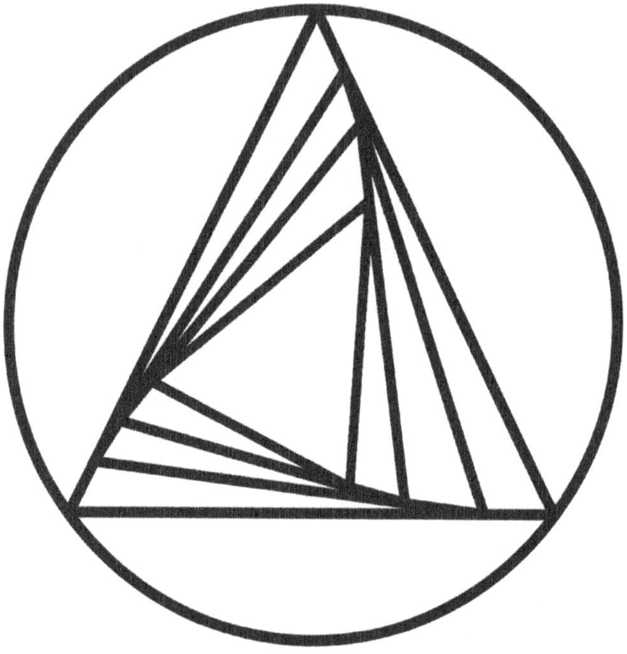

THE COLOURS BETWIXT

D. I. Richardson

Published through CreateSpace Independent Publishing

Copyright © 2017 by D. I. Richardson

All rights reserved. This book or any portion thereof may not be reproduced or used in any manner whatsoever without the express written permission of the publisher except for the use of brief quotations in a book review.

Typeset in Baskerville and Sketchtica.

ISBN: 1539149714
ISBN-13: 978-1539149712

This novel is dedicated to

Emily Yuill

"Time heals all wounds.

But not this one.

Not yet."

— Marie Lu, *Champion* —

PART ONE
The Bright

Part 1
Chapter 1

The New Year

I have a talent. You know what that talent is? Never getting hangovers. I've never, not one single time, had a hangover in my life. While all my friends are groaning and popping Tylenol and swallowing water like air, I'm over there frying bacon with a smile on my face. Fiona, on the other hand, suffered from hangovers a little worse than everyone else, but that's mostly because her pain tolerance isn't very good. And she's a giant baby. But she's my giant baby, and I love her.

That brings us to New Year's Morning 2017. We had hosted a party at Fiona's house, like we usually did, and Fiona and I had passed out on the floor of her room (naked, as per usual). I sat up and pushed my hair out of my face. I don't know why I kept the top of my hair long, it always ends up in my face, so I have to constantly push it back and put products in it to keep it back.

I stretched my shoulders, arms, and back out a little as I yawned and looked over to Fiona. She was still naked on the floor, passed out on her stomach, arms out wide as if she were trying to hug it. Her long, wavy, brown hair was seemingly thrown out in all directions, which made it seem like a small circular rug. The sun peeking through the window lit up her tanned skin and made it look almost golden. She's a masterpiece of a human, that's for sure.

I ran my fingertips up and down the dimple of her back that her spine created. She flashed a sleepy smile at me as she turned her face to look up to me. "Good morning," she mumbled, her voice husky and *very* full of sleep. Her light brown eyes peeked at me behind her heavy eyelids.

"Good morning," I replied. "Happy New Year, babe." I smiled at her and then leaned down to kiss her cheek. She half-assed an attempt to kiss mine too, but she was far too sleepy and far too hungover.

Fiona rolled onto her side and let out a loud groan. "Fuck! My head is splitting right now."

"Just try to go back to sleep," I said as I stood up. "I'll go to the store and get you some Tylenol and some food."

"McDonald's breakfast?"

I frowned at her. "It's past noon, babe," I told her as I started pulling on my boxers and pants. "I'll get us some lunch though."

"You're a saint. You're too good for me."

I smiled at her and pulled my shirt over my head, struggling slightly to get my limbs in their proper place. I've never been good at shirts. I leaned back down over Fiona and kissed her cheek again. "I love you, dork."

"I love you too," she mumbled.

I picked her up and lifted her onto the bed. I wrapped a blanket around her and rested her head down on her softest pillow. I kissed her on the forehead and gathered my phone, keys, and wallet. I walked downstairs and tiptoed through the house. I didn't know how many people would still be asleep.

Derek, best friend, probably would be. Marshall, other best friend, would probably also be asleep.

I walked outside and narrowly avoided slipping on the ice of the driveway as I made my way to the end of it to where I had parked my car. It's a little gunmetal grey hatchback sedan. It wasn't the worst car ever, but it wasn't the best one either. It got me from A to B and that's the important thing.

I got in and stuck my key in the ignition and turned it. My car whizzled and whirred to life. The engine on this stupid car was so underwhelming. But like I said, it got me from point A to B, so that's what matters. Or at least that's what I tell myself (because sometimes you gotta lie to yourself).

I backed out of the driveway and headed down the wide and winding streets of the suburbs that Fiona lived in. I loved the neighbourhood she lived in, to be honest. The houses, while all similar, were all still somewhat unique. The residents here at least made some kind of effort to separate themselves from all the rest of the copy-and-pasted houses on the street.

It wasn't that I hated the houses of most of the suburbs, it was the lack of colour. Life should be vibrant, and these soul-sucking white homes that line the roads all take away from that. So it's nice that the families here have put the effort in to stand out a little. It helps put my mind at ease from the monotony of suburban life. I know, what a cliché, a white young male, bored of his First World life, I get it. I don't have a lot to whine about, but yet here I am, still bored of life, bored of things without life, bored of things that lack colour.

My first stop was the drugstore for Tylenol. That was pretty uneventful. After I got that good good for Fiona, I made my way over to the McDonald's and got myself and Fiona a quarter pounder each, not the meal. I had to go to Wendy's for the fries. Fiona likes Wendy's fries better, so I always make the extra stop for her. It's (sort of) on the way back to her house anyway, so I don't mind it. Plus, it makes her super happy because she always loves the little things I do for her like that. It's worth it in the end.

I made the trip to Wendy's and got our fries and drinks and then headed back to Fiona's. I parked in the driveway and noticed that all the same cars were still here. I guess nobody wants to go home yet. They're probably all on the floor, wrapped in blankets, whining that their heads hurt. Poor saps.

"Edwin!" Derek shouted out at me as I walked into the house. I looked over and noticed my dear friend on the floor, sprawled out and craning his head around at an inhuman angle to look up at me.

"Hey," I said, walking over to him and peering in to the room around him. "Y'all look dead." Time to give you the rundown on Derek. He's a black dude. Whoa, a white dude and a black dude are friends? Crazy. He grew up in a "white" neighbourhood, so he likes to make jokes about being an Oreo, you know, black on the outside, white on the inside. He's good people. He's a year younger than me (so he's nineteen). He's pretty tall too. Hair always in a near-buzzcut style. He's also one of my classmates. He also always wears button-up shirts. He probably shops exclusively at Old Navy or something. And him and I played hockey together, so I knew him since before college.

"Could you so kindly, sir, sauce this dying boy a water?" he requested.

I sighed and shuffled to the kitchen, dropped the bags and drink tray onto the counter. I went into the fridge and grabbed a fresh, cold water bottle for my boy Derek. I walked out and dropped the water next to him and he winced. Even a bottle on carpet was too loud for him.

I went back to the kitchen and grabbed the food and drinks and walked back up to Fiona's bedroom. I opened the door quietly and then shut it just as quietly. I looked over and saw Fiona passed out on the bed, which was evident from the snoring I heard as I stepped into the room. She shuffled and rolled over as I sat on the bed.

She rubbed her eyes and looked over at me. "You're back already? That was fast."

"I was gone for at least a half hour," I replied. "Had to make a stop at Wendy's for our fries."

"Aww, you love me." She stretched out her legs in the bed and yawned. "Okay. Tylenol?"

"Right here." I pulled the bottle of Tylenol out of my sweater pocket. I then took off my sweater because her room was way too hot for sweaters right now, or even clothes, and her being naked still made me want to get naked again. I watched her down three tablets and then she handed me the bottle back and I tossed it, along with my sweater, over to the corner of her room that was designated for any and all of my shit.

Fiona sat up on the edge of the bed and pushed her hair out of her face and then smiled at me. "You're looking pretty darn cute today."

I gave her a once-over and smirked. "You're looking pretty darn cute yourself." *Well, of course she looks cute, she ain't got no clothes on, dummy.*

She smiled and blushed a little. More than six years together and she still blushes when I call her cute, now that's love. She reached over me for her drink and then took at least half of it back within three sips of the straw. "Damn. Now *that* hits the spot."

"So will this." I handed her the quarter pounder. "Eat up, dork."

"Thank you," she said, grabbing the box from me. She pulled her top bun off the burger and picked the pickles off and placed them on top of my quarter pounder box. She hated pickles on her burger, but she always tells me to keep them on instead of ordering her burger without pickles. She does it so she can give me her pickles, since I (a normal person) love pickles all day every day.

We ate together in relative silence. I liked eating with her because we ate at the same speed, so we always ended up being finished around the same time. There was no awkwardness while one of us waited for the other to finish the last third of their meal. When we were done, I ran all our garbage to the kitchen and by the time I made it upstairs, Fiona had hopped in the shower. I don't blame her for not waiting for me.

I shuffled into the bathroom and undressed myself before popping into the shower with her. She turned and smirked at me. "Hey, dork."

"Hey," I said, reaching past her for the shampoo. I scooted her over a little and got my hair thoroughly soaked. I quickly washed it once, twice, and then that's it. You rinse and repeat. No need to repeat and repeat.

She pouted at me and pushed me out of the stream of water with a little huff. "Freezing my ass off over here."

"Sorry." I placed my hands on her bum and squeezed a little. "I got it now. It'll warm up."

She smiled and shook her head. "Here. Soap me up." She handed me some body soap and a loofa.

"Fine," I groaned. Sure, washing someone else sucked, but not so much when the someone else was *Fiona*. The girl was a goddess in every sense (at least in my eyes). I'd do anything to keep my hands on her forever. That being said, I soaped up the loofa and then absent-mindedly washed over her body with it as my mind raced with thoughts of her. My mind is always so full of her. Ever since I first set eyes on her eight years ago, she's all I had wanted, and then six years ago, I got that; I got her.

"Gimme," Fiona barked, grabbing the loofa from me. I didn't look down, but she was washing her more intimate areas. I don't own the same parts, so fair to be said that I can't clean them the right way (but also fair to be said that it isn't that hard to just soap and scrub). I went over my body with the loofa as she used some peppermint face wash stuff to exfoliate her cute little face and make it all soft.

She handed me the face wash and I rubbed it on my face. It was pretty refreshing. It made my skin soft, cleared up acne, and it made me feel like there was a cool breeze on my face, even though we're in a climate-controlled living space with zero air current. Either way, I liked it.

We got out of the shower and headed down to the kitchen to make coffee/tea. Derek was sitting at the table, face hovering over a bowl of corn flakes. He looked up at us and mustered a small smile. "Hey," he spoke, quick and simple.

"Hey. How ya feelin'?" I asked, walking over and sitting across the table from him. He blew a raspberry, frowned, and then stuffed a spoonful of corn flakes into his mouth. I don't even think they were frosted flakes, just plain corn flakes, no sugar or fruit or anything.

"That bad, huh?" Fiona chimed in from over by the coffee maker.

"Very," Derek replied. "Why do you kids let me get so drunk?"

"You yell at us when we try to cut you off. You always do," I stated.

He shrugged. "Whoops." He took another bite of cereal. "Suppose I just like my booze a lot, then, huh?"

"Fair to be said, yeah."

"Head's thumping something fierce," Derek mumbled. Poor kid always drinks more than he can realistically handle.

"Incoming cereal," Fiona shouted at me. My head snapped up and I managed to raise my hands just in time to catch a box of frosted flakes that she had hurled towards me. I waited and watched patiently as she sauced a bowl over to me. I snagged it out of the air and dumped some cereal into my bowl as Fiona came over with a bowl for her, spoons, and a carton of milk.

Fiona sat next to me and swapped the milk with me for the cereal. I poured milk over my frosted flakes, not corn flakes, because Fiona and I aren't savages like Derek over there. I slid the milk over to Fiona and scooped some flakes into my mouth. They're more like chips, aren't they, though? Ah, whatever.

Fiona and I ate in silence for Derek's sake, sneaking the occasional glance at each other and rustling our feet together under the table, because no matter what anyone tells you,

you're never too old for footsie. I looked up at her and smiled, and she smiled back at me.

The colours betwixt her lips were of happiness, purity, bliss, hope. And corn flakes a little. She was still chewing.

Part 1
Chapter 2

The Portrait

As soon as possible. Her words floated through my mind as I raced over to her house. It was freezing cold tonight and there was a light snow, thank God it was only light. I didn't wanna be rushing to Fiona's house and have to worry about sliding off the road every two seconds. That would be a little detrimental to tonight's mission: Make it to Fiona's house alive and preferably in one piece.

Fiona hadn't told me why I *needed* to go over to her house, but who was I to complain about her needing her hero boyfriend to save the day. Although it's a Sunday night, and we don't usually spend Sundays at each other's house because it's laundry night and gear-up-for-school-tomorrow night, so her demanding me to come over was a little out of left field.

I pulled into Fiona's driveway and parked behind her car.

I grabbed my backpack from the passenger seat and a plastic bag full of clothes for tomorrow from the floor in front of said passenger seat. It was extra heavy because I had stuffed an extra sweater in there for Fiona to wear, because girlfriends love their boyfriend's sweaters.

I walked up to her door and walked right in, because that's what I do. I'm here enough and I come over enough that I can just walk in. Like, shit, I even have a spare key to the front door *and* a spare key to the back door. I closed the door and slunk myself up the stairs into her room. I didn't wanna risk bumping into a sibling or a parent.

I stepped into her room and looked over to her. She was sitting on her bed with a PS3 controller in her hand. I looked over to her TV and noticed a brightly coloured game being played. It was the homie Spyro. Fiona was playing *Spyro: Ripto's Rage*, but of course she was, that was her favourite game growing up, so she bought it from the PlayStation Store so that she could play it whenever she wanted.

"Hey, dork." She didn't even turn away from the TV screen to acknowledge that it was me in her room and not her mom or dad or whoever else it could have been.

"Hey." I walked over and sat on her bed next to her. "Why'd you want me to come over?"

She paused her game and turned to me and then wrapped her arms around me and tightly hugged me. "I missed you," she mumbled into my neck. I always loved that. Her words felt as if they melted into me.

"That's the reason you called me over?"

She nodded. "Problem?" She pulled away from me and looked up at me.

I smiled and kissed her forehead. "No. I was missing you something fierce too."

"Mm, also," she said, pulling away from me and unpausing her game, "you still have all your old art shit in my closet. I found them earlier when I was digging out that brown jacket I wore that one time to that thing."

"The one with the front pocket that had a broken button?"
She nodded. "Yeah, that one."
"Why'd you need that jacket?"
"Not important. Anyway, yeah, you should get back to painting and stuff. You still have a few canvases left, so get on that."
"The 24-inch ones?"
"Yes." She hesitated a second to think. "Yes," she repeated, "they were the 24-inch ones. I think."
"Oh, shit. Sorry. I've been meaning to take those home. Sorry for clogging up your closet."
Fiona shrugged. "Doesn't bother me. I don't really keep anything I used often in the closet, so like, not really a big enough problem to apologize for."
"Well," I said, getting off her bed and walking toward her closet, "I don't like the thought of me cluttering up your room or closet. That's all."
"If you were cluttering up my room or closet, I would personally deliver all of your shit to your bedroom door." Fiona turned and smiled widely at me. "So you good... for now."
"For now." I scoffed. "Like you would care if I kept my shit here forever." I pulled a few canvases out of the closet and pulled out the easel from in the back. As I yanked the easel out, it knocked a bag of art supplies off the small shelf in her closet. I leave too much art stuff in places I shouldn't. At one point, Fiona's closet was literally just my art supplies. I had taken all her clothes out and turned it into a personal Edwin strorage.
"Yeah, and you left your paint and some brushes here. I thought I would tidy them up for you because you also left your art bag here." Fiona glanced over at me and sighed. "I really feel like you purposefully leave shit here all the time."
"Gives me a reason to come back, right?" I walked back over to her and set up the easel on a 45° angle to her. "I'm gonna paint you, alright?"
"Yeah. Go for it, homie." She smiled widely as I set up my canvas, brushes, and paint stuffs. She glanced over at me and

11

dropped her smile. "Never mind. I can't smile that wide for that long, it was starting to hurt a little. Just paint my concentration face as I fuck up Gulp's day." (Gulp is a boss in *Spyro: Ripto's Rage*, just an FYI.)

"That'll make a better portrait anyways." I walked over and kissed her cheek. I grabbed the foldable chair from her closet and dragged it over to the easel so that I'd have somewhere to sit whilst I paint.

Fiona yawned and stretched out and then assumed her position. She probably did that on purpose so she wouldn't have to move while I was painting. That was subconsciously thoughtful of her.

I began my routine of observing the subject. It was a habit to just look at them for longer than what was probably comfortable for them to deal with, but I wanted to soak up all the details of their form. The lines of their faces, the folds in their skins, the colours of their cheeks, the glimmer in their eyes, the freckles on their nose, the red-pink of their lips, the tones of their skin. I wanted to take in as much as I could, because attention to detail is a good thing, that and I like pretty things, and I can find something pretty in most anything.

Sometimes, I zone out when I'm looking at Fiona though. I just get lost in thoughts of our future and of our past. It's just insane to me, that I can look at this human being and know that she's the only person I need in life. I can live without everybody else. But her? No. I would be an empty shell, a husk. She's my vital signs, my heartbeat, she's the air in my lungs. It's terrifying too, looking at this girl and knowing that she holds so much of my happiness and sanity in her hands, knowing that at any minute, if she changed her mind about me and us, then she could twirl my world around and throw it away with a flick of her fingers.

"Earth to Edwin," Fiona half shouted.

I snapped back into reality and blinked at her a few times. "Yeah?"

"You zoned out. Get painting, ya dink." She turned back

to the TV and crossed her legs on her bed. Hmm, I hadn't noticed before that she wasn't wearing pants. I scanned her over and watched as the reflection of the TV light danced around in her eyes. If only more people could see what I could see right now.

I sighed softly and started painting. My paintings were always full of colour, not in the typical sense, but they were heavy in contrast and I used as many colours as I could to give them abstract feels, almost watercolour in essence. I just really like colour; life would be so boring without it. Fiona likes the colours, she says that it "adds depth," whatever the hell that's supposed to mean. Depth of emotion maybe? I dunno, I never asked, I just sort of pretended like I knew what she meant.

Depth. Of what? Depth of character? Depth of artistic value? Depth of design? It confused me, and I could ask her what she meant by it, but it was long enough ago that she had probably forgotten. Besides, I needed the confusion and mystery about it, wondering can be good.

By the time my brain clicked back into what my hands were doing, I had painted half of the canvas with colours that roughly looked like the scene of Fiona on the bed with her legs crossed and a controller in her hands. I ogled her a little and then went back to painting.

I'm really happy that Fiona has gotten used to me occasionally ogling at her. She actually likes it because I must really like her face to ogle at it, and like her face I do. I loved watching the way lights floated around in her light brown eyes the most. They were a melting medley of colours and I loved getting lost in them, especially watching the reflection of city lights flash by as she drove.

After a while, I had used all of my brushes and paint was starting to get dried in them (because I use different brushes for different colours because I never remember to get a cup of water to rinse out the old colour). I walked into the bathroom and rinsed the brushes in the sink. I walked back into the bedroom and sat back at my artist chair.

"Took you long enough," Fiona chirped. "I was starting to get worried you weren't showing up."

I scoffed. "Not like you moved at all anyway."

"Shut up." She furrowed her brows. "I'm tryna beat these losers."

As I made myself comfy in the chair, I glanced over to see her spearing enemies in her game with the horns on Spyro's head. Fucking savage. I picked up my brush and began painting the canvas some more. The painting needs more detail and whatnot before I can be satisfied with it.

I've never been satisfied with anything I've done artistically. There's something left to be desired because only after something is finished can you sit back and see what you *should* have done instead of what you ended up doing. I might not be satisfied with the end result, but that's just art. I love the process, I love creating, but I don't ever *like* what I've created. I think, as an artist, I'm not supposed to like what I create, probably because I know it so well and I've spent so much time looking at it.

I could never be a novelist, for example. I think I would go crazy because I'd never feel like I filled the pages of that novel with meaningful words that opened eyes and changed lives. I even feel like I can't fill a canvas with soft and precise brush strokes that display the essence of something greater than us. I could never write a song with beautiful melodies that make you feel more connected to the person sitting next to you. And that's why I love colours. Colour lets people know what to feel, lets them know how I feel, how I felt. Colour can convey things that we simply cannot.

I studied Fiona's face a little more as I went over the painting and sketched in some grey shadows with a pencil. I liked the contrast of colour with little sections of grey overlapping. I also used the pencil to make darker lines where I wanted them. I never used black paint in anything I painted or drew, ever. It's a rule. Black is the absence of all colours.

"Is it done?" Fiona asked, stretching out her arms. I guess

she noticed that I had stopped painting.

"It's done-ish, I guess." I set all my utensils down on some pieces of paper on the floor. I didn't wanna track paint through the carpet. I'm not a savage.

Fiona paused her game and frowned a little at me. "What do you mean done-ish?"

"Like, it's done, I guess, but it's not perfect."

"You say that about everything."

"And I've been right about them all so far."

She shrugged. "Matter of perspective. I, for one, find your art very beautiful."

"I find you very beautiful," I retorted.

She smirked. "Knew you were gonna say that. Can I see the painting now, ya dink?"

I shook my head. "Let me make sure it's *done* done first."

"It's never gonna be done." She pouted softly.

"Give me some time." I pouted softy right back at her. Two can play at that game.

Fiona sighed and unpaused her game. She zoned right back out of reality and into the colourful world of a fire-breathing dragon and his glowing dragonfly partner. Sorry, I have to stare at this painting until it sickens me. Only then will it be "complete." Well, no, it still wouldn't be, but I just give up on it.

"Is it done yet?" Fiona grumbled.

I sighed. "Sure." I looked the painting over, giving it one last stamp of good enough before letting Fiona see it. "It's done now."

"Can I see?"

I turned the easel so it faced her. She paused the game and then scanned over the canvas. I don't know how much she could see in the low light. It certainly looked like she was straining her eyes. She could have just turned the light on. I watched her eyes dart around, scanning the colours and the lines and the overall portrait of this beautiful creature playing a video game on her bed. She smiled softly and looked over to me. And then she closed her eyes and took a deep breath, nodded, and immediately went back to playing her game. The nod meant she liked it. And I'm glad she liked it. I pretty much like anything she likes.

I'm so dependent on her, if we're being honest. I feel as though I've lost myself in the colours of her. All my colours have been mixed and blended with hers, and there's no definition on who either of us are as people on our own. I mean, there was an Edwin before Fiona, but now there's only an Edwin *with* Fiona.

The colours betwixt the edges of the canvas portrayed a scene simpler than the lines made it seem, a scene of something beautiful, not to many, but to me.

Part 1
Chapter 3

The Planning

Fiona stepped back into the room with a pot of tea, which was wrapped in a very thick woolen tea cozy. She set it down and the four of us took our turns filling our cups with tea. Sometimes we like to be fancy. Not all college kids are aggressive drunks. We like tea, we have manners, we're polite.

"What's the plan, boys?" Fiona asked.

Marshall sighed. "Shit, you got me. Not like we're gonna do the same thing we've done for the past couple years or anything."

"The cottage, yes, of course, how could I be so silly?" Fiona chimed, smiling widely. "Weather's pretty ass lately, are we sure we wanna risk the drive?"

"It won't be so bad," Derek stated. "It should be pretty clear for when we'll wanna go. Should be fine."

"This weekend?" Fiona asked.

Derek shrugged. "We're supposed to get hit with a snowstorm. If we can make it up there before it hits, then it'll be fine."

"When does it roll in?' I asked, blowing lightly on my tea. I don't really think it helped cool it down any though.

"Saturday," he replied. "So if we head up on Friday night, we should be good. Might get snowed in, but that just means more cottage time for us." Derek grabbed the teapot from the table and went to pour himself a cup, but he filled it to the brim and then some. We watched as it spilled over the edges of the cup and across the table. "Dammit!" he groaned.

"Accidents happen," Fiona said as she quickly got up and ran to the kitchen. She came back in with a towel and handed it to Derek. "Maybe next time, pay attention to the level of liquid in the cup."

Derek started mopping up the mess. "Yeah. I got carried away. You guys know how excited I get about tea. I just wanna drink all of it."

"So I'll start off by saying that these planning meetings are stupid," Marshall stated.

"Seconded," Derek and I said in unison.

Fiona gave each of us a variant of her *fuck you guys* face. "We have the pre-plans planning sessions to iron out any wrinkles in the plan, and because it's an excuse for us to have tea and hang out."

"It's just useless," Derek stated. "We're gonna be doing the same thing this year that we did last year and the year before that."

"Yes, but this year is different." Fiona smirked. "This year, we don't have any chaperones. We're going up alone."

"Like last year," I pointed out.

"No, but alone the *entire* time. My parents won't be up to drop by for the week." Fiona took a sip of her tea. "So basically, this is gonna be a really fun week. And Derek, feel free to bring a *flute* of your choosing."

"No, no flutes for this guy," Derek stated. "This week is one about getting away. I don't wanna drag somebody that's gonna be whiny or cause drama."

"Yeah, ditto," Marshall chimed in. "This week is for the three amigos... and Edwin."

"I'm the main amigo. I'm this group's Beyoncé," I chirped. "You three would be nothing without me."

"Yeah, yeah," Fiona said, raising a hand to shush me. "So we need people to take on some responsibilities here. One of us needs to be in charge of snacks, another in charge of first aid and the like, and someone else needs to be a trooper and take all the bedding things up with them."

Derek raised a hand. "I volunteer my services for bedding and first aid and whatnot."

"I'll do snacks," Marshall said.

"Good," Fiona beamed. She turned to me. "And you'll be the unpacker and putter-awayer."

"And what will you be?" I asked her.

She shrugged. "I'll be project manager."

"Which is a nice way of saying you won't be helping us out?"

"I own the cottage, bitches. I do what I want."

I sighed. "That's a fair point, I guess. Let's start putting together some lists of things we want to bring."

"Like an inventory checklist?" Derek asked.

I nodded. "Didn't have one of those any of the times we went last year and we ended up forgetting to bring some stuff. So let's make sure we get everything we need."

"Smart thinking," Fiona said. "And while I still remember, Edwin, you're also in charge of setting up the TV and consoles."

"And what do I get for doing that?"

She winked at me and then turned back to Derek and Marshall. "Marshall, don't just load up on junk food. We need real food for the week too. Get some frozen pizzas and pasta and eggs, you know, *actual* groceries."

"Yeah, got it," Marshall said. "I wasn't going to just stock up on Doritos and chocolate. I know we need food. You guys can shoot me a text later on in the day with a list of stuff you want." I don't think I've introduced Marshall yet. He's pretty average. He has dirty blond hair that he always keeps slightly shaggy. He has very noticeable icy blue eyes, like, that's the first thing you really take notice of with him. He's about my height, but he's a bit chubbier than I am. Him and Derek are close because I spend so much time with Fiona, so they go hang out and hook up with random girls and all that together. Well, not like *together* together in the same room, unless they're into that. I don't know and I don't really wanna know either.

"And where do I get the bedding from?" Derek asked.

"My storage out back," Fiona replied. "I'll find the key later for you. Oh, and when the time comes, you can just back your car up into the yard and load the stuff into it."

"Well, duh," Derek said. "I'm not in the business of carrying things up and down a driveway *and* a backyard."

"Anyways," Fiona said, scoping the room, "I call not it on the pizza run!"

My 4-door hatchback sedan and all its shimmering glory carried Derek and I to a pizza shop, as him and I both had the hesitant fortune of going to get pizza for the four of us to eat. Usually, Fiona would shoehorn those two into going for pizza while her and I go up to her room for a quickie. But today, I offered to go with Derek. I wanted to change things up a little bit. As much as I love nutting in my girlfriend, I love hanging with my best friend the same amount.

"How nice of you to volunteer your services on this ride," Derek chimed as we pulled into a parking lot.

"It was the least I could do," I said. "Besides, we never get alone time, the two of us. And like, I miss having alone time with you, yanno?"

"Yeah, usually one of those other two dusters are tagging along."

"Are you saying I'm a duster?"

"Maybe."

I scoffed. "You got some bad beaks, you plug."

"Hey, fucking watch it, buddy. I'll clap you one in the chiclets." I pushed his shoulder playfully as I stopped the car in front of the pizza shop. "Shut up and go place our order."

"Aye, captain." He got out and walked into the store as I parked the car.

I walked inside and saw Derek sitting at one of the tables with a little slip of paper in his hand. "What'd you get us?" I took a seat next to him.

"Two pepperonis and a three-cheese."

"Are you gonna teef one of those pepperoni pizzas for yourself?"

He nodded. "Sure am, bud." He stretched his arms out and sighed. "Long semester coming up."

"Final trek," I said, resting a hand on his shoulder. "We'll make it. We're almost finished."

Derek smiled softly. "Yeah, it's just crazy, looking back at how quickly it seems life can change."

I nodded. "It is pretty crazy. Five years ago, I could have never guessed I'd be where I am right now with the people that I'm with right now." I sighed and lifted my hand off Derek to rest my arms on my knees. "But that's life, you know?"

Derek smiled at me. "Anyway, are you as excited for the cottage as I am?"

"Yeah, but definitely not as much as Fiona is," I said, laughing softly.

"No kidding. She loves that place."

"She spent a lot of summers there growing up, so of course she does."

"I don't blame her. It's nice up there."

"I hate going up in the winter," I stated. "Roads are always so ass up north during this time of year."

"That's true. We should dodge the brunt of that storm though," Derek noted. "At least, like, I hope we do. I don't wanna get stuck hours from home in the middle of a freak blizzard."

"We won't. Make sure you have winter tires on though, you know, just in case."

Derek stood up and started to walk over to the pizza counter. "Winter tires are ass."

I chuckled and looked out the window. I squinted to see past all the brightness of the outside world that was busy and bustling and full of life. I framed the world through the two black bars that held the windows in place.

The colours betwixt the pillars reflected a world of life, a world devoid of grey.

Part 1
Chapter 4

The Colour of Night

Her hands always gripped the steering wheel too tightly. You could see the pressure building up in the whiteness of her fingers. She had good reason to be gripping so tightly tonight though. We were in the midst of a raging snowstorm (just like Derek had warned us about), but that had never stopped us before. Fiona *was* a pretty good driver, and she had a lot of winter driving talent.

Her parent's cottage was an hour and a half away, but in this weather, it was more like three hours. And that's okay, just more time I get to spend in the front seat next to her, granted, it was pretty quiet in this car's cabin. She had turned down the heater a half hour ago because it was like blankets in here, way too warm and cozy. She had turned the music down to "focus better on the road." And she had stopped replying to my half-assed attempts at conversation because, well, she was focusing on the road and keeping us on it and not wrapped around some tree.

I didn't mind the silence. Just being in her presence was good enough for me. Usually, we just flick on music and then at the end of every song we tell each other that the other person is cute and that we love them and then the next song starts. And I did love Fiona, so much that even these long stretches of quiet were amazing.

"We need to pull over for a bit," Fiona muttered. "This is taxing on my brain. Can you find the nearest gas station or Timmy Ho?"

"Yeah, sure thing," I replied. I pulled my phone out and tapped the Maps app open. "If you take the next road, um—" I looked at my phone's screen. "Dew Drop Road, that one should take you up to the 41. There's a Timmy Ho to the north."

"How long does it say it'll take to get there?"

"Um." I clicked the little arrow on the top left of the screen and the Maps app calculated a route for us. "It says it should take us fifteen minutes, which would be in good weather, so I'd say we'll get there in twenty-five or so." I looked over her face. It was so focused on the road, staring blankly into the white roads and falling specs of ice that swirled around in her headlights. "Do you want me to drive for a bit?"

"No. I'm fine. I just wanna stop and get something to drink and just not have to stare at all this fucking snow." She smiled. "Love you, dork."

"Love you too, dork." I smiled back, though she didn't see it. We trudged along in her little red car. The snow crunched under the tires and I could feel us slipping every once and a while. We really shouldn't even be driving right now. It's definitely not safe to be out on these roads. This much snow having fallen so quickly didn't give any time to the plows and salting trucks to do their job.

We made it to the Tim Hortons in twenty-seven minutes

from where I had first checked the map. That wasn't so bad, considering how shit the roads were. Highway 41 wasn't so bad though. More cars drive along it, so that helps keep snow down, but there was still a pretty gnarly build-up of white snow and brown slush on the asphalt.

We got out of the car and walked through the snow and wind to the front doors of the coffee shop. The snow stuck itself all through Fiona's hair and eyebrows. Her face was already turning red from the cold. I could only imagine that mine must have been tomatoes right now too.

"Fucking Derek and Marshall are probably all cozy at the cottage while we're still making our way through this stupid storm. Why did I have to work late tonight? If I had got off at a normal time, we would have dodged the brunt of this stupid snowstorm," Fiona grumbled as we got inside and shook out our coats and hair.

"Doesn't help that they have a 4x4 Jeep and we don't. Derek should have driven you up here. I coulda taken my car with Marshall," I said as we took a spot at the back of the line. They had decided to load up a Jeep to carry everything, rather than go up separately. And they needed the company, it's a long drive.

She shrugged. "Eh. It's whatever. We'll get there… eventually."

"Eventually is better than dead and not at all."

She smirked. "A good point does the Edwin make."

I pulled my phone out of my pocket as Fiona stepped up to make our order. Two coffees, one cream each, simple enough. I flicked through the Maps app and looked at our route. She had driven these roads a few times, and a bunch more if you count the times when she wasn't the one driving. I felt her kick my shoe and I looked up at her. She had an impatient expression on her face as she held up two coffees. I took one and mumbled a thanks as I followed her over to a table. She gets real salty if I don't take a coffee right away, I guess because she always wants to drink hers and she can't really do that if I make her carry *both* coffees.

"What're you looking at?" she asked, peeling back the tab of her coffee lid.

"The route," I replied, doing the same to my lid.

She sighed. "So many hills and valleys, and twists and turns. I hate driving these roads, even in good weather." She groaned. "We'll probably have to park at the lodge and hike the rest of the way to the cottage." We had to do that last year in the winter too. There had been a huge snowfall and the dirt roads that led right to her cottage hadn't been cleared of snow, so we had to park at the Everwoods Lodge and hike an hour into the woods to get to her cottage. The lodge was run by a family friend, so they never care if we park in their parking lot.

"Should we call the lodge ahead of time?" I asked.

"No. We'll go in and say hi for a bit."

"Yeah?"

"Yeah." She took a sip of her coffee. "Oh, ow, fuck. That's hot. Really hot."

"Yeah, you are!" I winked and clicked my tongue at her.

"I just wanna be curled up on a couch with you already," Fiona grumbled. "That fireplace is gonna be so blessed later. I'm already warmed by the mere thought of it."

"We gonna eat some charcuterie?"

She scoffed. "Duh."

I took a sip of my coffee and winced a little. It was piping hot, which was nice, considering that it was −21°C outside tonight (and that's without factoring the wind chill). "So how long do you wanna stay here?"

Fiona shrugged. "Just till the coffees are done, I guess. I don't wanna be here all night."

"Well, yeah. I'd also like to be curled up by the fire with you as soon as possible."

"There's so many hills and turns on this stupid road," Fiona grumbled, looking at the Maps app on her phone.

"Take her slow."

"No shit," she sassed. "If we pick up speed on the hills though, 'cause slippery, then we're in for a fun ride, and by fun, I mean terrifying."

"We'll be fine. Just gotta go slow and pump the brakes lightly. Most of the turns are long ones anyway, so you can just drift it."

"I-I don't think cars work like you think they work." She grinned a little at me. "Some of these hills are pretty intense though." She sighed. "I'm not looking forward to the stress of driving through this shit again."

"I'll drive," I offered.

She scoffed. "Babe, you freeze up when it rains in the city. There's no way you could drive in this much snow. Sorry, I love you and all, but driving makes you uneasy enough in good conditions."

"A good point does the Fiona make. And, of course, how will I ever get better if I don't study the master?"

She laughed softly. "You're a dork."

"Yeah, but I'm *your* dork."

She smiled and blushed a little. "All mine."

"All yours." I smiled back at her and then pointed at her, poking her lightly in the cheek. "Mine."

"Yours," she stated. "All yours."

"You're cute."

Her mouth dropped and she gasped, giving me a wide-eyed look. "You're cute!"

"You." I pouted at her subtly from behind my cup of coffee as I took a sip. We sat in quiet company for a while as we sipped are coffees intermittently. We watched the snow falling outside and the hurried cars driving by on the 41. We watched the line dwindle and build back up. Pretty busy here for this late in the evening on Friday in a snowstorm. But then again, who doesn't love snowstorm coffee.

Fiona tapped her empty cup on the table and stared at me with a sombre, nostalgic expression. "It's all gone." She puffed her lip out and mimed a cry.

"We can make more when we get to the cottage," I told her. "I promise."

"Good. We'll be plenty of cold after that hike, so we'll need something warm. Maybe a hot chocolate or tea, something nice and cozy."

I nodded. "Agreed. Tea would be lovely."

"You're lovely," she quipped. "Did you finish your coffee yet?"

"Nah. I like to actually enjoy my coffee. I don't just scarf it all down like you do." I gave her a cut-eyed look. I enjoy throwing some shade sometimes.

"Shut up. I drink it fast 'cause I *need* the caffeine, bro."

I eyed her over and smiled. Out of all the dorks in this world, I get this one all to myself. "You're so adorkable."

"You!" she said, giving me a feigned pout as she pointed to me.

And then we stood up and walked back to the doors, tossing our cups into the garbage along our way. We stepped outside and braced ourselves as best we could against the wind and snow as we trudged through the snowy parking lot to the car. The snow stuck all through her hair again. Fiona doesn't believe in hats. She always says that we have hair to keep our heads warm.

We hopped into her car and she let out a loud groan. She turned over to me. "Which way would be quicker, do we take the 41 up and then cut across the back roads or do we go back down Dew Drop and continue the normal way?"

"Taking the 41 would be quicker and safer, but the back roads are probably a lot worse off than the normal route."

She started the car. "I'll drive slow. What road do I have to turn down? Will you keep an eye on the GPS tracker and let me know when we get close?"

"Yeah, of course."

"Okay, good." She sighed as she turned around to back out of the parking spot. "Flick on some tunes though." She turned back to face forward and pushed the "prindle" to drive.

"I don't like driving on highways without music."

I pulled my phone out and closed the Maps app and opened the Music app as I connected the aux cord to my phone. All in one fluid motion, like I had done so many, many times. I flicked on the *Reimagine EP* by Hands Like Houses. It's one of my favourite EPs ever, so it's a good thing that Fiona also quite much enjoys it.

She turned on the highway and started picking up speed until we were going ten kilometres per hour under the limit. Generally, when it snows, people go under the limit as a safety thing, which is nice. Nobody wants to total their car or get killed.

I stared out the window and looked at all the little flecks of white blurring by the car as we drove. Watching the snow fall from inside a moving car is the only good thing about winter driving, the actual driving part sucks. I glanced down at the phone to check our route every 30 seconds or so. I wanted to make sure we took the right road. "It's the next road after this one," I told her as we started approaching a fairly busy intersection.

She slowed down (as you do with stop signs) and the car slid halfway into the intersection. "Oh, shit," she muttered, quickly pushing her foot on the gas and getting through the intersection. "Thank God there was nobody driving. Coulda got T-boned. Scary."

"Yeah, no kidding," I said, trying to get my heart to stop racing.

"You said it was the next road, right?"

I nodded. "Yeah, next road on your right. You'll have to drive slow, this one's got lots of turns."

"So, like, if we had died right there, my last words would have been me griping about driving on the highway without music," she stated. "That's pretty lame."

"Yeah, but what would you rather your last words be, then? Huh?"

She thought for a split second. "I love you."

"Yeah?"

"Yeah." She nodded. "I love you, Edwin. I love you so much. You are my light, my stars, my fresh pot of coffee." She turned to smile at me. "I love you."

I smiled. "I love you too, Fiona."

She smiled and squinted into the distance to see the road she had to turn down. She started braking a lot earlier than she had with the intersection. She took the turn and clicked her high beams on. I turned the music down so she could focus on keeping us on the road and not in the thicket of trees that had just swallowed us up. I enjoyed forest roads… usually.

The trees just looked like blackness next to me. The ones in front of us, speeding through our views as we passed, those ones all looked pretty intimidatingly thick and tall. The road stretched upwards and then crested into a fairly steep hill with a few curves down it. This was probably the first of a dozen hills like it. The entire stretch of road was pure white. Not very many people had driven down this road, so all the snow that had accumulated had just sat and stayed untouched for us to plow through. I did see a flicker of headlights behind us. They were moving far slower than we were.

The road just got worse in front of us. The snow was deeper. I had banked on this road being cleared, seeing as that it was a pretty popular road to drive down, but no. There was no plows down this road in the past few hours, and I don't think there'd be one for quite some time.

And then, the car, obviously, started to slip and slide its way down the downhill slope. I could see the helplessness in Fiona's eyes as she tried to keep us straight down the hill. A part of her looked like she had accepted what was happening, another part of her was fighting like hell. One small movement left or right had caused us to start wobbling all over the road. My heart started getting jumpy when we were basically drifting through turns going at a higher speed than this road should be driven even in good weather. My heart leapt into my throat and pounded like a kick drum.

And then all at once, everything was nothing.

    Time stopped, but it rushed by in a blur.

    And then I was looking down at her.

    She didn't speak.

    She couldn't.

    But she mustered up a smile, small and soft.

    Her eyes had glossed over.

    They were calm.

    Unblinking.

    Peaceful.

The colours betwixt her iris were of naught, and they reflected only that of flashing lights and silent screams. A tranquil silence overfalling her body.

Part 1
Chapter 5

The Colour of Lack Thereof
{One Year Prior}

The car came to a stop in the snowbank/ditch and suddenly the warm air of the car erupted with Fiona's laughter. I turned to see her smiling wildly at me, her eyes lit up like a Christmas tree (metaphorically).

"Did you see that?" she shouted. "We did a hundred doughnuts!"

"Well, maybe if you were a better driver," I chirped her. I was still trying to calm myself and reassure myself that we hadn't slid into a tree and died. But the car was resting in a snowy ditch and we were very much alive, though the car might freeze to death tonight. The snowbank had covered up most of the hood and most of my door, so I doubt this car is going anywhere.

"Excuse me?" She was glaring into my soul.

"Sorry," I said, "it's a joke. I'm joking. You're a wonderful driver."

"You're damn right I am."

"How much further to the lodge?"

She shrugged and blew a raspberry. "Maybe a mile or two. I think we can walk that far. Just watch out for other cars sliding off the road."

"I'll be sure to get on that." I let out a loud and very obnoxious groan. "Fuck, Fiona, we have to walk *so* far."

"Shut up. This is why we have coats."

"Are you gonna call for a tow?"

She sighed. "Yeah, I'll let my dad know where the car is and he can get his tow-truck buddy to come and haul the car out tomorrow or something."

"I can't get out my side, just so you know."

Fiona scoffed. "All well. Climb out my side. You'll be fine, you big wuss." Fiona zipped her coat up. "You might wanna bundle up though. And make sure your boots are tied up nice and tightly. We have a pretty good walk to the lodge, and then some more to the cottage."

"I don't wanna."

"Too bad. Bundle your cute little ass up and let's get to it already, huh?" Fiona wasted no time in pushing her door open, and as soon as she did, a flurry of snow floated its way into the new opening. Fiona climbed out of the car and then I did the same.

I did my best not to jerk around too much on my way out of the car, but it was on an angle on account of it being in a ditch. I got out and slammed the door shut. The last bastion of warmth, or so it felt.

"Okay," Fiona said from behind me. "Let us begin our long, cold, and very dangerous trek into the wilderness."

"Shut up," I muttered as I zipped my coat all the way up to my neck.

"Don't be rude," she barked as she clicked her key fob to lock her car. The headlights lit up quickly to signal that the car was locked and it lit up the snow in front of the car. "I'll push you into a snowbank."

There was snow everywhere. In my sleeves, my socks, my boots, my pockets. Fiona's hair had clumps of snow strung throughout it. It was cold and messy out tonight. The fact we made the drive was a miracle. Should have let her parents drive us up when the roads cleared, they're coming up anyway. I think next year's cottage getaway will be just Derek, Fiona, me, and Marshall. I guess I'll have to bum a ride off Fiona, unless I get a car in the next year (doubtful).

"It's about time you two benders showed up," Derek said as Fiona and I trudged up to the front of the Everwoods Lodge. This is the first time we've had to park here and hike to the cottage. I don't mind, it's for reasons like this that we bring our biggest winter coats.

"Roads were bad. Sue me," Fiona barked back to him. "Let's go inside and warm up a bit before we take this journey." The group of us followed Fiona's lead into the lodge. The Everwoods Lodge is a hunting lodge, but during the winter months, it's a cozy little hotel just off a semi-main road. It was a massive building that was hidden from the world by the thick boreal forest that surrounded it on all sides. The nearby lake was just a quick walk down a pathway behind the building.

"Hi, Fiona," an elderly lady said as she came over. She was the platinum blond-haired owner of this lodge. Her husband was the one who ran the hunting parties during hunting seasons, but she was the boss for the "hotel and B&B" season.

"Hi, Laurie," Fiona said, walking up and hugging Laurie. She was a friend of Fiona's grandma. Laurie was like Fiona's godgrandmother or something.

"Would you guys like a pot of tea?" Laurie asked, turning to the rest of us.

"Yes," I replied. "That'd be great, thanks."

"Yes, please," Derek and Marshal answered in unison as Laurie turned to them.

"Come with me to the dining room," she said, turning and walking through a doorway to the left. It led us down a large hallway and into a cafeteria-sized dining hall. It had three nearly room-long tables set up with dozens of chairs. A lot of people came here during hunting season. There were a few people along the tables all eating some dinner. The four of us took a seat at the end of one of the tables as Laurie went off into another room, presumably the kitchen, to prepare us a pot of tea.

When she came back, we had a few cups and chatted amongst ourselves and periodically with Laurie when she would walk by us. After an hour or so, we were all warmed up and ready for the hike to Fiona's cottage.

Though "ready" is a very loose term. I don't think we've ever been ready, nor will we ever "be" ready for walking through a foot of snow for an hour or more. Nobody's ready for that kind of journey.

I tried to prolong our stay at the lodge for as long as I could, but eventually Fiona won out and we had to pack up and be on our merry way.

I never knew air could hurt so much. Or snow. Everything hurts. My legs hurt from hiking over such shit terrain, my lungs hurt from breathing in so much cold air, my arms hurt from carrying bags, my face hurts from the cold and snow, but I can't complain about it, at least not openly. No one else has complained about it, so I'm sure as hell not being the first. We were more than halfway there already anyway. I could manage.

"How much further?" Marshall whined. "My face is frozen

and I feel like my legs are gonna fall off." I can finally complain! I sort of already knew that Marshall would cave first. He's the one that's least in shape. Derek and I both played hockey since we were seven and eight, respectively. We played in a league until college. We wanted to play hockey for college, but we didn't wanna play with college kids, we just liked to do it for fun, so we just decided to play shinny at local rinks instead of varsity. Fiona's in shape because she jogs a lot and plays varsity soccer and volleyball (which does absolute wonders for her figure, if you know what I mean).

"Puck up," Fiona chirped. "You're a Canadian, all this cold is good for us."

"That's just a lie we tell ourselves to deal with the cold," Marshall muttered. "It's like we all have Stockholm syndrome or something."

"Ottawa syndrome," I chimed in. "It's when you lie to yourself about liking the cold because the cold is all you've known."

"Ah, you think the cold is your ally?" Derek asked in his all-too-perfect Bane (from *The Dark Knight Rises*) impression. "You merely adopted the cold. I was born in it, molded by it. I didn't feel the warmth until I was already a man, by then it was nothing to me but searing!"

"I'd give you a slow clap, but my hands might shatter," I said. I always enjoyed when Derek busted out the Bane impressions. They were probably my favourite Derek impression. He does a good mating cat impression as well (that is, he shrieks and hisses).

"The cottage isn't that much further," Fiona said as we crested a small hill. "Although, I really should invest in one of those sleds to carry things. I don't like carrying all this weight on my back. It's not good for my posture."

"Your posture is fine, relax," Marshall stated.

Fiona scoffed. "Yeah, for now, but I'd like to keep it that way. I don't want arthritis at twenty, for Christ's sake."

"Take Epsom salt baths, then," Derek chimed from behind

us. He had fallen behind a fair bit. "I used them all the time after hockey and I feel just fine."

"Do you though?"

"I do," he said, glaring at her.

"Then why are you the one trailing so far behind?" she quipped as she stopped walking. "Give me the bag." She pulled the backpack off of Derek's back and swung it onto her back and then started walking again.

"Thanks," Derek muttered as he wrapped the strap of the bag he was carrying in his hand around his shoulder. That should quicken him up. I don't know how Fiona is such a pack mule though. She's got a backpack on her back and two bags in either hand, and none of these bags were *light* by any means.

We all trekked through the snowy forest for another twenty or so minutes. And then we finally arrived at the cottage. I can speak for myself when I say that for the past hour, since we left the lodge, that this cottage was all I could think about. All I wanted was to be warm again and to drop all the bags and shit. I just wanted to collapse onto the couch while Fiona cooks us dinner and Derek and Marshall play pool just to the left of the TV I'd be watching.

Fiona led us up the front porch and we all collectively let out a sigh as we dropped the bags to the wood beneath our feet. Fiona looked around and scoffed at us as she dug around in her coat pocket for her keys. "Bad news, guys. I think I left the keys back in my car by the lodge." She gave a half-frown to the group of us.

"You're fucking kidding, right?" Derek grumbled. "You can walk back with Edwin. I'm staying right here."

"Just kidding!" Fiona shouted, lifting a jangly bunch of keys from her pocket. "Did you idiots really think I wasn't gonna remember the keys?" She pushed the key into the lock and turned. The sound of the tumblers releasing was like music to my ears.

I pushed right past the others and got inside the cottage. It wasn't warm in here, since nobody's been here in a while, but it was mountains warmer than the air outside. I basked in the warm chill of the cottage and let out a sigh as I dropped the bags I had been carrying. I dusted myself off as the others came inside. Fiona shut the door behind us and turned over the deadbolt to lock out the outside world.

"Before you body-check any more of us, I'm gonna head to the bathroom," Derek said as he dropped everything he was carrying. "I gotta rock a wicked piss."

"Yeah, same, so hurry up," Fiona barked at him as Derek trudged down the hall.

"Use the downstairs bathroom," Derek chirped back.

Fiona scoffed. "Not in this lifetime." The downstairs bathroom was pretty disgusting. It's a half-finished toilet room, and that's best-case scenario. It just has a toilet and a rickety sink. The light flickers a lot. The walls are exposed. The floor is cold cement. There's always some kind of bugs on the floor, because even in a cottage this nice, you have to be reminded that there are savage things in nature. The reason why the downstairs bathroom is ass is because it was halfway through a renovation when the previous owners of the cottage just sort of stopped renovating it and then decided to sell it. Fiona's parents just say not to use it, it's not worth the money to fix it at this point. The upstairs bathroom has a toilet, sink, bathtub, full shower, and all the rest of that jazz. It just sucks when you're sharing it between 4 or more people.

"Well, I gotta piss, so wish me luck," Marshall said as he laid his stuff down and headed down the stairs toward the forsaken downstairs bathroom.

"I guess we're waiting," I said as I walked over to the kitchen and flicked the light switch on. I should clear up that the downstairs is technically the basement, but it has a back door to the backyard because the cottage was built into a hill.

"I guess so." Fiona came in behind me and went to the fridge. "Not a lot to eat until the rents come up with the good food." She opened up some cupboards and started rifling through them to find something for our dinner. She pulled down a few boxes of mac and cheese from the top shelf of one of the cupboards. "I dunno how old these are or when they expire, but it's food, and it's pretty much all we have."

"Do we have butter?"

Fiona scoffed at me. "Do we have butter?" She mocked. She walked over to her backpack and unzipped the biggest pouch and pulled out a small Tupperware container that had a stick of butter smushed inside.

"Put the water on."

"Don't tell me what to do," she barked as she walked over to the sink. She turned the tap on and nothing came out. She let out a loud groan. "Water must be off." She turned to me and sighed. "Okay, you go get the heat on and I'll get the water figured out, hopefully soon. I don't want used toilet water stagnating."

I grumbled as I stood up to walk over to Fiona. As I did, she opened the drawer in front of her and handed me a flashlight. I headed downstairs and opened the janky door that led into the furnace, water heater, and fuse box room. I replaced the filter on the furnace and clicked the marked switch to give it power. I went back upstairs and toyed with the thermostat until the furnace roared to life beneath the floorboards.

"Got the dragon working?" Derek asked as he walked by me and into the kitchen. "This place better warm up soon. It's freezing in here."

"Did you try to flush the toilet?" I asked him as I sat down at the table.

"Yeah, but I forgot that the water wouldn't be working just yet. I was in there trying to figure out what the hell I did wrong, but then I remembered and came out."

"I guess Marshall isn't as bright as you, then?"

"He probably went to help Fiona."

I nodded and looked out the window of the kitchen. It was still snowing heavily outside, blanketing the ground in a thickening layer of cold white blankets, the kind of blankets you'd like to avoid sleeping in. If we had left even a half hour later than we did, it might not even be safe enough to drive. If one of us had worked late, one of us could have ended up dead on the side of the road, resting finally in that thickening white blanket.

 The colours betwixt the melting layers of white would be one of deep crimson, a tranquil silence overfalling the victim.

PART TWO
The Grey

Part 2
Chapter 1

The Wake-Up
{Present Day}

There was a thin layer of whiteness all around me. Not soft, not cold, but bright and warm. The walls and ceiling seemed more like they were made more of paper than of drywall and wood. Everything was opposite to the way I had lost consciousness. When I blacked out, things were cold and dark, and now that I'm awake, everything is bright and warm and welcoming again. I could swear I heard the chirping of birds outside, but of course that's not right. It's the middle of winter, the birds have all gone south, but not owls.

Owls don't migrate. That's why I have a tattoo of an owl on my calf; because owls are stubborn and powerful animals. Fiona has a tattoo of a small bird, a migratory bird, a symbol that she likes to always be on the move. Where I stand in the north, she watches from the south. Ever vigilant, my little bird.

The whiteness became too much for my tired eyes to stare at. I shut them tight and pushed myself with all my strength (which wasn't much at this point). I opened my eyes again and looked around the room. *Hospital,* I thought to myself, *Why the hell am I in a hospital?*

Nothing came to me. Nothing but darkness and cold. What happened? What day was it? Can I even be sure that I'm Edwin right now? Maybe my entire existence as him was a lie? Before I could existentially brain-fuck myself to comatose, a nurse came in the room and picked up a clipboard from beside my bed.

"Edwin Flowers," she read aloud. Okay, so my name is Edwin. I wasn't in a coma. This isn't me waking up to find out I'm not who I thought I was. "How are you feeling?"

I went to speak but my throat felt like rusty chainsaws, so all that came out of me was a raspy whine. The nurses nodded and walked out of the room. She couldn't have been gone longer than twenty seconds by the time she reappeared in the doorway with a glass of water. She handed it to me and I threw it back like it was my first shot. I've never been more thankful for the existence of water in my entire life.

"How are you feeling?" she repeated her question.

I nodded. "Better now." I handed her the cup back. "I feel sore all over."

"You should feel lucky," she said, flipping through a few pages on the clipboard. "You didn't even break a single bone."

"Why would I have broken a bone?" I asked, silently praying that she'd get me another glass of water, or an entire lake's worth of water.

The nurse turned to me and sighed. "The details will come back to you, but you were in an accident. The car you were in spun out and slammed into a tree. It wasn't anyone's fault but the snow."

"How long have I been out for?"

"Less than a day," she replied. "You came in last night

around eleven. And right now it is—" She paused for a moment as she raised a hand up and checked her watch. "—four PM."

"Shit," I muttered. "Was I with anyone else?" I can't believe I don't remember anything about yesterday. I could only remember waking up yesterday and eating cereal in my kitchen before going to class.

The nurses nodded and gave me a small, sympathetic frown. "You were with a girl. Fiona. Do you remember Fiona?"

I nodded. "Of course I remember her. I remember everything except for last night."

"Of course, sorry." The nurse jotted some stuff onto the clipboard and went to speak before being interrupted by a doctor walking in from behind her.

"Edwin, you're awake," the doctor pointed out as he took the clipboard from the nurse. "You're feeling alright today?"

"Just sore," I replied. "And thirsty, very thirsty."

"Well, the X-rays came back. You didn't break anything, there's no internal bleeding," he stated in a monotone voice. He was clearly just reading notes from the clipboard. "You just hit your head real good. It knocked you out for a good while."

"Where's Fiona?" I asked.

"We're going to go and call your friend in from the waiting room," the doctor stated, dodging my question. "I think he said his name was Derek."

I nodded and watched as he and the nurse exited the room. I was alone with the soft beeps of nearby machines, the distant echo of cars on the streets outside, and hurried footsteps pacing through the hallways. I heard two sets of footsteps grow close to my room and then Derek appeared in my view, behind him was the nurse. She walked back down the hall and Derek stepped into the room. His eyes were a mess, like he had been without sleep for days and crying heavily the entire time. I shot up and stared at him. "What happened to you? You look like dusty shit."

He coughed up a small laugh and wiped his eyes. "How long have you been awake?"

I shrugged. "A couple minutes. Why?"

"They just caught me at a bad time, is all. I was hoping maybe you'd have been awake longer so I could explain to you."

"Why's it a bad time?" I asked him as he pulled a small chair over to the side of my bed. "I'm fine. Fiona's gotta be fine too, right?"

He looked up and gave me a pained smile. "They didn't tell you."

"Tell me what?"

"Fiona," Derek whispered, "she passed away this morning."

"Stop." My voice was low but firm. My body welled with heat, but it was the pins-and-needles heat of bad news and anxiety. It wasn't anger, it wasn't jealousy, it wasn't embarrassment. It was a heat that radiated from something not of my flesh and bone. I shut my eyes and begged myself to remember what had happened. I begged myself to wake up and feel Fiona clutching my sweaty body as I trembled in the moonlight on the edge of her bed from this nightmare. But nothing magical happened. I opened my eyes and my vision was blurred from the unforced tears freely flowing out of my eyes. Derek was there, his hand on mine, trying to comfort his best friend.

"There was nothing any of us could do, Ed," he said. He hadn't called me that in forever. "Come here." He scooted the chair closer and wrapped his arms over me and hugged me, not one of those lame one-arm hugs, a full-on hug.

"She can't be gone, Derek. She can't be," I mumbled into his shoulder. "She was just with me last night. She was *just* with me. I had my hand on her thigh. She smiled at me. She was alive."

Everything came rushing back to me in waves. My eyes drowning of their own accord, I relived memories of what had happened in my head, blocking out the noise and light from the world around me.

"*I love you, Edwin. I love you so much. You are my light, my stars, my fresh pot of coffee. I love you.*"

Her final words rung in my head like the loudest of bells. How could someone so full of life and love die so young? She was not ready to fly south. She didn't want to, and she didn't deserve to. I had offered to take the wheel and she had refused. Should I have pressed my case more? Should I have made her take a different road? Should I have made her drive even slower? Does it even matter what I *could* have done? Maybe it only matters about the things I *didn't* do. But she was just as alive as I was after the crash. She smiled at me, a soft smile. She blinked at me too. She was alive. Her eyes were glittering in the flashing sirens. She was alive. She was alive. She was alive. She has to be alive. She has to be. She is alive. "She's alive," I thought aloud.

Derek pushed me back and looked me deep in the eyes. "Ed, I know this is a lot to swallow, but I would never lie to you about this."

"She has to be alive."

"Edwin, she's not. She's gone. They tried like fucking hell to save her. I promise you." Derek handed me a napkin so I could wipe my tears off my face. "They just couldn't. She was originally declared dead on arrival, but they detected a weak heartbeat and thought they could save her. They just couldn't. I'm sorry. They're sorry. We're all sorry. None of us know how hard this is for you, and none of us are going to pretend we do." Derek helped me sit upright properly. "I love you, man. She did too, so much, all the way to the end. I know you were the last person she was thinking about."

"She can't be gone," I mumbled, collapsing back into the arms of my friend. Fiona was everything to me. She was the sole reason I tried in life. I wanted to be the best Edwin I could be for her. I wanted to grow old with her. I wanted to watch her succeed in life. I wanted to be right by her side through every battle lost and every battle won. I wanted to help her through it all and hold her up higher and higher each day. She was my little bird, and I was the little branch that she could stand on.

Derek rubbed my back a little and stood up. "Do you wanna go and get some lunch?"

I shook my head. "I want to see Fiona."

"You have to eat," Derek said, grabbing my arm and pulling me out of the bed. "Come on. It's burrito night."

"Yeah, but I don't want to." I sighed as he led me out of the room and into the disgustingly bright hallway. Derek kept ahead of me, walking slower than he wanted to just to make sure I was still keeping up with him. My whole body was stiff and sore. I was achy all over. I might not have broken anything or punctured any organs, but that doesn't negate the fact that bodies can be bruised and battered.

"Do you want a wheelchair?" Derek asked once I had stopped walking and started leaning on a nearby wall.

I nodded and slumped down on the floor as Derek walked off. He came back a few moments later and helped me into a wheelchair. My body was too tired and sore to move on its own accord. Derek pushed me down the halls and to the cafeteria.

"I texted Marshall," he told me. "He's on his way. He was taking all our stuff back to Fiona's place. You woke up just a little while after he left, actually. Bad timing on your part."

I chuckled softly. "Sorry... my bad."

"Good to see your sense of humour is still in tip-top shape." Derek smiled at me as we went over to the serving area. He pulled a tray off the stack and put it on my lap.

"I still refuse to believe that she's gone, Derek."

"I know. I refuse to believe it as well." Derek began putting food items on our trays. "But life goes on."

"Just not for Fiona," I said, looking down at my lap. I pushed the wrapped burrito over and sighed. "She can't be gone, Derek. She can't be."

Derek turned and gave me a small smile, nothing more

than an acknowledgment that he had heard me, a subtle agreeance that he, too, did not want to believe that Fiona was gone. How could we? She was the most radiant beam of light on this planet, and for her to be snuffed out so suddenly, not with a bang but a whimper; it was rude.

The colours betwixt her eyelids were a fleeting memory, following the sound of her voice out the doorways of my mind and into the emptiness.

Part 2
Chapter 2

The Return to Routine

The car creaked to a stop at the intersection, the snow steadily falling around in the slowly blinking yellow light overhead. It was a caution light, a light that let others know it that there was a stop sign here for the small street that crossed the regional highway. Fiona put the car in park and let out a sigh.

"Why'd we stop?" I asked her.

She shrugged. "I just need to take a break. We've been driving in this shitty weather for so long." She ruffled a hand through her long, wavy hair. She smiled at me. "It's not like we have anywhere important to be other than with each other? Right?"

I nodded. "Right."

Fiona put the car in reverse and backed onto the shoulder so we were out of the way, not like it mattered much, there was nobody on the roads.

Not a single distant headlight, no distant horns, no sirens, nothing but serene, quiet, snow-covered farmland and fields. Fiona turned the car off and popped open her door. "Come on. Let's go for a walk."

I unbuckled my seat belt and got out of the car. The air was warm, but snow still fell around us. The flakes of snow were cold on my cheeks as I walked to the front of the car. Fiona waited there for me with a small smile on her face.

"Come on," she said, raising her hand to me.

"Where are we going?" I asked as I took her hand in mine.

She turned and smiled at me, her hair blowing in the wind. "For a walk." So we started walking. We crossed the empty intersection, putting distance between us and the car, between us and the blinking yellow light. The world was illuminated only by a brighter-than-normal moon and a starry sky, which begged the question: where was the snow coming from?

"We're getting pretty far away from the car," I pointed out. I let go of her hand and turned around and looked at the small pinprick-sized flashing yellow light in the vast dark horizon behind us.

She shrugged. "We'll go back in a bit." She grabbed my hand again. "Now let's walk some more, please."

"Fiona, you're acting strange." I looked down and noticed she didn't have any shoes on. "You're barefoot right now? It's snowing. There's snow all over the ground. Come on, let's go back to the car. You're gonna get frostbite."

She wiggled her toes in the snow, her black nail polish getting covered by white snow just for more snow to push it off. "It feels refreshing, the cold in between my toes."

"Refreshing or not, you'll lose your foot if you don't go put shoes on," I stated. I tugged on her arm, let's go. Come on."

"No," she said.

I turned back to her. "Come on. This isn't a joke, Fiona."

"No."

"Fiona!"

"Edwin, I said no!" She turned and started walking again.

I let out a low groan and begrudgingly followed behind her. Minus the frostbite, there are still a lot of coyotes and bears out in the sticks. The forests were just on the other sides of the fields all around us, it wouldn't take much coaxing to get a pack of hungry coyotes after us. Where was

Fiona trying to take me?

"Fiona," I called up to her. It seemed as though she was walking twice as fast as me now. She was in the distance, walking further away from me. "Fiona! Wait up!" I called to her as she became smaller and smaller in my eyesight. I saw her turn around and look at me for a moment before running off into a cornfield. "Fuck's sake," I muttered as I ran up to edge of the cornfield. I looked around and couldn't see any movement from within the corn.

I walked into the field and pushed stalks of corn out of my way as I walked through, looking up and down the slim rows where there wasn't any corn. Thank God humans love neatness. If this corn was planted haphazardly, I'd already be lost. "Fiona!" I shouted into the stillness of the air. There wasn't a reply, just the soft sounds of the corn brushing into each other with the occasional breeze.

I pushed through more rows of corn. I wasn't any closer to finding Fiona out here. Fuck her, why did she run off like this? Why did I let her take me out of the car? We were already so far away from the car when we entered the cornfield. God only knows where we'll end up now. But regardless, I wasn't going to just leave Fiona out here. I don't know what's come over her tonight, but I refuse to abandon her, no matter how annoying this is or how much it pisses me off.

"Fiona!" I shouted after walking another minute through this godforsaken cornfield. No reply, no evidence Fiona had passed through this area of corn, no footprints in the mud, no dishevelled stalks of corn. I was beginning to get more than frustrated at her. Why did she just run off? "FIONA!" I bellowed into the night air. "ENOUGH GAMES, I'M GETTING COLD. LET'S GET BACK TO THE CAR!" My voice filled the silent night air, but nothing but more silence was returned to me. My voice didn't echo, no animals made any scurrying. It was just complete and utter quietness.

I started walking down one of the sections where the corn separated a little wider than usual. I followed it until I ended up on a road. I hadn't turned around either, so now I was even further from where I wanted to be, which was the car, and by extension, the cottage with Fiona. I pulled my phone out of my pocket to check the time, except that all the numbers looked like gibberish, and they were cycling through even more gibberish the longer I looked at them. I blinked a few times and put my phone back.

Okay, Edwin. Just get back to the car. This is how a horror movie starts, I thought to myself as I started walking back toward the east-west road that we had stopped at. I could take this back to the intersection the car was at... hopefully.

I reached an intersection of road, but I couldn't see very much. My way was still only lit by the bright moon in the sky. I turned around back the way I came and squinted into the distance. A slowly flashing yellow light had appeared in the air 100 or so feet behind me. I walked over to it and noticed a car, Fiona's car. How the hell was I back at the car? We walked far away before Fiona ran into the cornfield. How did I get back here so fast?

I walked over to the front of the car and Fiona got stepped out from her door. "Where the fuck have you been?" she shouted. "You were supposed to be taking a piss, not going for a hike! Get in the car."

"Me?" I asked, walking over to her. I looked down and noticed that her feet were now dressed in a pair of moccasins. "You're the one who ran into a cornfield after dragging me for a hike."

"I've been in the car waiting for you," Fiona shouted at me. "You said you had to piss, so I pulled over so you could go in the bushes because we're nowhere near anything."

"What the fuck are you talking about?"

She glared at me. "Just get in the fucking car, Edwin!"

I listened to her and got into my side of the car. The seat was still warm. The heat was still on. The windshields were fogged up a little bit. And the air around the car was just as still and calm as it was when Fiona dragged me out of the car for an impromptu hike. Was she just playing games with my head now for fun or something?

"Fiona, I didn't get out to go pee, I swear," I told her. "You stopped the car and started walking down the road, and you walked way far."

"I didn't though," she said, her face tense and voice irritated. "I stayed in the car because I stopped so you could take a piss, like you said you needed to. It's cold outside, why the fuck would I go for a walk?"

I sighed. "Give me your foot," I said, remembered that Fiona hadn't been wearing any shoes when we went for our walk.

"My foot?" She raised an eyebrow as she lifted her leg up and put it on my lap. She was practically sideways in her seat. "What are you doing?" she asked I shimmied off her moccasin. "You're not gonna suck my *toes or something are you?"*

"No, what the fuck? No." I placed a hand on the bottom of her foot. It was warm. She must not have removed her shoe at all. I gave her leg and moccasin back to her and she put it back on her foot and then made a grumbling noise before putting the car in drive.

I could have sworn that I had chased her through those stupid fields. I fucking know I did, so how was the sole of her foot so fucking warm still? It's snowing outside. It's not like she could have dried her foot and gotten them warm again in the time it took for me to follow her back to the car. No way. Something's so off about all of this.

I sighed and looked out the window. Empty fields and dark skies. I turned to look at Fiona as we pulled through the intersection only to be blinded by a set of headlights from a large truck barreling at us. The collision was almost as instant as the realization of what was happening. I opened my mouth to scream, raised my arms to shield myself as best I could...

I jolted upright and looked around my room. Sweat covered my body. The time displayed on my alarm clock blinked at me in the morning-lit room. 88:88. The power must have flickered during the night. I picked my phone up from the nightstand and checked the time. It was only 6:03. I still had plenty of time to get ready, more time than usual. My alarm was set for 6:45, so I'm awake 42 minutes earlier than I budgeted for. I'm okay with that.

I got off my bed and got dressed. I piled everything into my backpack, the one I had emptied last night of all the stuff I was going to bring to the cottage, had we made it there. I sat back down on the bed and ran my hands through my hair, trying to make sense of that mess of a dream. Is this going to be my life now? Having confusing dreams about Fiona until I one day forget her entirely?

Ridiculous. I could never forget Fiona. This would be my life; waking in cold sweats and heavy breathing. Perhaps they won't happen every night. Some days will no doubt be better than others. There will be gaps of time where Fiona eludes my conscious thoughts, but she'll always be there, looming in the back of my head like a storm cloud in the distance, she's there; waiting.

I gathered my composure and once the sweat was dried on my skin, I went and washed my face, washed my hands, brushed my teeth, and tried to resemble a fully functional human being (that just so happened to be made of aching and rusted parts). I walked downstairs and then outside and then to my car and then I opened the back door and put my backpack on the seat. I got in and started the car. I let out a small sigh as I looked behind me in the mirror and backed out.

I got to school an hour early for class. An entire fucking *hour* early. I got myself a coffee and walked to class and sat there in the emptiness. What a metaphor for my life, an empty classroom, something usually bursting with colour and noise, and now it sits empty. I pulled my laptop out of my bag and started going over notes from last week's class. I know we're not gonna have a test this week in class, but it's still nice to review things.

As the minutes ticked by and the start of class grew near, more and more people began to come in and take their seats. Having heard of Fiona's passing, a lot of them gave me looks of sympathy (more like pity; there's the boy with the dead girlfriend, how tragically melancholy of life to do that to him). I did get a few looks from people that I knew genuinely cared for either Fiona or I. Those looks stung, the ones from people who really did know her.

Class trudged on and I drudged through the work for that day. I hated going home with things to do for any class. I always tried my best to finish it before I left. I work better in a classroom anyway, too many distractions at home for me to focus on homework.

This was my routine: I would wake up and come to class and then when class was over I would check my phone to see where Fiona would want to meet up. I'd go meet up with her and we'd do a late lunch together and figure out what next, who had to work, what we'd do if neither of us had a shift that night. We'd call Derek or Marshall and figure out what they were up to. At the end of the day, Fiona and I would sleep in a bed together at my place or hers. Repeat four more times for that week.

    My routine was now broken. Instead of calling or texting anyone, I drove to a coffee shop, got a bagel and coffee, then drove back to my house and went to my room. I closed the door and turned some music on. I blanked the world out of my foreground and into the background. Nothing felt normal, nothing felt real, nothing felt like it should. Everything felt so empty and unfamiliar now that Fiona was gone. I'll never say she's dead. To admit that is to admit that she really is gone. Because, in the wise words of Carolina from *Red vs. Blue*, "Never say goodbye. If you don't say goodbye, then they aren't really gone, they just aren't here right now." So I refuse to say goodbye.

    I find myself wondering if goodbye would ever even fit into my life. Am I even capable of letting go? Do I want to? Will I ever want to? Maybe, but maybe not. And will I ever want the colours betwixt of before and after Fiona to be anything but grey?

Part 2
Chapter 3

The Day of the Funeral

A closed-casket funeral. I guess I'll never get to see her face again. Regardless of that, I can remember clearly from the night I last saw it. No sanded-down mahogany casket was going to block out the view of her, bleeding and dying in the wreckage of her car. I rested a hand on the casket, a few inches of wood separate me from what remained of the girl I had loved irrevocably for years.

Fuck. I just miss her so goddamn much. It doesn't even feel like she's gone. I had all of her and now I have none of her. I just wish I could take her back to the night we met, just to be able to relive every moment with her once more. God, I would kill for one more minute with her. I feel like such an asshole now, for every time I told her "No," when she wanted to hang out. I should have seen her every moment that I could have, because now it's too late. I'm never going to get another minute with Fiona, never. Every minute that I could have been around her that I wasn't feels like a fucking eternity, and that eternity feels like the weight of the universe sitting on my chest.

I snapped back to the real world when I heard a cough nearby. I had heard others whispering their goodbyes to the casket earlier. But not me. I refused. I whispered a quick apology and admission of undying love to her and then walked back to my seat for the rest of the ceremony. And then we buried her. And everyone wanted speeches from those closest to her (her parents, her best friend, her boyfriend (me)). I couldn't stomach speaking a word about her though. My eyes stung and my stomach churned just thinking about the fact that the funeral around me was indeed Fiona's, and that she was, in fact, gone.

The day began to slip by and once people left the service, I returned to the inside of the funeral home and sat in the pews, somewhere in the middle, waiting for Derek and Marshall. They had gone to get food for us to eat at Derek's and I had stayed because I needed some me time. Watching the casket that my girlfriend now called home get lowered into the soil was mentally draining and emotionally exhausting.

The large doors that served as the entrance to the funeral home's largest room opened behind me, the creaks echoing through the empty room. I turned my head and saw Derek walk in, still wearing his suit from today. I thought he would run home and change before getting food, guess not.

"Glad to see you in the same place I left you," Derek said as he walked over and sat down next to me,

"I wasn't about to walk across town in this cold," I said, scoffing a little. "And besides, you're my ride and source of food for the night."

"Right." He nodded. He pulled a small flask from within his suit. "Whisky. I thought you might need something to make you a little numb. I'm not normally one for vices, but in this case, I'll give you an exception."

I took the flask and smiled softly at him. "Thank you." I twisted the lid off and punched back a solid shot or two worth of whisky.

"So, what do you say? Let's go get drunk and eat Chinese food until we puke?"

I managed to crack a smile as I nodded. "Yeah, for sure."

Derek's house had always felt like a second (third) home to me, ever since I first walked in. Every wall was a dark colour that felt warm and inviting. Walls were trimmed with stained oak. His kitchen counters were dark granite and his cupboards were the same stained oak. His floors were a brighter stained wood, not sure which kind. Anything metal was kept shiny. He had an electric stove with an all-black top. It was very a nice, upscale, welcoming home.

The three of us made our way to the basement recreational room (I'll call it a rec room from now on, sorry) with our bounty of Chinese food and booze. I took my seat on the couch and Derek took his seat in the recliner chair at the other end of the couch. Marshall sat on the couch at the other end. The coffee table was now overflowing with Chinese food boxes and glass alcohol bottles. What a beautiful sight it was though. Before we dug in, Derek ran upstairs and grabbed us three tumblers with ice.

Derek opened a bottle of whisky and poured each of us a glass. He raised one and looked back and forth at us. "Though she may not be with us in flesh, she'll always be with us in spirit and in heart. To the most beautiful girl I never made out with, one of the most amazing people I could ever wish to have the pleasure of getting to know. To Fiona."

Marshall and I raised a glass and we all clinked cups as we spoke all at once, "To Fiona!" And then we took a long drink, each one of us seemingly wanting to take a longer, deeper drink than the others, to drown whatever sorrows were trying to cough themselves out of our mouths. And then nobody spoke for a while. It was silent lest the ringing hums of the lights and TV that sat displaying a blank HDMI input screen.

"Sorry," Derek said after a few moments. He reached for the Xbox controller and turned the console on. "I didn't mean to kill the mood of the room like that."

"It's fine," I said.

Marshall nodded. "Yeah. It's not your fault. It's just that she should be here with us. We should be toasting her because she did something amazing, not because she isn't here."

"Toasting herself is something she'll never be able to do," Derek added.

"Not just that," I said, feeling a welling of something heated in my chest, spreading slowly to my veins and seeping through my bones. Was it a sense of pride in explaining that Fiona would miss so much more than just a toast? That she would miss *everything* that would ever happen from this moment forward.

"What do you mean?" Derek asked.

"She won't miss just this," I said. "It's not that she'll never be able to raise a toast to herself and accomplishments. She won't ever get to have things to accomplish." I ran a hand through my hair and let out a sigh. "She'll never get the chance to do so many things. She'll never get to be a mother. She'll never get to see another sunset or get to wade through waves with her toes in the sand. She'll never be able to ride her favourite rides at a fair again. She'll never be able to graduate college. She'll never own her own house. She'll never get wrinkles. She'll never be able to sing in the shower again." I stopped myself short of continuing because my emotional minutiae had caught up with my words and I found myself choking for a breath.

"Edwin." Marshall's hand rest on my back as I seemingly collapsed into myself. My head rested in my hands.

"This isn't fair," I muttered. "Why was it her? Why not

me?" I stood up and clenched my fists. "Why did it have to be her?!" I screamed at the ceiling. "It could have been me, it s*hould* have been me!"

"It could have been both of you!" Derek shouted. "You could have both been left for ghost on the side of the road. It hurts that she's gone, but you're still here. And it hurts now, but you'll grow around your scars."

I turned to him and glared. "I don't wanna grow. I want to go back to that night and redo everything that led us to be on that road. It's not fair that she had to die. She wasn't even done schooling. She didn't even truly start her life. It's not fair!"

"I know it's not fair, but there's no sense in blaming yourself," Derek said, getting up and over to me. He rested a hand down on my shoulder. "There was nothing you could do to save her. You loved her while she was alive, and that's more than she could have ever asked for. You loved her so much, so fiercely. I can still see it in your eyes that you love her, a piece of you always will." Derek smiled softly at me.

"Nobody's asking you to move on within the month after her passing," Marshall chimed in. "We just don't want you to blame yourself for something that was out of your control."

"But it was in my control. I could have told her to take another road," I rebutted. "I could have made us stay longer at Tims. I could have made us not go at all because the weather had gotten so bad by the time we left her house to go up there. I could have done so much more than just sitting in a passenger seat fiddling with the heat and radio. I fucked up."

Marshall gave me a half-frown. "You didn't have control over the outcome, Edwin."

"No, but I should have." I sat back down. "Let me rewrite that night and I'll tell you what I *should* have done."

"There was nothing else you should have done," Derek said. "Trust me."

"I'm always going to feel like I should have done something though." I groaned. "I'm going to blame myself for her death for the rest of my life."

"Can I give you a word of advice?" Marshall asked. "Don't. Seriously. Do whatever you need to do to absolve yourself."

"I can't."

Derek sighed. "You can. You will. You feel like this now because it's fresh, but as time moves forward, you'll realize that you had no say in how things turned out. You weren't a paramedic that didn't try hard enough or a cop that didn't get there fast enough or a surgeon that didn't stop the bleeding soon enough. You were just a passenger, a victim, a person that survived a crash. You're not at fault for what happened, you never will be. You're the only person blaming you for any of the events that night."

"It's all so stupid and meaningless in the end anyway."

Marshall handed me my glass of whisky from the table. "Then drink up, because life is only as meaningless as you make it out to be."

"I make it out to be pretty fucking meaningless right now." I took the glass from him and drank it down.

"That's good, he said 'Right now.' I guess that means he expects life to be meaningful again," Derek said, smirking a little bit as he poured more whisky into my glass. "Also, we're gonna get you nice and fucked up tonight. It'll help keep your mind off things."

"I guess it's better to think about nothing than to think about her, huh?"

Derek frowned slightly. "No. It's better to think about nothing than to blame yourself for things that were out of your control. Now come on. Grab a controller and stuff an eggroll in your gullet. We've got zombies to murder."

After many hours and many drinks, I found myself on the floor behind the couch, staring at the ceiling fan as it spun around

and around and around and around and around. My eyes were training on a small crack in the ceiling behind the fan. My ears were fixed on the rapid button clicks of Marshall and Derek from just beyond the other side of the couch. The room was spinning above me, opposite to the way the fan was spinning, oddly enough.
Spinning.
    Spinning.
        Spinning.
My head felt full and my limbs were just *there*, not doing much of anything other than being attached to the rest of me. I lie motionless, stuck in a recurring thought: That no matter how many times someone tells me that there was nothing I could do to have stopped Fiona's death, I would never believe that. As human beings, we can always do more, because that's what sets us apart from the animal kingdom. We crowned ourselves king and acted with morals and ingenuity; we can always do more. I could have forced her down any other road. I could have told her to go back home when the roads started getting too bad. What happened to Fiona was a direct causality to every unknowingly wrong choice I made. But I should have known. I should have had some foresight to think about the worst-case scenario, not just the best-case scenarios, because life doesn't care about the best-case scenario, not even in the slightest. Nature always sides with the hidden flaw.

    I rolled onto my side and stared at the back of the couch. I rolled to my other side and stared at the wall. I blinked once, twice, three times, four times, five times, six times… on and on, and that was all I could do. I was too drunk to move, not drunk enough to pass out. I stared at the empty slightly yellowed white baseboard as it fuzzed in and out of focus.

    The floor around me felt less like a solid and more like a concept, something to hold me in place, never letting me move even though I could; static to a visual or hissing to a sound. Perhaps never moving would be the most beautiful idea I've ever had. I could lay in wait until my time came to be with

Fiona again. But people were never meant to be static. And yet, that's all I feel. My insides fuzzy with the cold white noise. My ears full of empty ringing.

So I lay, staring at a blank wall. The colours betwixt the floor and the ceiling reminded me of a fleeting happiness, something distant and something far gone.

Part 2
Chapter 4

The Colour of Denial

My mouth stretched into a yawn as my eyes began fluttering softly as I forced them open. My head was throbbing and the whole world felt like a swirling vortex of static and loud ringing. I looked around and found the source of the ringing: my phone. I had set an alarm because I didn't want to sleep in past 10, so I guess that makes it 10 in the morning right now. When I clicked the sleep button on my phone, I was practically blinded by the light that erupted off of the screen. I should have turned the brightness down before going to sleep last night, but I'm not a smart man.

I dropped my phone to the floor and sat up on the couch. Marshall was sleeping in the guest room and Derek, obviously enough, was sleeping in his own room. I had requested the couch because Derek's couch is (and this is a true fact) the most comfortable couch in existence for sleeping on. I sat upright and stretched out. I had nothing to do today. I had no plans, no objective for the day. I don't think anybody expected me to either. I had just attended a funeral for my deceased girlfriend just yesterday, so I think I've garnered myself some free passes for the day.

I picked my phone up and squinted through the brightness until I managed to down it. Once the screen was more bearable, I checked my social media accounts, text messages, watched a little bit of porn (just kidding about that last thing… maybe). But my alarm had gone off, so I knew I was the first one awake. There's no way either Derek or Marshall would be awake yet, not after how much we drank last night. They're both probably still ripped right off their rockers at this point in the morning.

There was still so much day left today. Why did I think it'd be smart to wake up at 10 in the morning? When is that ever a good idea unless you have class or work to go to? I've become a proper mess without Fiona. She's only been gone a couple weeks, barely long enough for everyone on the street to have finally shovelled their driveways from the storm that caused our crash.

I grabbed my socks from the table and slipped them back onto my feet. I slid my shirt over my head and stood up to stretch, smoothing out the shirt as I did. I put my phone, wallet, and keys back into the pockets of my jeans (and yes, I slept in jeans; sue me). I stretched out and headed upstairs. No sounds. Everyone was either already gone for work or still asleep. Perfect.

I slipped out the front door and headed down the driveway to my car. I got in and started the car, turning the heater on full. The air inside (and outside) of the car was frigidly cold and painfully dry. I could feel my skin cracking as I wrapped my fingers over the steering wheel.

The roads all look the same. Every house looks the same. They don't, but it just feels that way. Everything was a blur around me. I didn't even have any set destination. I was just driving, driving, driving some more. Driving out of Derek's neighbourhood, driving past my neighbourhood, driving out of the city, parking at a small café that was the last building for the next hour or more down the road. The road was infamous around here for being so desolately long.

My car shuddered to sleep and the cold snapped back around me, almost instantly. I rubbed my hands together to create a small bit of warmth. I placed my keys in my inner coat pocket and got out of the car. I walked in and ordered myself a coffee, and another two coffees. I got back in the car and headed back into the city.

I drove until I arrived at Fiona's house.

My fist knocked four, five, six swift knocks on the wooden door of Fiona's house. My knuckles wrung from the knocking. The cold always amplifies pain and discomfort. I shook my hand out as the door in front of me unlocked and swung inward to open. I was greeted by a woman of small stature, long brown hair and welcoming amber eyes with an equally welcoming smile stretched on her slightly wrinkling face. Fiona's mother, just as beautiful as Fiona was (though she had a good 30 years on Fiona).

"Edwin," she spoke, her voice low and soft, "what are you doing here? Not that I don't want you here, just that you usually call if you're coming by. Everything okay?"

I nodded. "Yeah, I just wanted to drop by and bring you guys some coffee." I lifted up the tray of coffees I had got from the little café (my favourite café, by the by). "Have you guys gone through Fiona's room yet?"

She shook her head. "Haven't had time. We've been busy, and we've been trying to stay that way."

"I understand." Of course they'd want to be busy. I wanted to be busy too. None of us wanted a prolonged period of time to think about just how *gone* Fiona really was. "Do you mind if I come in?"

"Not at all, dear. Come in." Fiona's mom, Carol, stepped out of the way and let me in. I kicked my shoes on the small step into the house to rid them of any loose snow. I pushed them off my feet and followed Carol into the kitchen. Her house wasn't anything too different than Derek's or mine. All the houses in this town were basically the same.

"Is Brian around?"

"No, he's out shopping."

"I'll just put his coffee in a thermos." I opened a cupboard and pulled out a silver thermos. I took the lid off Brian's (Brian is Fiona's dad, by the way) coffee. I slowly poured the coffee, careful to only spill five drops on the counter. I mopped it up with my coat sleeve, fastened the lid back on the thermos and took my coat off and hung it around the backrest of a chair at the table.

"So what brings you around?"

"I wanted to grab some stuff from Fiona's room." Her name stung as it passed through my mouth.

My heart winced at the sound of it coming from my voice, like I had somehow betrayed myself by saying her name. It wasn't a bad word, not by any stretch. It was the best word, the most beautiful one I could ever hope to think of, and it pained me to know that I would never be able to speak it without being panged by hurt.

"Yeah." Carol nodded knowingly. "Take whatever you need. Whatever helps."

I gave her a small smile as I picked up my coffee. I turned and headed to Fiona's room upstairs, a set of stairs I had gone up so many times before, but a set of stairs that now felt more like a mountain, each step another one closer to a summit of disappointment.

I edged myself forward, each step seemingly taller than the

last. And then, finally, I was atop the stairs. A minute victory for me, but a victory nonetheless. I walked to the most familiar door in the hallway—Fiona's. I put my hand to the handle, even though the door was ajar, light seeping from her room and the window in it. I took a deep breath.

A deeper one.

And one more as I pushed the door open.

Her room was exactly as I expected it to be. There was a clean clutter everywhere. Clothes strewn on the floor. My painting of her from the other night when she had been playing *Spyro* and I had been watching her. Things were so much happier for me then.

If only, I thought, *I could just jump into the painting and go back to that moment. If only I could warn her, warn me. If only I could have a second chance at saving her, at loving her.* I felt a sting in the corner of my eyes. Tears, almost on cue, spilling over the edge of my tear ducts.

This isn't fair.

You're supposed to be *here.*

With me.

It should have been *me.*

I sat down in front of the painting and looked at it for longer than I should have. It wasn't like it was a good painting. It wasn't a work of art. There was nothing special about it to anybody but me. It was the last painting I would ever paint with colour, that much I know. When Fiona left, she took my colours with her.

A promise that I'll never love again, never see colour, never feel the warmth of the sun in the same way. But that's a promise everyone breaks, isn't it?

Colours retract for a short while, but nothing stays grey forever. Or does it? And what happens when you can't remember their face anymore? When the person you lost becomes a distant memory, a trace, a far-off echo? Then what? Do we move on? Is that when we finally let go of the weight that person shackled onto us when they passed? Or do we carry the

weight forever? Do colours stay faded forever?
Even here, in this room, so full of vibrancy.
Everything felt dull.
Felt nonexistent.
Felt like Fiona—

She was still here.
She has to be.
She can't just be *gone*.
I refuse to believe she's gone. She's just out studying, she'll be home soon. This has all just been one huge mean prank. We'll all laugh and I'll be pissed at her and her family and friends and be impressed at the lengths they took to pull one over on me. They'll apologize and say it was all in good fun. We'll have a few drinks. We'll laugh. The night will wear on. The colours of the sky will blend into the colours of her eyes and we'll unwrap each other of our clothes and fuck on her floor, the same floor where I now sit, staring at a painting of her—one where she looked more alive than ever before.
But that's fabricated.
That's a story.
She's gone.
She's beyond gone.
She's never coming back either.
She's *just gone*.
"Fuck you," I muttered. To myself. To the painting. To her. To the road. To the snow outside. To this room. To the world. I wiped some tears from my face and tried to remember how she had sounded that night.

"Hey, dork." She didn't even turn away from the TV screen to acknowledge that it was me in her room and not her mom or dad or whoever else it could have been.
"Hey." I walked over and sat on her bed next to her. "Why'd you want me to come over?"
She paused her game and turned to me and then wrapped her arms

around me and tightly hugged me. *"I missed you,"* she mumbled into my neck.
"*That's the reason you called me over?*"
She nodded. "*Problem?*"

And just like that, a wave of something indescribable swept over me. Something more than sadness, but not quite as desolate of a feeling. It was almost warm.
    I felt happy, almost, not quite fully. But I was happy to remember her so vividly, to remember the way she spoke to me, the way she smiled at me. I was so happy to have remembered.
    But sad.
    Sad because I might never again remember her this clearly.
    But of all the things I could ever forget about her, I know that the one thing I could never forget, that I would never *allow* myself to forget—her last words. Those words, spoken just minutes before she died, would remain etched into me so well and for so long that even my fossilized skeleton will be able to recite them to those that ask (and to those that don't).

"*I love you, Edwin. I love you so much. You are my light, my stars, my fresh pot of coffee. I love you.*"

Her words were an echo. They'll never be as clear as when she spoke them. It'll never be her voice that says any combination of those words ever again, but those words were hers. Those words were her last words. She'll never say anything more than that.
    But she can't really be gone, of course. I'm just being stupid. I'll wake up tomorrow and it'll be back to normal.
    I'll wake up in tears, covered in sweat, screaming about this dream in a frenzied panic as Fiona listens intently. But I've woken up several times since she *left*, and it hasn't been me waking up to that scene. It's just been me waking up to this new world that was minus Fiona.

I sighed.
I took a breath.
And another one.
And another.
And another.
And another.
And another.
And another.
And another.
And another.
And another.
And another.
And then I was sure I was awake.
I was alive.
I was awake.
I was existing.
Without her, I was existing.

And the colours betwixt the edges of the canvas reflected all my failures, every failure I ever made to Fiona—my failure to kiss her first, my failure to show up on time to our first date, my failure to save her life in any way close to the way she saved mine.

Part 2
Chapter 5

The Colour of Nostalgia

I packed away my stuff—the stuff of mine I took from Fiona's—into my closet. I wouldn't really say I packed it away, actually. What I did was closer to haphazardly stuffing things into positions where it wouldn't all collapse (I wish I could do the same thing with my life). I shut the closet door tightly. I should just clean my room and throw away things I have no use for, but in reality, I have no use for most of the shit in there. I just like to keep some stuff for its nostalgia factor.

I picked up my phone from my bed.

No notifications.

That was good. I guess my friends knew I wouldn't want to be bothered. I had taken off before they even woke up, so they'd have either blown up my phone with calls asking where

I ran off to, you know, to make sure I didn't go kill myself. I hear that's a thing that some people do after losing someone close to them—the pain gets too much and the weight of it all drags them down.

But they opted to believe that I just needed space—which is the truth... for a while anyway. At least they understood that sometimes to heal from emotional anguish, people need to be alone and overthink about things. Granted, too much alone time can be just as equally devastating as not having any. I'm walking a thin line here.

I dropped my phone back to my bed and looked around at my room. This small, cramped room that I don't think I've cleaned even once since I turned fifteen.

So maybe I should.

After seventeen minutes of rummaging through half-packed boxes of stuff like a cumbersome sorting robot, I pulled out a photo album and collapsed down onto my floor. I pushed the box away from my feet and set the album down on the ground. I had put this album in the box on Fiona and I's fifth anniversary. She had taken so many photos of us over the years.

The album was large, leather-bound, and dusty, so very dusty. I had never closed the box. I had always meant to add more albums. Below this album, several more (less dusty) albums sat, untouched for years. Those ones were just full of old family photos—road trips, camping, fairs, amusement parks, new pets, birthdays, graduation from elementary school, first days, last days, tears, my life before Fiona.

I opened the cover of the album and looked at the first photo. It was a vertical photo shot on her phone from the night of our first date. We were both smiling ridiculously wide. We must have been, what, 14 or so. Our faces were round, not yet defined by puberty. She had braces, freckles, a hairband pushing her hair back, and a white sundress. I had one of my dad's old button-ups that was far too big for me. I remembered that I had to tuck in so much shirt, and that I had to roll the sleeves up pretty far too. We looked so geeky, but we were happy. I smiled at the memory and it was almost like I was right back there.

She smiled brighter than I thought anyone ever could. She was ungodly amounts of beautiful. And even as she sat here in front of me, in the candlelight of the restaurant's table, I couldn't believe that she was really here, with me of all people.

"Is this what a date is supposed to be?" Fiona asked.

I shrugged. "I guess. I've never been on a proper one. My only experience with stuff like this is from movies and TV."

She smiled. "I suppose it doesn't matter either way, as long as we both enjoy it, right?"

"Right," I nodded.

A waitress stepped up to our table and smiled widely at each of us. "Can I get you guys some drinks to start?"

"Just water, please," we both replied. The water here came with a slice of lemon in it too. I swirled the ice and lemon with my straw and watched it spin. We ordered crab-stuffed mushrooms and cheese-covered garlic bread for our shareable appetizers.

When the waitress came back for our food orders, I ordered an eight-ounce steak with a twice-baked potato for my side. Fiona, being the pretentious little shit she was, ordered something weird. I think it was called quinoa arancini. *Fiona didn't know what she ordered, but it sounded fancy, so it must taste good.*

She's so beautiful. Her skin is glowing. She's a goddess. I'm literally the luckiest boy on earth to be on a date with her.

I'm so lucky. So, so lucky.

That was such a nice night. I can still remember loading up on cologne and triple-checking to make sure my hair looked nice. I was so nervous and she was so beautiful. I'd give anything to go back to that, to feel that rush of nervous energy all over again, to know where it would all lead.

I flipped through a few more pages of photos. I didn't want to get all caught up in nostalgia all night. I love each one of these photos, and I'd love to look at how happy we are in all of them, but there's only so much reminiscing I can take before the weight crushes me. I paused when I saw a very special photo.

It was a photo of her and I, lying in a bed. I was topless (I was actually naked, but you could only see the top of my chest to the top of my head), and she was wrapped up in a blanket. It was the night we lost our virginities.

My legs were on fire from pedalling so hard and fast and for so long. The hills of the country roads get pretty steep once you're out of the city, but it is quite nice to glide down the other side of the hills, also a little terrifying when you can't see if there's anything ahead of you that could send you tumbling into the gravel on the shoulder of the road.

"Fiona!" I shouted up at her. She slowed to a stop and looked over to me. I pulled to a stop next to her and took a minute to catch my breath. "How much further?"

"Ten more minutes," she replied. "Tops."

"Probably not an issue for you." I scoffed. "You got the lighter backpack." I fixed the positioning of the bag on my back and started pedalling again. Fiona, however, was faster at pedalling than I was, and she shot past me to keep leading the way to wherever it was she was taking me.

She opened her arms wide as I dropped my bike to the grass at our feet. "Ta-da!" Her voice seemingly rumbled through the forest and sky around us. I looked up and saw stars. I looked around and saw trees. I looked in front of Fiona and saw the lights of the city we had just biked away from. I looked to Fiona and saw my happiness.

"Now you have to help me set up the tent," I said, tossing my backpack to the ground. She pouted and unzipped my bag. We set up the tent in record time for two teenagers in the dark. Once inside, we set up a light to shine down on us so we could see. She unzipped her bag and pulled out two small pillow and a fleece blanket.

"Now"—she turned to me—"what do you wanna do first?"

You, I thought. "I dunno," I spoke.

She smiled. "Got anything cool in this bag of yours?" She grabbed my backpack before I could even react and then she was rifling through the smaller pockets. She gave me a wry smile and then pulled something out, something in a small square packaging.

"*It's just in case,*" *I blurted out.*

"*Somebody thought they were getting lucky tonight, huh?*" *She twirled the condom in her fingers a little.* "*I was thinking of something similar, which is why I was smart and put myself on birth control a few months back.*"

"*You did?*"

She nodded and tossed the condom aside. "*Come on, Edwin, you don't really think you have a say in when you get to fuck me, do you? I get the say. The girl always gets the say. You have to physically penetrate my body, therefore, I get the say. And I said many months ago that I did want you to fuck me, just not right away. I wanted to wait until I was ready, but I got on the pill just in case, and so that I could be ready for when I was ready.*"

"*And, um, uh, y-you're— you think you're ready now?*"

She nodded. "*Oh, yeah.*" *;)*

I smiled softly. I remember that night. How could I forget it? That was the night that Edwin the Boy became Edwin the Man. She took that picture after our breathing returned to normal. Once we took the picture, we shut the light off for the night and talked for a few hours until falling asleep, curled into one another.

Her skin was so soft, every inch of it. I just remember that I couldn't get enough of it. I wanted to drink her in, soak her up, breathe in every particle she exuded.

I shook her out of my head.

No more of those thoughts.

I want nothing more than her.

Right now, I need her.

I could feel tears welling in the corners of my eyes, but I wasn't going to just sit here and cry, no matter how much I miss her right now, no matter how much I need her to just come up and sit down next to me and kiss my cheek and hold my hand, no matter how much I need her to make me feel okay.

I shut my eyes and flipped to a new photo and let out a small laugh. It was a picture of me, holding up a boom box in Fiona's yard. This was taken after our first major fight, the first fight we had that involved screaming and crying.

I pushed the slider to ON, but nothing happened. It wouldn't turn on, no matter how much I pleaded for it to just work. This stupid two-bit boom box. I knew I should have just gotten an iPod and a speaker. I pulled the cover off the back and pulled the batteries out and replaced them for the fourth time.

I swear to God, if I have to spend one more minute behind this bush, I might just go insane. And then the boom box crackled to life. It was soft, it was barely audible (because I had the volume set low), but it worked. I turned the volume up and listened to the soothing sounds of Death Cab for Cutie.

I took a few deep breaths and then willed myself to pick up the boom box and walk across the street to Fiona's house. I walked across the yard, reached into my pocket, pulled out some pebbles I had collected earlier, and then I hurled them in a frenzy to her window. I quickly picked up the boom box and switched to the song that was our song. *Death Cab for Cuties'* I Will Follow You into the Dark *began playing as Fiona opened her window.*

I smiled up at her and she rolled her eyes at me. "What are you doing here?" *she called down.*

"Apologizing," *I replied. The music wasn't loud enough to obscure us from talking.* "I'm so sorry. I'm a total asshole. Let me make it up to you."

She rolled her eyes a little less noticeably this time.

"Please," *I said.* "I love you, Fiona. I don't want to lose you over something so stupid."

"You're playing our song," *she noted.* "The one we were listening to when we first kissed."

I nodded. "Yeah."

"You're pretty cute, Flowers."

"Say it to my face." *I smirked. She closed her window and came down. She kissed me and we made up in the only way star-crossed lovers knew how—fucking until her parents pulled into the driveway.*

I can't even remember what the fight was about. All these years that I've been with her, we've had one fight that almost tore us asunder, and I can't even remember what it was that brought it to that point. I suppose it doesn't matter because we worked things out in the end.

I flipped to a new picture and looked it over. It was a picture of Fiona in the driver seat of her car. I was in the passenger seat, leaning over on her and making a goofy face. This was the day we went and got her car. She was so excited about being able to drive around on her own.

But then another picture caught my attention.

It was a picture of Fiona in bed with a cloth on her forehead and a thermometer in her mouth. She had been really sick that night and I made her pose with the thermometer to make it *look* like she was sick. I guess she got me hooked on capturing stupid little moments to reminisce about.

I rushed into Fiona's room and closed the door behind me. I was biting down on a wet cloth with my teeth and carrying a bowl of soup, a cup of peppermint tea, and a thermometer in my hands. I set the soup and tea down on a small bedside table that I had pulled closer to her. I set the cloth on her head and smiled at her as I gave her the thermometer.

"You're taking my temperature?" she asked. She looked at the thermometer and turned it in her fingers.

I nodded. "I just wanna make sure your fever isn't bad. High fevers could be dangerous."

"I feel fine," she mumbled.

"You don't look fine," I said, pushing some hair out of her face and flipping the cloth for her. I took the thermometer from her hand and put the end in her mouth. "Hey, stay like that for a moment."

"What are you doing?"

"Documenting." I stood up and walked to the other side of her room and picked up her camera bag. I pulled the camera out and walked over to the bed. The light from her TV was good enough for a quick photo.

She groaned. "Edwin, stop. I look like shit."

"You feel *like shit," I corrected her. "Smile." I smiled behind the*

camera and she looked up at me as I clicked the button. I set the camera back in its bag and then smiled at her. "You look beautiful, trust me."

"Just promise me something," she muttered. *She rolled her eyes a little as she looked over to me.*

"Yeah, anything."

"Promise me you will never show anyone that picture of me, ever. Seriously. Never."

I nodded. "Anything else?"

"Yeah," she said. "If I die before you, you have to burn that picture. I don't want that thing living a day longer than I do."

"Sorry," I whispered, "but I can't burn this photo. I need every memory of you." I smiled a little as I flipped the page. Fiona might be mad at me for not burning the photo, but I know some part of her would be happy that I'm keeping it. I shut my eyes for a moment as I closed the photo album, letting myself wallow in the nostalgia for just a moment more.

The colours betwixt the past and the present blurred together to form an incoherent string of tearful memories, each one making me long for her more than the last.

Part 2
Chapter 6

The Refresh

My face was on fire. The heater was blasting hot air right at my face, but I didn't care. It was freezing outside and the warmth was welcome. I loved my car's heating system (because it actually worked). And that's about where my love affair ends. Most cars are the same to me, nothing more than a way to get around, but cars with heating and A/C systems that work are unequivocally better than cars with either of the aforementioned systems not working.

Which brings me to today.

I was driving out of town to check and see if this one old red muscle car was still for sale (don't bother with the make and model, I've never been good with remembering car names). Fiona had seen it once and swore she wanted a car just like it. I jokingly said I'd buy it for her, but now I wanna go see how much it's worth because, well, I might buy it for *me*.

I had been saving up for a while now to get a new car anyway, but I was looking into something new, not pre-owned, so I'm sure I'll have enough to buy this old car that's been sitting on a driveway for God only knows how long.

I parked my car across the street and walked over to get a better look at the car. It was freshly refurbished. The interior was completely redone (because there ain't no way that a car from the '70s would look that good without work). The red paint on the outside had been completely redone as well, and by the looks of it, it was all done fairly recently.

There was a sign in the window with a number in it. I pulled my phone out and dialled it. It rang a few times and then a woman answered the call. "Hello."

"Hi, I'm calling about the car you're selling," I told her, looking up the long-enough-to-be-a-road driveway at the house. I imagined whomever was on the phone would be walking to look out the window and see my shape in the distance.

"Are you outside now?"

"Yeah. I stopped by to get a look at the car."

"Okay." She paused and shuffled something around. "I'll be out in just a moment."

I switched every couple seconds between watching the driveway and the road where a few cars would drive by once and a while. The lady who had answered the call, I assume, appeared down the length of the driveway, walking up to me. She seemed fairly old, definitely post-50.

"Would you believe that you're the first person that's called?" the lady asked. She was elderly alright. Greying hair that once could have been a shimmering brown. Her smile was bright still though. Her hair was tied back and she was wearing a wool cardigan.

"I would not," I replied to her as she got closer. I noticed her bright, popping blue eyes.

"Smart kid." She smiled. "So what brings you all the way out here to look at a car?"

"My girlfriend wanted this car. She saw it sometimes when we would drive to and from our trailers or cottages."

The lady nodded and looked around, like she wanted to see if I brought the aforementioned girlfriend, which I would have, but coffins are far too heavy for me to carry alone.

"So why are you selling it?" I asked, trying to escape the silence that had settled in around us. Not that it was awkward, just that I came here intent on buying the car.

"It's my husband's car. He just finished fixing it up, but he can't drive it. He can't see very well anymore, so he isn't allowed to drive, but he loves tinkering with cars," she explained. "I had to talk him up to selling them. We just sold an old Jeep last month."

"How much are you asking for it?" I asked.

"Ten." She eyed me down, knowing a kid like me would most likely not have ten grand lying around for a car.

I exhaled sharply. "Well, I have five on me. Can we do five?"

"I'll go as low as eight," she said.

"I can give you seven and a half."

She half-frowned. "You got yourself a deal, then. I've had all kinds of people not willing to go higher than four."

"I really do only have five on me though." I pouted a little. "What if you give me the paperwork and I'll come back with the rest when I come get the key?"

She hesitated for a moment to think it over. "You seem trustworthy enough."

"Just a sec," I told her. I walked back to my car and pulled out a small envelope from my glove compartment. I walked back and handed it to her. "Five thousand in fifties."

She took it and counted it as she walked back to her house. She motioned for me to follow her, and so I did. She lived in a typical farmhouse, nothing too out of the ordinary. She went inside for a couple minutes and then re-emerged with a folder of papers. "Ownership, proof of your purchase, car facts, make and model information. Everything you need to know about the car is right here." She handed the folder to me and smiled. "You can come back a week from now. I'll be home then. Same time too. Makes it easier on both of us."

I nodded. "Of course. Have a nice rest of your day." I smiled at her and turned around.

"You too," she called out as I walked away. I headed back out to my car. I got in and started my car up, looking over at the other car that would soon be mine. I smiled a little, remembering Fiona always gawking at the car as we drove by it.

We rounded the curve and we were officially out of city limits, off into the sunrise, the golden hues swamping over the horizon, lighting up the dirt on my windshield.

"Edwin," Fiona beamed, "did you see that car?"

I glanced over at her and saw her rubbernecking behind us. "Nah, I missed it. What was it?"

"I dunno, but it was gorgeous," she told me. "And, best part, it was for sale."

"Is it the red one that's been sitting on the the edge of the driveway for the past few weeks?" I asked.

She huffed at me and pouted. "You knew about this for weeks?"

I shrugged. "Yeah, I mean, I've driven past it before."

"Why didn't you tell me?!"

"I didn't know you'd want another car."

"Yeah, 'cause I wanna drive around in a sedan my whole life." She scoffed. "Come on, Edwin."

"I need a new car, not you."

"So buy that car for me and you can have mine." She pushed her seat back and put her bare feet on the dash. "Think you could avoid the potholes? I wanna redo my nail polish."

"You brought nail polish with you?"

"Yessir," she said, fishing a small bottle from her purse.

I smiled softly and glanced over at her. I love this girl so much, beyond reasonable understanding. Fiona, Fiona, my happy ending. "Why didn't you just paint them before we left?" I asked as I eyed her trying to delicately apply a fresh coat of nail polish to one of her toes. It really is an art form sometimes, this nail-polish-applying thing.

"*Because some jackass woke me up early to go and get breakfast with him.*"
I smirked. "*Oh, right. Forgot.*"
"*Pfft.*" *And with that, she went back to focusing on colouring inside the lines.*

My lungs were going to collapse, that much I was sure of. Riding uphill was the worst part of biking anywhere. My legs were tired and the tires kept slipping in the slush (because slush never really goes away in the winter, it's always there). My backpack was riding up my back and bunching my shirt under my coat, which made the whole ride quite uncomfortable.

I dropped my bike in a ditch beside the house where the car was. I walked up to the door and knocked. The upper-middle-aged lady answered the door. "I'm here for the car," I told her.

She smiled a little. "Of course." She stepped inside and turned to me. "You can come in if you'd like. I just made a pot of tea, you're more than welcome to have a cup."

"Uh, sure, that'd be nice. Thanks." I stepped inside and closed the door. Nearly instantly I was awash in warmth and of the smell of farmhouse. You know the smell. If you've ever been to a house in the country, they have a certain *smell* to them. I can't pinpoint it, but it's distinct enough to be noticeable. I followed the lady into her kitchen and sat down at the table with her.

"So are you buying the car as a gift to your girlfriend?" the lady asked me as she poured me a cuppa. I watched the steam rise out of my cup.

"Oh, no. I'm buying it for me."

"Sorry. You just mentioned last week that your girlfriend wanted the car." The lady smiled at me.

"She did," I said, mixing in some sugar to my tea. I could tell I confused the lady with that answer.

"Does she not want it anymore?"

"You could say that," I said. I paused a mixed some milk into my tea. I gave a quick smile to the lady. "My girlfriend passed away recently. That's all."

"I'm sorry, I shouldn't have been prying."

"It's okay." I chuckled a bit at her getting flustered over it. "You didn't know. No harm." I pulled my backpack around and pulled out an envelope. "I have the rest of the cash here for the car." I outstretched my hand to the lady.

She eyed my hand and the envelope and then pushed it away. "You keep it."

"Are you sure?"

She nodded. "Yeah. Just make sure you take good care of it. My husband would lose it if he saw you wreck that car after the hours he put into it."

"I can promise you that I'll look after it." I stuffed the envelope back into my backpack.

The lady pulled a keychain from her pocket. A key, a small coin, and a key fob. "My husband wanted to modernize the car a bit. It has electronic locks." She handed the keys to me.

I smiled and looked at the coin that was tied to the keychain by a small piece of string. One side was engraved with the outline of an owl head, the other side was engraved with the outline of a fox head. An owl and a fox, two beautiful little woodland creatures. "So what's with the owl-and-fox coin?"

"Owls and foxes are wise creatures, very clever." She smiled. "It's to help remind you to keep your wits, no matter what hour of the night it is."

"That so?" I looked it over. It was old, but it might just need a polish or two.

"My husband and his friends got them made years and years ago. My husband had a bunch of extras, so he sometimes gives them away, attaches them to things and whatnot."

I sat and drank tea and listened to this lady talk about her husband for at least an hour more. It was nice. I like listening to people sometimes. The world is full of self-centred people,

people who only listen for their turn to talk, instead of listening to hear what other people are actually saying. So after two cups of tea, I was on my way into the cold day. I got in my new car and drove home. My parents were pretty impressed, impressed enough to denote the car a steal. Which it was. Five grand for a fully refurbished classic muscle car? Fucking *steal*.

And then it was off to sleep.

Tomorrow was a new day.

Another day to live.

Another day without Fiona.

Another day the colours betwixt ever so slowly fade away.

Part 2
Chapter 7

The Colour of Depression

All there ever is these days to do is think. Think about this and think about that and think about Fiona and how I want her back. It's all bullshit. It's repetitive. It's stupid. It's senseless. It's all worthless, not worthwhile in any way. I can think about her all I want, but no amount of thinking can bring her back. I can pray (regardless of faith or how religious I may or may not be) and nothing will change.

It's all fucking empty.

It's all fucked up.

My fist was still balled up in the hole I had punched into the back wall of my closet. *That's nine*, I thought to myself as I looked at the other holes I had punched over the years.

The realization was finally hitting me. Maybe because I

didn't have anyone to hang out with today or anything to go and do, so I had nothing to do but think. So the realization swept in like a current and washed me away.

And nobody ever plans to be depressed or to have a panic attack, but all of a sudden you can't breathe. You're on the floor with a tear-soaked face, begging for the hurt to stop, but you don't even know what's hurting.

You cry.
You beg.
You cry some more.
You beg for it to stop.
It never does.
It just gets worse.

You start to blame yourself, you blame the world, you ask the ceiling what the fuck it expects you to do. You explain to the empty room that you did your best, that you're still trying. You sob on the floor about how it's not fair and how you should be better than you are, but nothing changes. It just leaves you feeling exhausted.

It sweeps in.
It takes you over.
It destroys you.

And then it leaves, with the door wide open; all of your questions unanswered, unheard, unvalidated.

My eyes were clammy, drowned in tears. My mind was foggy, clouded in sadness. My fist was throbbing. I had hit a stud on the first punch.

Fuck you, Fiona. Fuck you for not staying alive. Fuck you for letting me live while you died.

It's not fair that either of us should have to live without the other, to lose one of us is to lose half of who we were. It's not fair. I did everything right. I loved her and treated her like gold. Sure, we'd fight sometimes, but dammit if that isn't just a part of being human.

I'm not sure I'm really ready to accept this new reality, the one without Fiona. I don't have to either. There's no one around to stop me from taking too many pills or driving my car into an oncoming truck. But that's stupid, of course, because there's no guarantee that killing myself would fix anything for me, and it certainly wouldn't fix anything for my friends and family.

I gritted my teeth and slunk to the floor. A sobbing mess, I've become. How did I ever let myself think for even a minute that I could hold this back? Was I stupid enough to think that I could just deny her death for the rest of my life? Was I really that naïve?

Maybe I was. I at least hoped I could have been. But I'm not stupid. I'm not naïve. It just took a moment of silence, a moment of still, a moment to reflect, a moment to call her phone even though I know she wasn't going to answer.

And why did I call her?

Because humans are habitual creatures. I called Fiona because that's what I'd do any other time I was bored and wanted to go do something. Derek and Marshall are off at work. My other friends aren't close enough to me to hang out with on such short notice. Fiona was always there though. So it was habit, and that habit was what made me realize that she's really gone, for good. There is no bargaining, praying, or pleading to get her back; she's gone, eternally gone.

The tears stung as they flowed out. I shut my eyes as tight as I could, but the tears found their way out, seeping through my eyelids if that's what it took. My face was now the world's saddest waterfall.

I shut my eyes tighter.

Tighter than I ever have before.

I balled my fists. Tore at my hair.

My throat dried.

I began walking without a clue where I was heading. I began running a bath, letting the bathtub fill up with water. I wiped away the tears that remained on my face.

For a moment, things were calm. I focused on the sound of the water filling in the tub, collapsing and splashing in on itself. A metaphor for my life, to be honest. Once the bathtub was full of water I closed my eyes again.

A deep breath.
And another.
And another.
And another.
And another.
And another.
And another.
And another.
And another.
And another.
And another.
And another.
And another.

I dropped to my knees and grabbed the edge of the tub and lowered my head into the water, eyes still tightly closed. I let out the most powerful scream that I could, the water erupting into bubbles around me from the air I was exhausting.

She placed her hand on my back. It was warm, always was. I turned and looked up at her. She smiled back at me. She rubbed my back in small little circles until I turned around and sat back on the cold tile of her bathroom floor.

I wiped my face and sighed. "I feel better."

"I'd hope so," Fiona said. She scooted over to the toilet and made a disgusted face before flushing it. "At least you made it to the toilet."

I pulled my head out of the water and took a deep breath, deeper than I needed to. I grabbed a towel and patted my face and dried my hair. I leaned against the wall and let out a sigh. Of all the memories to remember, why would I remember her flushing my vomit down the toilet?

Whatever. I won't even pretend like I know what's going on with my head these days. All I know is that my head hurts and that I'm tired. I drained the tub and walked back to my room. I jumped into my bed and stared at the ceiling. My eyes grew heavier. Then there was a cozy silence. And then nothing.

And then suddenly, I was awake again. I was in a car. I turned my head to the left and saw Fiona sitting in the driver's seat. Had I nodded off? Had her death been a dream? Fuck. I really need to get a regular sleep cycle. I feel like I'm perpetually tired and always nodding off at shitty times lately. I sit upright and sniffle to clear my nose.

"'Bout time you woke up," Fiona said once she noticed me moving around.

"Sorry. Are we almost there?"

"Another twenty minutes or so, tops."

I let out a quiet sigh. Maybe the past few weeks had been a dream. Maybe this was real life. Or was I tricking myself. "Where are we going, anyway?"

"Cottage," she said. "We've had it planned since last year. You know, the annual cottage getaway thing we do. Is your memory slipping? You're too young for dementia, Edwin."

I nodded. "Right, sorry. Just disoriented. I'm still half asleep."

"More like fully." Fiona pulled the car to a stop at a stop sign. "Get it together, babe."

"Sorry. Just gimme some caffeine and I'll be A-okay."

"Ha," she laughed. "You're not getting my last energy drink."

I looked in the back seat and poked around for a bag. My hand found the plastic bag behind my chair. I pulled it onto my lap and pulled out an energy drink. "Looks like I have one left anyway." I knew this one was mine. She doesn't like this flavour, and there's another one in the bag of a kind she likes.

"Hmm, lucky you, then."

I cracked the can open and took a sip. "Yeah, lucky me indeed." I looked out the window and up to the sky. It was bright outside for nighttime even though the moon was well away from view behind a far-reaching cloud cover. I turned back to Fiona. "Hey, how long was I out for?"

Fiona shrugged. "Couple hours, I dunno. I wasn't really paying attention to you napping. Trying to drive, so…"

"Yeah, you're right. Sorry. Why'd you even let me fall asleep?"
"Have you ever met a tired version of you?" Fiona asked. *"You turn into such a brat, you're so whiny."*
"Yeah, again, you're right." I looked out the window. "Sorry."
"I can forgive you if you feed me some of that beef jerky we have."
"We have beef jerky?"
She nodded. "In the bag you got your drink from."
"Didn't see it." I reached into the back and grabbed the bag. Sure enough, there was a bag of beef jerky in the plastic bag. I pulled it out and opened it. I took a piece out and bit some off before sticking the rest in Fiona's mouth. Her teeth were pearly white and her lips, just the perfect shade of soft pink that made you think nothing else but how it would feel to have them pressed against yours. (For the record, it's warm and soft and she tastes nice and smells good. It sends fireworks through the entirety of my body and soul.)
"Ahh!" She groaned. "I fucking love teriyaki beef jerky."
"So where are we going again?"
"Cottage." She raised a hand to me and snapped her fingers for another piece of jerky. I pulled one out and gave it to her. "You really gotta try to remember things. I've told you eighty times."
"Pretty sure I've only asked once or twice." I took a bite of jerky. "I'm just sleepy. It didn't stick." I sighed. Cottage. We're going to the cottage. I can remember that, sure. Too tired, Edwin, I thought. That's all, you're just too tired.
"Have any dreams about me?" she asked.
I shrugged. "Can't remember. Sorry."
"You just woke up." She sighed. "Whatever. You suck."
"I know, I know."
"So I was just thinking, and brace yourself a little because it's morbid, but your life is in my hands."
I cocked an eyebrow. "How so?"
"Because I am the driver of your life," she replied. "Think about it. I'm driving you literally right now, but I'm the reason you do a lot of what you do. You do a lot for me, with me, or because of me. Without me, who would drive *you?"*
"I would," I said, feeling mildly offended that she would be implying I can't find my way without her.

"Or would you find another driver?"

"No. I would drive myself."

Fiona shook her head. "Not how it works. Nobody drives themselves. We all need someone to push, someone to guide. We can't live on our own. That's just not how it works."

"But I can be just fine. I'm independent enough to get by without you."

"Sure," she said, "if that's what you'd call getting by."

"Why are you going on about this?"

"I'm worried about you."

I paused a minute and thought about what to say next. "Why are you worried about me?"

"Because what if something happens to me and I'm not around?" she asked. "I wanna know you'd be okay, and I hope you would be, but I just don't think you would be. You'd be lost, confused. I just don't think you'd be able to drive yourself."

"I think I'd be able to."

She turned and smiled at me. "We'd better find out, then, huh?" She reached over and unbuckled my seat belt. I tried to tell her to stop, but no words passed my lips, they got caught on something intangible in my throat. I grabbed at the seat belt, but my hand refused to grip it. I turned back to Fiona... and watched helplessly. The car sped up and sped up and she closed her eyes, gently guiding the car into the oncoming lane, in which there was a large truck barrelling towards us.

And then a moment of impact...

I was back in my room, blackness all around me. It must be well into the night. There weren't any sounds from anywhere in the house or outside. The world was calm.

The colours betwixt my room were muted and black.

Part 2
Chapter 8

The Colour of Fiona

Fixed my hair? Check. Shaved face? Check. Brushed teeth? Check. Cleaned bathroom sink? Check. Morning pee? Check. Washed hands? Check. Pants? Check. T-shirt? Check. Socks on feet? Check. Checked weather? Check. Jacket? Check. Keys and wallet? Check. Shoes? Check. Phone in pocket? Check.

 I find that checklists really helped alleviate the laziness and unmotivated-ness that depression had cast upon me lately. Before I made lists to get ready, I wouldn't even get out of bed until late afternoon, likely giving myself five minutes to get ready to leave for class or work.

 Today I was off to Fiona's house. I wanted to go over and get some of *her* things, stuff to remember her, stuff that she cared deeply for. I don't want her parents to just let these rot in boxes in a storage unit somewhere, unsure of what to do with them. Who knows, maybe I'll find some cool photos in some of her books that I've forgotten about.

Her house hasn't changed since I was here last, not that I was expecting it to. The Christmas lights were down though, that was the only change. I parked my car in front of the house on the side of the road. I walked up and knocked on the door.

The door opened and Carol, Fiona's mom, looked me over. "Fancy seeing you here."

"That's why I called yesterday," I said as I stepped inside. "I like to give heads-up when I can."

"Well, I'm going out shopping, so don't wreck up the place while I'm out."

I turned and gave her a playful smirk. "No promises."

"Phoebe should be back soon too, so don't get all worked up if you hear someone making noise." Carol shuffled around her purse, assumingly making sure she had everything she needed. "And if anything comes up, just call me."

"Sure thing, *Mom*," I taunted. "I'll be fine. Get outta here."

"Yeah, sorry." She opened the door and smiled at me. "I'll see you when I get back if you're still here."

I closed the door behind her and watched through the window as she walked to her car, got in, started it up, and drove off down the street. I turned and let out a sigh. I don't think I've ever been alone in Fiona's house before. Even on times when her parents were out and she would run off to the store for fifteen minutes, Phoebe was still around, but not today. It was weird, to say the least.

I headed to the kitchen and pulled an energy drink from the door and then made my way upstairs to Fiona's room. It was barer than before. All her clothes had been bagged and donated to either her sister, Phoebe, or a charity. The bigger pieces of furniture (like her desk and dresser) were left empty, everything from them in boxes stacked in the corner.

The room felt different now, like I was *inside* a memory of Fiona. Everything was seemingly tinged in hues of sunshine yellow or lilac. Standing in the middle of her room and looking around felt like a tsunami of emotions from all sides, everything sucked out from underneath me just to be thrown back down on top.

I exhaled and cracked open my energy drink as I wondered where to start with everything of Fiona's that was left. I pulled the boxes out to the centre of the room and opened one of them. Inside was a collection of magazines. There were magazines from every facet of her life; magazines about toys, about sports, about celebrities. I could still imagine her sitting and reading these magazines on sunny days on her back patio, another thing she can never do again.

I pushed the box to the side, it wasn't that important to me. It's just a bunch of old magazines about stuff I was never really a fan of. The next few boxes were books from the feel of how heavy they were. I pushed them to the side. I'm taking the books with me. They all shaped Fiona in some way, so they could do the same for me.

I pulled a box over and opened it up. It was full of souvenir-type things. Postcards from trips to places out of the region that the two of us had gone on. Niagara Falls, New Brunswick, Montreal, Halifax, Algonquin, Yellowknife, Whitehorse. There were pictures that never found their way into our albums. A picture of her in front of a totem pole. A picture of her holding a fish (somewhere in Manitoba). A picture of her walking in a creek near her aunt's house just outside of Saint John, New Brunswick.

Poking around, I found more photos, enough photos to fill a small album. I stacked them and put them in a box of books to keep them straighter than they would end up if I left them in the souvenir box. There wasn't a lot in the souvenir box that I wanted to keep. It was full of things that were sentimental to

Fiona and no one else, and maybe that should be reason enough to keep some of the things, but it feels asinine to hoard things that have no value outside of her mind.

I pulled a box over and sifted through a bunch of notebooks, doodles and stuff. These are things that her parents would like to keep. I looked for school notes (she kept notes that she passed around in class). I found them and stuffed them into a binder to add to the pile of stuff I would take with me. Notes she passed around, her words written by her hand. I refuse to forget her.

And then finally came a box I was dreading, but one I knew I had to go through eventually. I pulled it over to me, not even needing to open it to know what was inside. It was the lightest box of them all, only a few small books inside, but it's what was inside the books that made this box the heaviest.

Journals. Seven small books outlining the major and important-to-her events of her past seven years of life. I sat on the carpet and leaned against Fiona's bed as I pulled the journals out of the box. The older ones would be safer to read, but the newer ones are the ones that hide all those secrets that she couldn't tell anyone. Anything could be in them. I was holding in my hands a secret guide to Fiona, a guide she would never have wanted anyone to see, ever, under any circumstances. And it was at this point that the room grew heavy and tense with the weight of intrigues. I know I shouldn't, but the curiosity was overwhelming.

A sudden janky noise from the hall made me shoot my gaze over to the doorway. I saw Phoebe waddling into view with a large gym bag. She looked over and dropped the bag. "Well, if it isn't the good man Edwin."

"Hey, Phoebe," I said as she walked over to the room. I set the journal down next to me. "How was the game?"

She shrugged as she walked into the light of the room. "It was okay, I guess." Phoebe was just as beautiful as Fiona or Carol. And Phoebe was a spitting image of Fiona, down to the way her face formed expressions. They could almost be twins except that Phoebe is much more toned than Fiona was. Fiona was slim and agile from volleyball, but Phoebe was denser and more physically built because she plays rugby, and she puts in work to stay in shape. She was in her rugby uniform still, I could see some pretty sizeable grass and dirt stains on her shirt. Also to be noted is that Phoebe is sixteen, Fiona's baby sister.

"Did you win?" I asked as Phoebe came over and sat down next to me.

She scoffed. "Yeah, duh. I'm on the team, aren't I?" She smirked at me. "So how are you? I feel like I haven't seen you in ages, man." Her voice was also deeper than Fiona's, huskier, I guess.

"Keeping busy," I told her. "What about you? Get up to anything cool?"

"Pffffffttftftft. Nope."

"Sounds about the same as everyone else lately."

Phoebe nodded. "Yeah. You're looking good though. Shaved and clean for once."

I chuckled. "Yeah, you're right." Light ribbing is normal between the two of us.

"So what brought you out here today? You've had a couple weeks to pop by and put yourself through this torture," Phoebe state. "Why today all of a sudden?"

I shrugged. "It just felt like it was time."

"Can't fault you for that."

"I could though. I've been feeling worse lately than at first."

Phoebe rested a hand on my thigh. "That, my good man Edwin, is because the longer something sits, the more of an impression it makes. Like a chair on carpet."

"You got that right." I sighed a little and took a sip of my energy drink. I don't feel any more energized than before I opened it. False advertising at its best.

"You want another drink or something?" Phoebe asked.

"You're too young to drink."

She slapped my arm. "Dumbass. Do you want me to go

make you a coffee or grab you another energy drink?"

"Coffee would be nice," I said. "Thanks."

"I knew you'd say that. I turned the coffee pot on before even coming up."

"How'd you know I was here?" I asked her as she stood up.

"Saw your car out front." She walked out of the room and then downstairs. I heard her footsteps fade away as she made her way to the kitchen. Within a few minutes, Phoebe came back upstairs with two cups of coffee in hand. She sat down and set a cup next to me. "It's still quite hot so be careful." She blew on hers before taking a small, slurping sip.

"Thanks," I said, doing the same.

"Is the coffee okay?" she asked.

I nodded. "Why wouldn't it be?"

"I always feel like I put too much sugar or too much creamer in it, that's all." She took another sip and grimaced slightly. She gazed over at me and raised her eyebrows at me. "Are you sure it's okay?"

"Yes, it's great. Thank you. Stop worrying so much. It's just coffee."

"Pfft." She took another sip and set the cup down. "It's weird that she's gone. Now that it's sort of settled in me that she *is* gone, it just feels weird. It's like losing a tooth or something, right, just takes time to get used to the new emptiness."

"It's weirder to spend time with you when she's not around."

Phoebe chuckled. "I guess you're right, we never really hung out without her."

"Nope."

"Don't make it weird, bro."

"Too late, it's weird." I took a sip of my coffee and sighed, resting my head back on the bed behind us.

"Are you doing anything tomorrow around noon?" Phoebe asked, sipping at her coffee, which was still steaming far too much for it to be drinkable, at least to her.

"Um, nope, don't think so. Why?"

"I was just wondering if you'd wanna take little old me to lunch."

I shrugged. "Can't see why not. Gets me out of the house at least."

"Yeah. That's the spirit."

"So why do you wanna get lunch with me though?" I asked her.

Phoebe sighed. "I dunno, man. You're the only person from Fiona's life that I actually liked having around. I don't wanna lose you just because she's gone. Like I said, I like you. You're cool and helpful and treat me like I'm not just a high schooler, which is nice."

"You're welcome… I guess."

"No, I mean it. You were nice to me when everyone else older than me treated me like I was just a kid."

"You were just a kid." I took a sip of coffee. "Are we forgetting that you were ten when I first met you?"

She shook her head. "No, not what I meant. I know I *was* a kid, but kids don't like being treated like kids, especially when they're trying to grow up and be a big kid."

"Fair point."

"Yeah." Phoebe stood up and sighed. "I suppose I should leave you to whatever it was you were doing. I have an essay to finish anyway."

"And a date tomorrow at noon."

"Yeah, can't forget about that. I'll meet you at that Italian place on River."

I nodded. "Sounds good to me." I watched Phoebe walk out of the room, cup of coffee in her hand, which reminded me of my own cup of coffee. I took a drink and swished it around my mouth for a few seconds. Not good for the teeth, but it's not like I really cared. I brushed twice a day, and sometimes I even flossed.

After I finished my coffee, I packed up all the things of Fiona's that I wanted to keep to remember her by. I kept her journals too, lest they fall into the wrong hands. I want her thoughts to be kept safe. I can stick them in the bottom of the box with our photo albums; the box *of* her—physically and mentally.

    I made my way home and put her things away in boxes and shelved them in my closet. I left the albums and journals box on the floor. I wanna add more to it, but I don't wanna have to move a bunch of other boxes out of the way first. I made another cup of coffee, this time in one of my own mugs, and then retreated back to my room. I turned the lights off, sat on my floor, and sipped my coffee until I was halfway finished and it had gotten far too cold to be enjoyable.

    I put the coffee down and sighed. The colours betwixt the lips of this mug reminded me so much of Fiona's eyes, a light and hidden brown, so lost to the world.

Part 2
Chapter 9

The Girl in the Stone

The ground was wet and damp with the fading memory of a snow that had come and melted. I looked over the etching of Fiona's name in the grey stone that stood over the spot where she laid. The daylight was fading fast and I knew I didn't wanna be in a cemetery too late into the night.

And so I began to dig a little hole in the spot where Fiona was buried. I had watched them lower her casket right in this very spot not that long ago, and the ground was still loose enough that digging wasn't as strenuous as I thought, even though it was damp dirt, which is heavier than dry dirt, I guess.

My hands were covered in dirt by the time I made the hole deep enough to be satisfied with it. I pulled over the box I had brought with me from behind me.

Inside the box were several small Fiona-esque items that I thought should have been buried with her, but generally people aren't buried with material items anymore, so none of these things were put in her casket. I took them from her room earlier in the day because I thought she should be united with them again. (And no, the hole isn't deep enough to see the casket or anything, it's not even a foot deep.)

I pulled out a small locket. I had gotten this particular locket for Fiona a few years ago, one she usually kept close to her at all times. For whatever reason, she loved it so much. It's just got a picture of us from our first anniversary date inside of it. It's gold and in the shape of a heart because when you're young, every cliché is beautiful and new and wonderful and gets your heart racing.

I put the locket into the ground and moved onto the next item. It was a 1967 bobcat nickel (Canadian) quarter. It's a very rare coin and was given to her by her grandfather before he passed away. Before that, it was her grandfather's most prized possession, so that's why it became one of hers.

The next item was a pair of socks. They had foxes and owls on them and were navy blue with a red ankle and red toes. It was slightly fuzzy to the feel and very soft. They were her sick day socks and her winter day socks and her "I just want my feet to be as cozy as can be" socks. I put them in the ground on top of the coin and locket. And I muttered an apology for letting them get all dirty. Fiona would have killed me if she saw me doing this to them.

I grabbed a book from the box. It was a copy of *If I Stay*, by Gayle Forman. It's her favourite book. She read it for the first time a year or two ago and since then has read it at least once a month. And so, I put the book in the ground to be with her and the rest of her things.

There were other items in the box I had brought too. Not as sentimental, but some of her favourite things. I brought a coffee cup from her favourite coffee shop. I brought her a chocolate bar because it was her favourite kind and a can of her favourite pop. I brought her a small packet of sugar (because when she was younger she would just eat packets of sugar like they were just candy). I brought a small paintbrush so she would remember me. And a hockey puck to remember Derek. And I brought a PEZ dispenser for her to remember Marshall (long story, but it involves a Secret Santa). And I settled all these things into the hole before reaching the last thing in the box.

I put three pictures into the hole: a picture of her and I, a picture of her high school graduation, and a picture of her family from the most recent family wedding they all went to. I figured that Fiona would like the people she loved and cared for most to be right there with her, even in death.

"There," I said, pulling the dirt from the hole back into the hole. I patted it down and it looked as good as it did before I had dug the hole.

The hole had disappeared in the dirt because it had moved to my chest. I forced a smile, to show that I was still capable of smiling, just in case she was somehow watching me from wherever it is that she was now calling home.

"I bought that car you had your eye on," I told her.

You did what!? That was my car! I hear her silent ghost cry out to me.

"I know," I said, "I'm a jerk. But you're never going to drive it and I thought that I should buy it in your memory."

Then she would huff and smirk. *I guess you're right*, she would have said.

The stone remained silent though. And I just waited and waited for her to say something, to let me know she was there watching over me. But she said nothing and did nothing and she wasn't there at all and she was dead and that was the end of it and nothing was going to bring her back.

I tried to focus on my breathing. I refused to let myself be reduced to tears again. I had cried enough tears to fill a river and I was getting sick of always crying.

Fiona was gone.

And I can't change that.

And sitting here while silently begging the girl in the stone to speak was fruitless.

I exhaled and stood up. "I love you."

I dusted my hands off on my pants, sending dried bits of dirt to the ground around my shoes. I turned. And I walked away. The colours betwixt the sky were getting far too dark and cold for me to be out much longer. And so off to my warm bed I went.

Part 2
Chapter 10

The Colour of Water

The key turned in the ignition and my car shut off. I stepped outside and shut the door, starting my trek to the front door of the Italian place that Phoebe wanted me to go to. To say it's weird to be going on a "date" with your dead girlfriend's younger sister is an understatement. It's completely deranged on a whole new scale, except that both Phoebe and I knew it was nothing more than a lunch where we could talk about Fiona without having anyone else privy to our topic of conversation.

There's something she wanted to tell me, something about Fiona that she didn't want to risk anyone else hearing and/or interrupting.

I found Phoebe standing in the waiting area. She turned

and smiled at me. "I thought you stood me up. I was about to leave."

"I'm three minutes past noon."

"You're supposed to be early. It's called good manners." I scoffed. "Shall we go and find a seat?"

"We shall." Phoebe led the way into the restaurant and sat at a small booth in the corner. "I already had this booth pre-selected for when you got here." She smiled, mostly to herself. "I'm pretty smart, if you couldn't already tell."

"Still can't tell." I smirked at her as I slid into my booth. She was wearing a cardigan today, which is odd, because I'm so used to seeing her in a sports uniform, whether it be soccer or rugby or hockey.

"Don't be rude or I won't share any of my cheesy bread."

"You already ordered a cheesy bread?"

"Duh." She took a sip of water from the glass on the table. "I got here early and didn't wanna just wait outside in the cold like an idiot."

"That's why you should wear a coat."

She lifted a coat from beside her. "I did wear a coat. Where's yours?"

"In my car," I told her. I didn't wanna wear it inside, no need. It wasn't unfathomably cold outside today, so I managed the barely twenty-second walk from my car to the restaurant.

"Because you didn't need it to walk into the restaurant?"

"Because I'm a Canadian and therefore am impervious to the effects of sub-zero temperatures." I took a sip of water from the other glass of water that was on the table. Restaurant ice water is the very best ice water that ever existed, by the way.

"So why'd you drag me out to lunch with you?"

"I wanted out of the house for a bit," Phoebe replied. "Well, that, and I wanted to talk to you without worrying about someone interrupting us."

"So what'd you want to talk about?"

She sighed. "I don't want you to call me a hypocrite or anything, but I would like to talk with you about—"

"Fiona," I interjected. "I figured as much."

"Yeah." Phoebe pouted a little. "Sorry, but I've never talked to you about her yet. And as far as I'm concerned, the two of us were the people that meant most to her in the entire world. We have a right to talk about her."

"What'd you want to talk about?"

"Her," Phoebe stated. "She just seemed *weird* towards her last few days. She was a lot more distant with me and the parentals. Did you notice anything?"

I thought about it for a moment. "I guess she was a bit quieter than normal, but it's happened before where she'll go through those depressive episodes."

"I dunno." Phoebe took a sip of her water and ruffled a hand through her hair. "I just feel like she somehow knew something bad was gonna happen or something. I dunno, she just seemed *off*."

I shrugged. "Didn't notice, really. She usually tells me when something's bothering her or got her down. And she didn't mention anything to me."

"Edwin," Phoebe said, staring me down, "she didn't even tell me. She's told me everything since I was fourteen. I know *everything* about her that there is to know. I even know more about you than I'd like to know."

"Gross."

"Yeah, but my point is that she would always tell me shit, regardless of what it was." Phoebe sighed. "She told me about pregnancy scares, when she was mad at you, when she was disappointed in herself, when she felt like the world was crashing down around her. I was the first person she would call for help with an embarrassing situation. I was her go-to clutch for the past couple years."

"So?"

"So? What the fuck do you mean 'so'? She told me everything, every time she had one of these depressive episodes, but now she decides not to. I'm worried that she…" Phoebe rested her head in her hands for a few seconds and then popped back up to look at me. "I don't know. Maybe I'm overreacting, but like I said, she always told me things. So whatever happened to her, it must have been bad for her to hide it from both of us."

"Are you insinuating that she wanted to kill herself?"

The waiter came by as Phoebe went to reply. He laid the cheesy bread down and asked for our orders. We both placed our order and then waited for the waiter to be out of earshot before resuming our conversation. She peered over me and then snapped her gaze to mine when the waiter was far enough away. "Look, I'm not saying she wanted to, but we can't rule out the possibility of it, right?"

"Why would she do it with me in the car?"

Phoebe shrugged. "Dunno, maybe she wanted to take you with her, maybe she didn't want to leave you alive to live without her. She knew you'd be hurt, obviously."

"I don't think she wanted to kill herself," I told her. "She was fine in the days leading up to it, just like any other day, really."

"Don't rule it out. You took her journals, right?"

I nodded. "But I'm not going to read them. Regardless of her being dead now, it's an invasion of privacy."

"But it would give you the answers. She would have written it in there, all her feelings. She would have." Phoebe outstretched her hand and placed it on mine. "Edwin, she's too good of a driver to have crashed by accident. But you need to know, I need to know. Please."

"Phoebe, I don't want the goddamn answers," I barked in a hushed tone. "If she killed herself, I'll just end up mad at her, and if she didn't kill herself, well, guess what, she's still fucking dead and buried. I don't need answers. What I need is to move on."

Phoebe nodded. "I get it. Sorry."

"And besides, that most recent journal of hers that I found was from four months ago, well before she got distant with you."

"Then she never took you."

I grabbed a piece of cheesy bread and eyed Phoebe over. "Took me where?"

"There's a lake she went to sometimes to be alone, to clear her head and think about things," Phoebe told me. "She kept a journal somewhere near there, a locked one, so you'd need the key to it. That's the journal that would tell you."

"Why don't I just give it to you, then?"

"Because if there's one thing I know about Fiona, it's that any letter she would write, it'd be to you."

"But if your theory is the truth, then she would have thought she killed me." I put the cheesy bread back on the plate. "I don't want to read the journal."

"Fine. But at least go get it."

"Why should I?"

"Because it's the last of her private thoughts, and it's better for you to keep it locked away somewhere than for some stranger to find it."

"And what about the key?" I asked. "If I ever changed my mind, where would I find the key?"

"There were two. One kept by Fiona somewhere secret, and the other one was the one she gave to you when she gave you *a key to her heart.*" I remembered that key. A literal key to serve as a symbol of her love for me, a metaphor for her letting me in, letting me make her vulnerable.

I took a bite of the cheesy bread I had taken and put back. "Where's the lake?" I asked through a mouthful of bread.

"It's a place called Emerald Cove. You're not gonna find it on any maps, but trust me, it's there."

"How do I get there, then?" I took another bite of bread while waiting for her reply.

She paused to think for a moment. "You have to go north to Highway 7 and then go east, towards Ottawa, there'll be a little dirt road called Slime's Grove Road. Take that and there'll be another little road called Green's Lane, that'll take you to a small dirt patch you can park at. Then follow the gravel trail to the lakeshore, and then bam, Emerald Cove."

"Are you going to come with me?"

Phoebe shook her head. "This is something you need to do on your own. Why? Because you were already probably going to tell me not to go with you anyway."

"You're pretty smart after all."

"Yeah, but don't go bolting off. Eat first."

I took another bite of bread and gave her an unenthused stare. "Because I haven't been trying to do that?"

Phoebe and I walked to the bus stop and I waited with her until her bus came, and then I headed back to my car. I started it up and plotted a course on my Maps app with the directions that Phoebe had given me. I'm not going to read the journal, but she made a good point about how it's better that it be kept with me and the rest of her journals rather than risk having some complete stranger stumble upon it.

And so, I headed north to the 7. I followed her directions to a tee, and eventually found myself driving at a snail's pace through a forest on a barely one-lane dirt road. I kept my eyes peeled for the Green's Lane road sign. And once I found it and drove down to the end, I parked the car, walked to the lakeshore, and for a few brief minutes, I took in the sights and sounds of the expanse of nature around me. No cars, no planes, no other people. I can see why Fiona would have loved this place, a place so delicately desolate and desperately isolated from the rest of the world around it. I guess it's a little analogous to herself as well. She was always her own thing.

I sat down at a small wooden bench that overlooked the lake and just rested a moment. I looked across the lake at the trees that jutted up thickly to create a jagged horizon. I had lots of time, it was still midday, the sun was high and bright in the sky, glistening off the water and reflecting off the snow on top of the trees.

I looked to my left and noticed a small shack. I got off the bench and walked over to it. I tried the door, but it was locked.

Of course. Maybe I needed the key to the journal to get in the shack too, but that wouldn't make too much sense. Maybe the key would be around somewhere, so I dug up some dirt around the little cabin and looked all over for anything that resembled metal.

If I were Fiona, I thought, looking around to get a fix on where Fiona might hide a key. I had tried all around in the dirt, leaving brown flecks in the snow that had found its way to the forest floor. No key, no shiny metal, nothing. Maybe the key wasn't even here. Maybe it was buried with her. Maybe it was thrown out in a box of her stuff that nobody needed or wanted.

At a loss, I called Phoebe. "I need a key."

"A key? Why?"

"The shack has a lock."

"I didn't know there was a shack."

"But you've been here before?" I questioned.

"Nope," Phoebe replied. "Fiona gave me the directions in case I ever needed to find her or if she was in trouble out there. Other than that, she strictly forbade me from going there under pretty much any other circumstance."

"Where would Fiona keep a key for this place?"

Phoebe blew raspberries for a few seconds as she thought. "I've no idea, Edwin. She would have kept two copies of that key though. One to keep with her other secret journal key and then she would probably have an emergency key up there for when she didn't have the other one. Think outside the box, Edwin."

"You're not much help," I mused.

She scoffed. "More help than you'd like to admit. Anyway, I got stuff to do. Call me later and keep me updated."

"Yeah, sure." I hung up and put my phone back in my pocket. I looked around once again. The afternoon was slowly slipping away and I was no closer to finding this journal. I didn't even want it, but yet here I am, compelled to find the last piece of Fiona.

I walked around the shack a few more times, looking for a hint. The roof was slanted away from the shore, towards a small slope. Maybe the key was on the roof. Worth a shot. I looked for a tree to climb up and uneasily made my way to the roof. The roof was quite stable, more stable than it should have been. *But that's a good thing, Edwin,* I thought.

I poked around the edges of the roof for anything other than leaves and dirt, but I found nothing. I looked around from on top of the shack. There was a large tree that had a single lonely branch resting above me. I looked closely and noticed a glimmering of metal; a key. I reached up for it and pulled the branch down. The key was tied to the branch with a small piece of string. I took it and put it in my pocket and then climbed back down to the forest floor. I stuck the key in the door and it unlocked.

The shack didn't have any proper lighting (because why would it?) but it did have an assortment of candles and flashlights. I picked up a lighter from a table by the door and lit some of the candles. I took a flashlight and started poking around through the shack. There were books and sketchpads and pencils and food wrappers and empty cans of pop and bottles of alcohol, some open and some not. Fiona had placed a potted flower, though it was fake, on a table by a window that looked over the lake. It felt like a small home away from home.

I searched the dresser and tables and cubbies for hours, covering every inch of the shack and getting lost in nostalgia. I imagined how she would have looked in here, probably sitting in a chair just under the window and reading one of her novels and eating chips. I get so swamped by it all that I almost forgot why I came here in the first place.

I gave the shack a one more good look around and sighed. The journal wasn't in any noticeable place, because Fiona would have put it in the floorboards. Because of course she would, it's the most non-secretive secret place to store things. I poked around the floor for a loose piece of wood. Eventually, I found it and yanked it up and out of the way. Inside was a small metal container, small enough to fit under the floor and big enough for a small book. I pried the lid off and inside was a locked journal.

I'd be lying if I said I didn't feel triumphant, because I sure as fuck did. I smiled and pulled the journal out, damn near wanting to kiss it like a long-lost lover. I spent hours looking for the last piece of Fiona's journals, and I found it.

And then the sadness swept in, because maybe this journal really did have the answer to the question: Did she want to die?

A question I didn't want to think about, much less know the answer to, at least not right now, not just yet. I wasn't ready to find out what her last private recorded thoughts were. And out of respect for Fiona, I won't ever know what they were. She kept these things private for a reason, I'm not to read them, just guard them. I put the lid back on the metal container and put the floorboard back in its place. I walked outside and sat on the hood of my car, looking over the cover of Fiona's journal.

I put it back in my car and walked to the shoreline. The water was most likely freezing to touch. I watched the sun's golden rays bounce of the waves of the lake. The sun was almost fully behind the trees now. It was getting late in the day. I should be heading home, I got what I came for.

But there was more.

There was a longing somewhere deep in me that cared only for being with Fiona. A longing that made me empty my pockets and place the items in a small pile on the hood of my car. And then I was there, shoeless and emotionally numb as I overlooked the lake.

Maybe Fiona did kill herself.

Maybe she wanted me to die too.

Maybe she's waiting on the other side for me.

I took a step and let the ice cold water flood my socks, freezing my feet almost instantly. It felt like a thousand small pinpricks constantly prodding my skin.

Fiona, I thought.

I took another step.
I'm coming.
Another step. And another, until the water reached my chin. My body was racked with the pain of being submerged in the water, water colder than I'd ever thought water could be. Colder than water ever *should* be.
I love you.
Another step, one more breath.
My only hope now is that the other side is heaven, a heaven where Fiona is waiting for me, smiling.
One more step.
I lost my footing.
One after the other, my legs gave way.
And I fell.
And then the colours betwixt became nothing.

PART THREE
The Betwixt

Part 3
Chapter 1

The Anniversary

"Time to wake up," Derek's voice rang out. He was always coming over and waking me up well before I was ready. I guess he doesn't understand that I work the night shifts now and that means I'm getting to sleep at seven in the morning (if I'm lucky) and that him waking me up at noon the next day is ass.

I mumbled something to him as I rolled over. I rubbed my eyes and tried to dig the sleep out of it. "Coffee?"

"Ah, yes, gotcha." He handed me a coffee and I graciously took it from him.

I pushed myself up and cracked the tab of the lid back and took a sip. It was the perfect temperature. "How cold is outside today?"

Derek shrugged. "Not too bad. Not as bad as yesterday."

"Blessed." I chuckled. "I swear I was gonna get frostbite."

"That's 'cause you wear sneakers in the middle of winter." Derek smiled wryly. "So that's a *you* problem, hoser."

I stifled a laugh. "Yeah, you right."

"I'll be waiting downstairs. Get dressed."

"Can we get another coffee?"

He nodded. "Sure. As long as you get up and get dressed, okay? Deal?"

I nodded to him and then stood up. While getting dressed, I glanced at the date on my phone. It stung, more than a day should. It stung because today meant that a full year had passed since Fiona did. I put my phone down and finished getting changed.

I had grown since then, grown since the night at Emerald Cove. I didn't feel as hopelessly lost now as I did back then, and thank God for that because I'm not sure I'd have lasted much longer beyond that night if I stayed feeling so low. Of course, though, it was still there, the aching and longing for her, but it was much less pronounced. That old adage of time healing all wounds isn't true, by the way. Time just helps you forget things. Time doesn't heal any wounds, physical or mental. It's all on you. You confront the things that hurt you or your body fights the wound and then you heal. Yes, it takes time, but so does everything. I haven't wanted to face that wound in my heart, my soul, wherever the wound is. I have not stitched myself back together. Fiona is still ripping my threads apart.

I pocketed my phone and wallet, grabbed my keys, then headed down the stairs to meet with Derek and Marshall (I got halfway down the stairs when I had to go back for my coffee).

"Good morning, gents."

The duo looked over to me from where they stood near the front door. "Morning," Marshall said.

I walked over and put my shoes on. "Shall we get going?"

"We shall," Derek said, opening the door. The world outside was bright and cold, just like a year ago. The three of us all got in our respective cars and began the drive. We were driving to a cemetery to pay our respects, because of course we would, we were her squad.

Derek had gotten the flowers and snacks for the three of us, Marshall was on alcohol duty for when we got back to Derek's basement later. They both insisted that today would be hard enough on me without needing to worry about getting provisions together.

The ground in the cemetery was covered in snow, and most of it lay untouched. Not too many people wanna venture out in this kind of cold for *good* reasons, let alone to a place that's going to make them sad.

"We'll give you a moment," Derek said, resting a hand on my shoulder. Marshall placed his flowers down and before I knew it, I was standing in front of a gravestone that read FIONA GRIER. I kneeled down, my knee crunching the snow beneath it, not that I cared or minded at all. The cold daggers of the snow didn't hurt anywhere near as much as seeing her gravestone, even if it was for the hundredth time.

"Hey, Fiona." My words floated like they were in a small unlit room, talking to her as if she were half asleep and lying next to me. "So it's been a year." I did my best not to shed a tear this time. It was too cold and the wind too stinging to have a wet face. I could be strong, strong for me and her. "I still miss you, duh, but it's getting better every day. I'm getting more and more used to you not being here. It's always gonna hurt. And I wish I had the guts to come to wherever you are, but it's not my time yet. But I think I need to move on, at least physically. I can't keep living like you still are. It's not healthy for me. I know you understand and I know you have no way of talking to me, but just know that I'll never love anybody the way I loved you."

And then I zoned out, talking to a gravestone about the good old days. Laughing to myself like *she* was the one telling the stories that I was reciting. It was cathartic in a way, I suppose, to just kneel in the snow and talk in stories until I cracked a smile at her memory. But it's just not the same, talking to a piece of stone. Nonetheless, it's a piece of stone that I'd never take for granted. I placed a kiss upon the top of the stone and wished it a pleasant rest of its day.

Derek came barrelling into the basement, a dog close in tow. He had bought a dog because even Derek gets lonely sometimes. It was a malamute, one of those big fluffy dogs that look like Siberian huskies. His name was Corduroy. I don't know why. I don't really bug him about it either.

"Down, Cord, down," Derek said as Corduroy slammed into the coffee table in front of me. "Damn dog doesn't know how big it actually is."

"Big-dog syndrome," I said, giving Cord a good pat.

Marshall walked down the stairs and set all the glass bottles on a shelf, out of Cord's reach. "Hopefully they stay safe up here."

"Stop it," Derek said. "Cord isn't that bad. It's just when he gets worked up about stuff."

"Which is constantly."

"Man's got a point," I noted. "Cord's a wrecking ball with ADHD."

Derek got down to Cord's level and rubbed his face a little. "You're not a wrecking ball, are you, boy? No, you're a good pup with some careless tendencies. You're kinda like Marsh."

"I'm not a good pup," Marshall chimed, selecting a bottle of rum from the shelf to get us started for the evening.

"Mm-hmm." Derek sat down next to me. "Anyway, let's get our drink on. NHL on deck." Derek picked up a controller. "And ice in the cups." Derek pointed to the cups on the table. "Every goal we score, we take a drink. Every goal scored against us, we drink twice. We drink three times for hat-trick goals. We drink twice for special team goals. If your player-controlled character gets called for a penalty, you drink one for a minor and two for a major." Derek clapped his hands. "Okay, let's do this."

The night (afternoon) wore on and as it did, our drink tallies kept rising. We eventually had to switch to energy drinks and then water (because there was a lot of scoring, penalties, and other sheningans).

"What are we doing tonight, ladies?" Derek said as our umpteenth game wrapped up.

"This?" I questioned. "What else is there to do?"

"Let's go clubbing, ya duster." Derek set his controller on the table. "We haven't gone out to any clubs lately."

"None of us are in"—I burped—"any position to drive."

"Mm, you right." Derek sighed. "Maybe next weekend or something. I miss tearing up house parties with you, Ed."

"Yeah, closing down bars with the Edwinner," Marshall chimed in.

"Stop," I barked. "My name is Edwin, not Ed or Edwinner. And as for closing down bars and tearing up house parties, I agree with you."

"You agree with us?" Derek asked. "Wow, okay that's, uh— I wasn't expecting this."

"I agree with you. It's not that hard to comprehend, is it?" I teased, then scoffing lightly. "And you're supposed to be the smart one."

"Right. Anyway, I don't wanna be an asshole about this, but Fiona died a year ago, and I know it's still hard on you, but you gotta live *your* life now. You've had time to mourn. It's time to move on."

"I know," I stated, taking a drink of the rum and Coke I had on the table. "Look, I'm not ever going to be the same person that I was before Fiona died, but I'm sick of doing nothing with my life. I'm letting myself waste away for no reason, and before you say it, I'm going to agree with you. Yes, I'm young and I have a full life ahead of me, so starting tomorrow, I wanna begin living *my* life again."

"That a boy," Marshall said, raising a glass in the air.

"Humans need to socialize and be intimate with one another, right? I'm sick of hiding away so much, I just wanna have fun. I just wanna forget about how much it hurts, you know?"

Marshall nodded. "There's a party going on for Valentine's Day in February."

"Valentine's Day?" I asked.

He nodded. "Yeah, why not? It's an excuse to get drunk."

"And hook up with cute flutes," Derek added. Oh, in case I haven't mentioned, Derek calls women he views as promiscuous *flutes*. I have no idea why, but then again, I dunno why Derek does half the things he does.

"Then it's a date," I told them.

Derek smiled widely. "This is gonna be epic. The three amigos, the three musketeers, the three… something else that comes in threes."

"The holy trinity," I added.

"Exactly." Derek smiled again. "We're gonna be the best damn team since, well, since ever."

"Still weird that the first party you want me to go to is a Valentine's party."

Derek shrugged. "Perfect chance for you to find love." Him and I exchanged vacant stares. "Just kidding, but there will be plenty of desperate people tryna get their freak on, so I mean, it's perfect for you. You won't even have to try, just show up and look pretty."

"Fuck you," I snapped. "I look pretty all the time."

"Edwin's shitfaced."

"Why do you say that?"

Derek chuckled. "Because you never have this much confidence sober."

"Fair," I said, resting back on the couch. "So this party, how big is it?"

"You remember when Sammy threw that rager last year?" Marshall asked.

I nodded. "The one where Fiona dived into the pool from the roof and we dropped a TV from the balcony?"

Marshall nodded. "Think even bigger and better than that."

"Who the fuck's throwing this party?"

Derek looked at Marshall and smiled. Derek then turned to me and smiled. "Patchy fucking O'Brien."

My mouth dropped at the mention of his name. See, in the history of my partying, I knew only three rules:

1) Never party at your own house.
2) Always bring more booze than you'll drink.
3) And that Patchy O'Brien's parties were legendary.

And why would Patchy's parties be legendary? Because the dude is rich, obviously. He has more money than he knows what to do with. Ever since high school started, the dude's been throwing ragers at his huge-ass mansion. It was just outside of town on a *massive* piece of property. It had a huge main house that had more rooms than you could count, and a pool bigger than most people's entire house. He had also done us partygoers the liberty of setting up small sheds for sleeping and love-making. He has several condom dispensers (yes, really) around his property as well. The dude was all about parties (and getting laid). Shocker to see why he was one of the most well-known dudes in the town for parties. And since he doesn't have any close neighbours, it takes an awful lot for the cops to get called on us.

"So you're in?" Derek said, looking at me as I sat with my mouth agape.

I nodded. "Oh, I'm so in. I've been dying to find my way back to a Patchy party."

"You gonna roll up in that sweet beaut of yours?" Marshall asked me.

"Duh," I replied. "What, was I gonna roll up in one of your beaters?"

"Hurtful," Derek butted in. "That's very hurtful. Our cars may not be as flashy and nice to look at as yours, but they have feelings, goddammit."

"Feelings that I don't care about." I winked at them and took another sip of my drink. I think things are gonna start looking up for me. Or at least I hope they were. I was drunk, so I couldn't really be sure about too much.

And so, the colours betwixt my ribcage beat a little brighter for the rest of the night.

Part 3
Chapter 2

The Colours of Tonight

Thirteen months was what it took for me to get back out there and live a life I could call my own. I refused to sit inside on sunny days any longer. I refused to sit inside when my friends called me to go out. Thirteen months since the day I lost my bearings, thirteen months until I was ready to let go and start trying to live again.

I lifted my head from the sink, staring back at my brown eyes in the mirror. Water dripped from the front of my hair and from the tips of my nose and chin. I grabbed the nearby towel and dried myself off. No doubt, Derek and Marshall would be waiting for me just outside my front door. I slipped my shirt on and fixed my hair. It's time to go and party like I'm not emotionally dead inside.

At least I can pretend to be a person for the night while I'm at Patchy's party. Drugs and drinks help with that I suppose (but do recommend). Also, I haven't mentioned it yet, but the reason Patchy is called Patchy is because when he was younger, he had a really bad rash and kids teased him, but he embraced it and started calling himself Patchy and it stuck. (I guess Patchy was catchy? I'm sorry. I'll stop now.)

"There he is," Derek said as I opened the front door and stepped out.

"And looking prettier than ever," I added. "So we gonna go do this?"

Derek followed Marshall and I followed Derek. Marshall's car pulled into the driveway and led the trio of us in. I gave the onlookers some courtesy engine revs as I pulled into an empty spot of lawn to park on. There were already a hundred or more people cramming themselves into this party. Tonight was gonna be big. I'd bet that half of the college kids in this town were gonna come out.

"Don't embarrass yourself too much," Derek said as he walked over to me.

I scoffed. "I've been to parties before."

He shook his head and laughed a bit. "Not what I meant, bro." I watched him head off and strike up a chat with a group of people near the front door of the house.

"Not too late for you to go home," Marshall said from behind me.

"No, no, this'll be good. I need to get out again."

He nodded. "Well, get in there and socialize. I'm sure some of those fine young ladies and gents would love to see you again."

I smiled at the thought. Maybe they would be happy to see me, maybe they finally gave up on pitying me for what happened, right? I'd like to think so. Anyway, I walked past the group of people and into the party. For how many people were already here, the place wasn't very cramped (again, this estate is pretty sizeable). I made my way out back and got a good look around.

"Hey," a voice from behind me said. "You're Edwin, yeah?"

I turned around and nodded. "I am," I replied, looking over the rather pretty young woman standing there.

"Derek told me to come over and say hi." She motioned to the front door where Derek nodded and smiled at me.

"Party's barely started and he's trying to get me to talk to girls?"

The girl smiled. "Apparently so."

"Well, hey, let's see if we bump into each other later on tonight, I'm gonna go talk to Derek." I went to walk away but then spun around on my heels. "Sorry, I never got your name."

"Amanda," she replied, smiling.

I nodded. "Amanda, I will remember that." I didn't. But I did walk over to Derek. "Why are you already sending girls my way?"

He shrugged. "Thought you could use a warm-up."

"I don't need one," I told him. "Especially not this early in the night."

"Have you had a drink?" Derek asked, handing me a cup. "If not, drink. If you have, drink again."

"I've been here all of twenty minutes, I was just walking around and enjoying the house."

"Drink."

I rolled my eyes. "Yeah, yeah." I downed the cup of beer he had handed me. "Do you have anything, I dunno, better than light beer?"

"Bar downstairs," a dude replied from behind him. "Hi. I'm Patchy." He stuck a hand out.

"*The* Patchy?" I asked, shaking his hand.

He nodded. "Yessir. The bar's downstairs, but it's locked off because you can never trust these savages. Derek says I can trust you though, so you get to be the barman tonight." He reached into his pocket and dug out a key and handed it to me.

"What do I have to do?" I asked.

"Bring up some good shit and then lock up the basement," Patchy said. "Also, you can keep the keys in case you need to go somewhere for a little *privacy*." He tapped his nose and smirked.

"What do you want me to bring up?" I asked him.

He paused for a moment and then Derek answered for him, "Just bring up as much as you can."

"Good idea, Derek," Patchy said. "Thanks for this, Edwin. I know it sounds like I'm making you do me an errand, and that *is* what I'm doing, but you'll thank me when you have somewhere to throw up in peace."

I nodded. "Good shit coming right up." I turned and headed down a long, dark hallway. At the end was the entrance to his private basement, i.e. the basement that the general public aren't allowed to visit (also, you know someone's rich when they have more than one basement). There were only three keys on this ring of keys that Patchy gave me. I guess one for the door to the basement, one for the private bedroom down there, and the third one for a second private basement. I dunno.

I made my way downstairs and began loading bottles of alcohol into an old laundry basket that I found on the stairs on the way down. I tried to get variety, but Patchy had more vodka than he did anything else. I should have recruited Derek or Marshall to come help me, 'cause this basket of alcohol was heavier than I thought it would be, but I refuse to put any bottles back. My pride's on the line with this right now.

When I made my way back upstairs, the party had quite emphatically started. There were people everywhere and the music was almost louder than the thoughts in my head. I shambled my way into the big room in the centre of the house to find a table to set the booze down. I must have made it fifteen feet from the basement when two dudes came by and took the basket of booze from me, not that I minded. I let out a sigh of relief and watched them carry the basket into the centre of a huge crowd of people.

I walked to the table they had put the basket down at and poured myself a tall of whiskey and cola. I turned and semi-consciously waded through the crowd to get outside to the cold air. I didn't see anyone in coats, but with this many people and the occasional heater, most of the outside patio would probably be warm enough not to need winter gear. I found a clear spot on the railing and leaned against it. I took a sip of my drink and looked up at the sky; empty and clear, a truly perfect night.

"There you are," Marshall said from behind me.

I turned and looked him over. "Already getting pretty drunk, huh? Pace yourself, it's barely past eight."

"Pace myself?" Marshall scoffed. "Dude, I can handle my beer, don't worry. What about you? How's your night so far?"

"I got sent on the bar run."

Marshall winced, as if he felt my pain. "Sucks, dude. Sorry."

"Maybe tonight wasn't such a good idea," I said, taking another sip.

"Why do you say that?"

I shrugged. "I dunno. I just feel melancholic, not happy. I just feel like I'm kinda *here*, but like, still invisible, you know?"

"Ah, okay, I want you to do me a favour." He handed me the drink in his hand. "Down this, right now. And uh—" He turned around and teefed a drink from someone walking by behind him. "And then down this as well. You need to loosen up. You're never gonna have a good time if you sip your drinks and stare at the sky. Tonight you party, tomorrow you can poetic."

"Not sure that makes much sense, but alright." I downed his drink and then handed him back the cup so he could give me the stolen one. I downed that one too.

"Okay, good." Marshall sighed. "Well, I guess I have to go

get another drink. Have you seen Derek lately?"

"Not since before I had to go get the booze from the basement," I replied. And with that, Marshall nodded and walked off.

Man, how did I ever function at parties before? I feel like a rookie all over again. Everything was suddenly lame and I was *too cool* to be here.

Give the drinks a few minutes, I thought. *All you need is for the edge to get taken off. You'll be fine.* I turned around to head inside and, *Speaking of fine. It's the girl from earlier tonight.*

"Hello," the girl said. "Seems we ended up bumping into each other again after all."

"Seems we have… Amy, was it?" I said. Shit, how did I forget her name already? "No, Amber. It was definitely Amber. You look like an Amber."

"Amanda," she said, sounding disappointed in me (I guess she can join the club called "Everyone Else in My Life").

"Sorry, I must have misheard you before. How are you?"

She smiled softly, forgiving me I suppose. "I'm good. And yourself?"

"Better now that I've had a couple drinks."

"Do you want a couple more?" she asked.

I shrugged. "Yeah, why not. What'd you have in mind?"

"I heard they're starting up the kegs by the pool." She smirked at me. "Up for a keg stand?"

I scoffed. "Please. I was born ready."

"Corny. I like it." She turned and led the way outside where a crowd was forming for none other than the keg stands. Patchy's keg stands were always fun because you did it over a pool on the diving board. If you did well enough, the crowd would cheer and you get to stay dry. If you did poorly, the crowd erupts with boos and you take a swim. Pretty simple game to play, and it's all in good fun, really. As we walked out, I managed to catch a glimpse back inside. There were still so many people in there doing their thing. I tried to eye out Derek or Marshall, but I didn't have any luck with that, too many dimly lit faces in the crowd to spot any one face in particular. I turned back just in time for the crowd around the pool to boo and have the girl up on the diving board get pushed into the water. The water must be freezing. I saw the girl swim to the side of the pool and get helped out by a few dudes with towels. They ushered her off to the house to warm up. See, all in good fun. We're not out here to hurt anyone for real.

I'd wager that an hour or more had passed by as Amanda and I watched the keg stands. Everyone wanted to last the longest up there, it was a sense of pride. I refused to go up there until Derek came by and offered to hold my things, and then him and Amanda cheered me on. And so I went up and did the keg stand. And so I drank, and drank, and drank. Eventually the crowd cheered and I was saved from the icy water below. I took a bow and headed back down, eyeing over the scrawny little dude going up after me. "Good luck," I wished him. He smiled and nodded. I followed Derek inside and he gave me my things back.

"Fucking brilliant." Derek beamed. "I'd have done it too, but there's no stopping the Edwinner, is there?"

"Edwinner?" Amanda asked. "Now that's a good one."

"Ah, nah."

"I like it," she said.

"We all do," Derek added. "So it seems you two are getting along pretty—"

"You're pretty cute. I think you'll do," a feminine voice said as I was suddenly being tugged away from the crowd and then down the hall.

"That's pretty fucking savage, Colby!" someone shouted.

After I was pushed into a small room, I shook the girl off my arm. "What the fuck are you doing?" I asked as she locked the door behind us.

"Hi. I'm Colby," she grabbed my hand and shook it without me raising my arm or shaking back. "It's so very nice to meet you."

"Do you know me or something?"

She shrugged. "Maybe. Do I? Do you know me?"

"No," I replied. "Why did you drag me in here?"

"It's dark in here," she muttered, flicking on the lights. "That's better."

And then I got a look at this mysterious kidnapper. She was average height, slim build, quite slender actually. She was pale, very much so. The black nail polish on her fingers stuck out because of the contrast. She had bright blonde hair and dark eyebrows. The slightest bit of freckling on her little perky nose. And a nose ring?! The slit of silver caught the light in the room and it glinted as she turned to me. (My mom always warned me about girls with nose rings, but I never liked listening to my mom all that much.)

I caught eyes with her hazel ones and she smiled at me and said, "Aren't you quite the looker."

"Are you gonna tell me why you dragged me off?"

Colby shrugged. "I thought people liked suspense and ambiguity and all that shit. If I just *tell* you why I dragged you in here, how will I know you'll help me?"

"You need my help?" I pried. "With what? And why me?"

"My friend's been on my ass about 'getting back out there' and meeting people," Colby stated, leaning against the wall. Only now was I realizing that we were in a small closet, just the two of us. "I, uh, had a pretty messy breakup a few months back and she's been pressuring me to just get back out there because, you know, I'll feel so much better about myself if I'm not just moping around my apartment."

"So why me?"

"It didn't have to be you," she said. "You're not special, you were just there. And besides, your face told me well enough that you didn't want to be with that girl you were talking to. It's not too often I see a dude look that bored with a hot girl in front of him."

"You know, you didn't have to drag me off like that."

"I didn't, no. But I'd rather talk in private than in a crowd with loud music and friends watching, wouldn't you?"

I nodded. "So, you just need me to keep you company for a bit, then, or what?"

Colby sighed. "Yeah. Could we also just *pretend* that we fucked? You know, if you would be kind enough to do so for the stranger that kidnapped you this evening?"

"Yeah," I replied. "I'll help you. I guess this'll be good for the both of us. My friends wanted me out and back in the game. You could say I had a messy end to things as well."

Colby smiled at me. "Okay, well, first of all, I don't like doing it in closets. Can we go get some booze and find a room with a TV or something?"

"I think I was a good choice for you to kidnap."

"Why's that?"

I pulled out the ring of keys Patchy had given me. "We get our own private suite tonight."

"Ha, I sure did pick the right one. Okay, let's go." Colby exited the closet and motioned for me to lead the way. I unlocked the basement door and locked it behind us. She went down and got the lights and TV turned on. "This place is pretty cozy," she said as I walked into the room she was in.

"Yeah, Patchy hired a professional decorator for every room of his house," I told her.

Colby scoffed. "What a lame job that woulda been." She took her shoes off and balled her socks in them. Her feet had the same black nail polish and the same paleness as the rest of her. Maybe she's a goth.

"What'd you wanna watch?" I asked as I walked back out of the room and toward the bar.

She came to the doorway and blew raspberries. "Fuck if I know." She looked around for a minute and then focused back on me. "Are you always this conversational with strangers that kidnapped you?"

"You didn't kidnap me, and you're not a stranger," I said as I pulled a bottle of vodka from the cupboard. "Your name is Colby, and I came willingly."

"Oh, we're not strangers because you know my name?"

she asked. "Funny, 'cause you haven't told me your name yet."

"Edwin," I replied. "All you had to do was ask."

She stuck her tongue out at me as she grabbed the vodka. She twisted the lid off and took a sip. "That's a familiar burn." Her face grimaced and she shook it off. "Anyway, do we have any snacks down here?"

"Dunno."

"I'll go look, you set up a movie. I'm into anything scary." Colby smirked at me. "And if you pick something scary enough, you might get a *I got really scared* cuddle."

"I'll keep that in mind." I took the vodka from her and headed into the room. I set the vodka down on the small table next to the bed and I picked up the remote. Colby had done the liberty of turning the TV on.

I flicked through the different selections offered by each of the video streaming apps until I found a movie that was one of the scariest ones I had ever watched. I suppose I subconsciously wanted to cuddle with this *Colby*.

She was gorgeous. I can't lie about that. And my half-drunk mind warped a vision of her porcelain skin curled into mine in the low light of this bedroom, the two of us panting on the bed. I shook myself out of it as quickly as it came. I shouldn't really be thinking about her like that. This is nice and all, but maybe tonight's not the night for any romancing.

I plopped on the bed and waited for a few minutes. I heard footsteps coming back to the room. Colby emerged into my view with a huge bowl of cheese puff snacks and a bag of dill pickle chips.

"Okay, well, let's begin this movie night, shall we?" I helped her onto the bed and she immediately got her legs under the blanket and propped the pillows on against the headboard. She stared at me and sighed. "Take your shoes off. Get your legs in this blanket." She placed the bowl of cheese puffs in between us and smiled at me, taking the remote from my hand and pressing play.

My eyes fluttered open, blurry from the amount of sleep stuck to them. I rubbed and rubbed, but it felt like sand had gotten under my eyelids. I breathed out sharply and tried to focus on the ceiling fan above me. Around and around it swirled. I focused on the dome in the centre, the light wasn't on, but it gave my eyes something to adjust to. After a couple minutes, I was fully awake and still staring at the ceiling, unmoved from where I had woken up.

I rolled to my right and got out of the bed. I slipped my socks onto my feet and then my pants. I grabbed my shirt from the end table and put it on. Again, I had left my coat in my car because it was easier than worrying about where I placed it all night. Once I had my head together, my clothes on, and then my things in my pockets. I turned to see Colby lying in bed. She was on her stomach, topless and snoring softly. The two of us had watched movies until we started getting a little too close and a little too cozy with one another. One thing led to another, obviously.

I tiptoed out of the room and pulled my phone out of my pocket as I closed the door. I went through my contacts and found an entry titled *Colby Claesson*. I guess that'd be her. I remember her saying her last name was pronounced [KLAHS-son]. I debated on deleting her number, because she's a one-night stand after all, but I didn't. She had my number anyway, and if *something* ever came up, it's best we be able to contact each other.

I made my way upstairs and into the common areas of the house. There were people still passed out on the couches and the floor. Anyone that was awake was mumbling about their head hurting, but not this guy. I have the gift of never getting hangovers, and it's a gift I wear proudly.

Once I got to my car outside, I realized I had left my keys in the basement room. I made the journey back in, not like anyone else really cared. When I got to the room, Colby was standing by the bed stretching. I coughed so she would know I was there. She turned to face me, still stretching out her arms a little, essentially puffing out her bare chest at me. "Good morning."

"Good morning," I said, walking over to the table. "My keys fell out of my pocket. Sorry."

"You didn't wake me up," Colby said as she sat down. She began putting her socks and pants back on. "Skipping out on me, were you?"

"Work," I lied.

"*Riiiight.*" She smiled at me. "Well, I had fun. Let's do it again sometime." She stood up, grabbed her shirt, and took the bag of chips that we didn't open from last night and then left the room. I peered out and watched her slip into the shirt and proceed to stuff chips into her face with all the grace of an actual angel.

I eventually got back to my car and started it up. I took a moment to soak in last night, trying to grab all the memories I could before any of them slipped away to the depths of my mind. Once I had a firm hold on what had happened, I started my car and drove off towards Derek's house so I could tell him that the colours betwixt were starting to look a lot less dreary than they had been before.

Part 3
Chapter 3

The One with Colourful Hair

Colby was a secret I had kept for a while. I dodged questions until one night before we were going out to a club, I slipped up and mentioned her in the context of having sex with her *again*.

"Again?" Derek asked, half shouting and nearly dropping his cup of tea on the floor. Derek was drinking a peppermint tea because that's his pre-clubbing/party ritual, apparently.

"You actually slept with Colby?" Marshall asked. "When?"

"Ah, fuck," I muttered. No sense lying now. "It was at Patchy's party."

"Liar," Derek said. "You just wanna sound like there's no pressure to hook up with someone tonight."

"There's no pressure regardless," I said. "But I did hook up with her. Sorry to disappoint."

Derek walked up to me and stared intently into my eyes. "Yeah? Describe it."

"It was just sex," I lied. It was amazing.

"Nice," Derek said, raising a hand for a high five. "I'm not saying I totally believe you, but I can't tell if you're lying or not, so I guess you're honest until proven otherwise."

"I believe you," Marshall added.

"That's good." I took a drink of my tea. "Anyway, when are we heading out? I wanna get a booth so we can eat some nachos before we get drunk."

"Oh, lemme just message our Wayz," Derek said as he pulled out his phone. Wayz is an app that lets you request rides from people that aren't taxis. It's an anyone-can-be-a-taxi program all done through the app. It's all paid for through the app too, via an online banking source or a credit card.

"Why do we even need a Wayz? Why can't we just drive there and crash on the floor somewhere like normal, upstanding partygoers?" Marshall asked.

Derek hushed him with his hand. "We're not soft-napping at every party we go to, Marsh. And I'm sure as hell not gonna be responsible for any of the three of us drunk-driving home."

"Fair."

I chugged back the last of my tea. "Okay, I'm ready. Is the Wayz on the way?"

Derek nodded. "Yes, ma'am." Derek paced around the kitchen for a few seconds before turning to Marshall and me. "Okay, let's just go wait outside."

This party was nowhere near the scope of Patchy's (which I didn't get to enjoy as much as I'd have liked because I was stolen away by Colby, but I digress). And, before I forget to mention it all, I don't really care about the partying itself, because I'm honestly just here to get drunk and maybe get laid because those things seem to take my mind off the whirlpool of other shit I constantly think about. The party we went to last weekend wasn't really noteworthy, just a gathering of friends in a basement, it was more like an indoor campout than a party. With that being said, I take you into the party.

"This place is crowded as fuck," I shouted to Derek over the blaring music. The party was healthily underway.

Derek nodded. "Yeah. Small house, lots of people. It's good for shenanigans, that's for sure."

"Okay, well, let's go get something to drink. I don't wanna be the only person in here without a cup."

Again, Derek nodded and led the way to the kitchen. Derek found the plastic cups and handed Marshall and myself one. Then he led us to the keg, because Derek is a born leader (and neither Marshal nor I wanted to wade through the crowd of people).

Derek handed me his cup, now filled with beer, and took my empty one. "Go. Go and mingle. You're here to cleanse your palate."

"Why is it that you're always getting rid of me as soon as we get to the party?" I asked.

He shrugged. "Habit, I guess."

"I came to party *with* you, not with strangers," I told him. "But if you're so desperate to get rid of me, I'll go mingle. Come along, Marshall."

"I'll find you guys in a bit," Derek said. "Have a few drinks. Have fun."

"He's always been too cool for us," Marshall said, laughing a bit as we made our way through the crowd.

"Let's find somewhere to sit," I said, looking around. "Or something to lean against that isn't a person."

"Good idea." Marshall used his slightly taller height to his advantage as he looked around for an emptiness in the crowd (and yes, all my friends were taller than me, but it's because they're tall, not because I'm short; I'm an average height). Marshall turned and nodded for me to follow him.

"Loud music, a shit ton of people, and crappy beer," I

stated. "Perfect night, really."

"I disagree," Marshall said. "A perfect night is a campfire with rum and seven or eight people, max."

"Yeah, yours is better." We exchanged a small laugh. "Do you even know anybody here?"

"Nah." Marshall looked around. "I don't party with these people often, so I've never made many friends."

"Edwin?!" a voice called out from somewhere behind me.

I spun around. "Colby?" I asked. "What are you doing here?"

"I could ask you the same thing," she said. "Well, maybe not. But I'm a DD tonight." She nodded towards a girl who was very much drunk. "I get to babysit my drunk roommate for the rest of the night, so I at least hope you guys are having more fun than me."

"Yet to be seen. We just got here not too long ago," I said. "Oh, and this is Marshall. Marshall, this is Colby." They shook hands and smiled at each other.

"Well, hey, I'm gonna get this mess out of here," Colby said, "but call me sometime. If you want, that is. Anyway, have a good night. Later, dudes." She picked up her friend and did her best to walk her out of the house with minimal disruption to the people around them.

"She's pretty cute," Marshall noted.

I turned back to him and shrugged. "Yeah, I guess she's a *little bit* cute." That was a lie, because she was immaculately gorgeous. The more I think about her, the more I seem to be building her up as some goddess sent from the worlds above our own. She's just some girl I hooked up with at a party last month, but yet she's a masterpiece of the human female form.

But those thoughts fluttered away from my mind as I heard a loud smashing sound. Marshall and I snapped our heads to see where the sound came from. Someone had knocked over a potted plant just a dozen feet from where we stood. The dirt spread across the hardwood very nicely, as did the shards of ceramic pot.

"I guess the party's gonna start getting rowdy now, huh?" I mused to Marshall. "We'd better get some drinks in us and join in on all the fun, eh?"

Over two hours, things were generally pretty calm, but then things started to get a bit more out of hand. I had also met a girl, a pretty little thing with blue, purple, and silver hair. She was cute, but nowhere near Colby, nowhere near Fiona either. I suppose I just have "high" standards, but that's not a bad thing. Everybody has different standards. What may be beautiful to one person, might not be to the next. That's one of the beauties of humanity.

"There you are," Derek said, jumping on my back. He tackled himself around me. "I've been looking for you."

"For me?" I asked. "Why?"

"Because, this place is getting real riled up." He looked around. "It's about to be a gongshow."

"Why's that?"

He nodded towards the stairs. "Apparently one dude walked in on two dudes fucking his girlfriend. So someone's about to catch some hands."

"Does that dude have a baseball bat?" Isabelle asked. That's the girl with the colourful hair that I've chatting up, by the way.

"He might," Derek said. "On an unrelated note, we should probably get ready to tear ass out of here. I'm pretty sure people have already called the police. And on a second unrelated note, one of those two dudes owns this house, so don't feel bad for smashing shit on your way out."

"The dude with the bat is your friend, isn't he?" I asked.

Derek nodded. "Sure is." He cupped his hands around his mouth and shouted, "Atta boy, Jeremy!" And with that, the party crowd all looked around and gave way to a small circle in the middle of the living room. Jeremy slammed the bat through the glass table in the middle of the room, causing it to smash into many, many shards.

"Dude!" a guy yelled as he ran down the stairs. "What the fuck?"

"Fuck you!" Jeremy shouted back at him. He raised the bat and slammed it into a nearby speaker.

Derek looked over at me, and stoically just said these few words to me, "Dude... I love college."

"Dude, stop!" The guy walked up to Jeremy and that was a mistake. Jeremy raised the bat and slammed it into the guy's thigh, causing him to double over in pain. That had to have been the world's worst charley horse. The guy howled in pain as he fell to the floor. The second guy that had come downstairs and watched this unfold, that guy just ran out of the house, because that's the smart thing to do. The girl was still upstairs, presumably.

Jeremy made his way through the crowd to find the second guy. Derek followed quickly behind, you know, to make sure Jeremy doesn't hurt the guy too badly. And as for the house, it was too late for the house. People were already rushing outside to try and get a glimpse of what was going to happen, and they were running. The TV got pushed onto the ground, the speakers got knocked over, pictures were pushed off tables. Everything was getting tipped over, pushed down, and smashed to make way for the horde of people trying to make their way outside. Myself, Isabelle, and Marshall were among that horde, because of course we wanted to see what was gonna happen next. We managed to get a look at Jeremy and the guy. They were standing in the street and shouting at each other. I couldn't tell what they were yelling, but they were yelling quite angrily.

"Derek said the cops were on the way, right?" Marshall asked.

I nodded. "Yessir."

"Alright, cool."

"That's it?"

"What?" Marshall asked. "Was I supposed to freak out and tell us to get out of here right away immediately?"

I shrugged. "I dunno."

"Okay, shut up. Things are happening," he barked.

I averted my attention from Marshall and back to the street. Jeremy and his *friend* were now exchanging some hands. It couldn't have been twenty seconds later that the police rolled onto the scene. They flashed their sirens and then the stampede began.

We all took off. Marshall ran ahead of me and I ran with Isabelle, my hand in hers. And we ran and ran, and so did everyone else. Derek was long lost though, not too sure where he ended up in the crowd. I'm sure I'll get a call from him in an hour or so asking if I got out of that stampede in one piece as well.

"So, that was pretty intense," Isabelle said. We had been walking for quite a while. We were far from the house at this point. Marshall was walking on ahead of us to let me and Isabelle talk some more, because he thinks we have chemistry, but I don't see (or feel) it.

"Yeah. I don't think I've ran like that in a while," I said. Not like I couldn't. I was fit. I enjoyed running, but that was a more like a full-on sprint.

"Um, so it's getting pretty late," Isabelle noted.

I nodded. "Yeah, we should be going home soon."

"Yeah, I was gonna ask if you wanted to maybe come to my place for the night?" she asked, smiling up at me like I would have said no if she didn't.

"Yeah, that'd be nice."

"Cool. We can grab a cab. I can make coffee or tea for us when we get there."

"That would be splendid," I told her. "Marshall!"

He turned around and let us catch up. "Yeah?"

"We're gonna grab a cab and split," I stated. "You should probably do the same, unless you were planning to walk all the way across town to get home?"

"Yeah. I'll just walk up to the next store and call a Wayz." Marshall sighed. "I'm fucking beat, man."

"Yeah, get home. Text me when you get there so I know you made it there safe."

Marshall nodded and walked up ahead, pulling his phone out. I turned back to Isabelle. She was on the phone, calling a cab to come pick us up.

"It shouldn't be more than ten minutes," she said as she put her phone back in her pocket.

"Good. I'm starting to get cold," I mumbled. I'd like to take this time to formally announce that I want to start a petition to make winter nights just a little bit warmer. Not a lot, just a little. Maybe warm enough to melt snow. Maybe if they were that warm, Fiona would still be here, not some girl I just met at a party. I fucking hate winter. I fucking hate snow. The colours betwixt the snowflakes can go *fuck* themselves.

Part 3
Chapter 4

The Strings

Days blink by. Nothing gets any better. Nothing gets any worse. It all just mixes and melts into a great big melancholy. The sun rises and sets, and the snow falls and melts. Spring gives a renewed life to everything from forests to people, but I still feel cold inside, like my bones haven't yet thawed from the passing winter.

Looking back, it doesn't even feel like I've been myself. It's like I've just been a passenger in my own body, enjoying what there was to enjoy and numbly going through the motions. Maybe it's just how I deal with moving on, because moving on is something I've never really had to do. I've had a solid life, a great girlfriend for so long that losing her didn't even feel *real*, so I refused to accept that it was for so long. I made my strings out of steel and nylon and some other space-age rope-type shit. I was unbreakable.

And over the few months since I had first slept with Colby (because I had to move on, at least physically if not emotionally) I had run up quite a rap sheet (i.e. a list of girls I've bedded). Colby's even added her name to that list a few more times lately. She's pretty cool, I guess. A bit eccentric sometimes, but cool nonetheless. I was having fun for the first time in over a year, but I suppose it's not healthy to just get drunk and have sex with different people all the time. It makes me feel like I'm breaking some unwritten human law about the search for love and the never-ending, undying quest of something bigger than us. I don't know. I don't care. I already finished my search for love, and I lost the prize.

I made my strings out of neglect for what I felt. It doesn't surprise me to think that they're all tangled up in my head, like when you put earphones in your pocket and pull out a wad of wire. I'm just a tangled ball of strings. I don't have any purpose anymore. I just work a shitty job and make enough to pay shitty bills at a shitty apartment where I live all by my-shitty-self. I go out to parties with friends that are increasingly worried about me and my lack of desire for anything more than the passing moments. Derek always says that I'm so busy living in the moment that I forget to think about the hour.

He's probably right.

Well, he for sure is, but that doesn't mean I was going to change, I have no real reason to. I'm not hurting anybody (though I can't promise all the girls I've slept with were single, but that's on them. I have a don't-ask policy). Derek and Marshall just worry too much, and besides, they were the ones who pressured me for so long about getting back out there and trying to have fun and living my life again. They didn't want me to just waste away in my basement or apartment, so instead, I'm wasting away my life in other people's basements or apartments.

I guess I'm just gonna waste away a little more before I get my life together. I'm too young to be feeling so hopeless. I have a whole life ahead of me. I guess it's just a matter of time before I have to start making conscious changes in my life to be better. Maybe I should go back to school for something that I want to do for the rest of my life. Maybe I should try harder at work so I can get a promotion or a raise or better hours. I haven't painted very much lately. Maybe I should get back into that, though most of my recent paintings have been pretty colourless (that's not like me at all, bad Edwin).

    I'm just stuck in the *betwixt*.

    The gaps between happiness are the betwixt, as in the thing between two things worth wanting. The betwixt is the void, that inescapable pit we all crawl out of to prove that there is something on the other side of all the melancholy and gloom. Somewhere where the colours betwixt don't make any sense simply because there just aren't any.

Part 3
Chapter 5

The "Not Cool, Bro"

Her name is Casandra. Not like that matters to me, she was just another girl, except that she wasn't *just* another girl. See, I have this friend named Anton, really cool dude. He's a first-generation kid, his parents are from Russia. He's a good dude, solid pal. Oh, why does Anton matter if this is about me fornicating with Casandra? Because she's his girlfriend.

"Not cool, bro," Derek said, glaring at me from across the table. Marshall sat down next to him in the booth and pushed a pitcher of beer to the centre of the table.

"Dude, what the fuck were you thinking?" Marshall asked. "That's our friend's girlfriend. You have to draw a line somewhere, man."

"Well, fuck, she was just as into it as I was!" I protested.

"Yes, and I'm sure Anton will have a similar talk with her when they break up because of you, you home-wrecking piece of shit," Derek chirped. "I'm not gonna bitch at Casandra because I'm not her friend, but I *am* gonna bitch at *you* because *you* are my friend."

"What he said," Marshall added.

"Was it worth it, Edwin? Was one night with her worth ruining a friendship? Was it worth ruining a relationship?" Derek questioned me.

I shrugged. "She felt good, so I guess so."

"Who the fuck even are you anymore?" Derek whined. "You've changed into some duster that doesn't care about his bros anymore. That's never been you."

I shrugged again and took a nacho off the plate and popped it into my mouth. "I guess I just don't feel emotionally invested with the whole *giving a shit about people* thing." I poured more beer into my mug and took a sip.

"You've crossed a line though, Edwin." Derek sighed. "It's time for an intervention."

"I don't need an intervention."

Marshall laughed. "Right. You have no respect for people anymore."

"I have respect for you two bench-warmers."

"You have a drinking problem," Marshall added.

I shrugged. "It's not a problem. I just drink a lot…most nights… you know, 'cause it's fun and I like it. It's not a problem if I like it."

"Yes, it is. That makes it even more of a problem because you can't see that it's a fucking problem, you idiot," Marshall barked.

"Not my problem," I said. "You guys are the ones taking issue with it. I'm fine."

"For now," Derek said. "You're fine for now. What next? What happens next in your life, Edwin? Don't you give a shit anymore, about anything? Are you happy working a dead-end job and rolling through the weekends with girls that are barely going to remember you anyway?"

"Yes," I replied flatly. "I don't really remember them either, so no hard feelings."

"That's not what I meant and you know it."

"What does it matter?" I asked. "I don't have a reason to do better for myself. Outside of you two, that is." Marshall raised a glass for that.

"*You* should want more for you. You shouldn't need a reason to want better for yourself," Derek stated. "First off, stop drinking so goddamn much. Secondly, cut down on the parties and the clubbing. Just focus on positive things in your life."

"Like my friends and family," I muttered. "Blah, blah, blah. I've heard this conversation before in movies and TV dramas. Fuck, I've even been on the giving end of this lecture. My problem is that I don't see how I could want better."

"What the fuck does that even mean?" Derek shouted. "Look, I don't give a fuck that you're sleeping with a bunch of girls, that's fine, that's whatever, not to mention you have a great streak with the flutes right now, but the issue is that you're just so fucking numb to everything around you. You need to stop for a while, you need to figure out who *you* are again. Fiona died well over a year ago, you need to move on from that. Let go of that anchor, Edwin."

"Well, that's easy for you to say," I barked. "You weren't in love with the girl. She was my everything, Derek. Not just a little notch in my bedpost, no, she was fucking *it*. She was the thing so many other men spend their entire lives trying to find. That is not something that is easy to let go off."

"Edwin, she was our friend too, you know," Marshall interjected. "Sure, we didn't love her the same way you did, but she was still basically family to us."

"And you know, all I hear is how I'm fucking up my life or whatever, but I'm not hearing suggestions on how to help me."

Derek sighed. "Dude, I dunno. Replace your alcohol habits with green tea or some other healthy drink. And what about that Colby girl? You still hanging out with her? She seems nice.

She might help you feel a little more like a... *person*, I guess."

"Yeah, I talk to her once in a while."

"Why don't you ask her on a date?" Marshall suggested.

"You guys seem to like each other."

"Yeah, because she's hot as fuck, so of course I like her," I stated. Man, these two can be a little stupid sometimes, huh?

"Okay, so wouldn't you rather be with one insanely hot girl for the *rest* of your life than have random half-as-hot girls for one night each?" Marshall questioned.

I blew a raspberry. "Fuck, that's a tough one. You got me there."

"Edwin," Marshall growled. "Stop being an idiot."

"We're just trying to help you," Derek added. "We're your friends, so it's kind of our job to make sure you never get too far off the deep end."

"I'm barely in the shallows," I told them. "But you know, you're right. I should probably do better by me so I can do better by someone else, right?"

"See, there's that old, altruistic Edwin we've missed so much."

I took a long drink of beer and sighed. "Okay, before I make any changes, we still have that party to go to next week. After that, I'll focus on being a better me for me."

"Hey, this actually worked?" Derek laughed a little. "Honestly, I'm just glad you're not as stubborn as you used to be or we would have been here all night."

"Too drunk to care," I stated, reaching for a handful of nachos.

"Did you drive here?" Derek asked me.

I nodded. "Sure did, pal. Relax, Colby's gonna drop by and drive me home."

"How's she getting here?"

"I dunno, bus or something." I munched on some nachos.

"Perhaps she will fly. I've heard angels can do that."

"It's past eleven, do buses even run that late on Fridays?" Derek asked.

I shrugged. "Beats me. I hope so."

"And you're gonna let her drive you home?"

"Yessir."

"And then what?" Marshall asked. "Are you gonna kick her out and make her walk home in the middle of the night?"

"No, you bender, I'm not an asshole," I stated. "She'll crash at my place with me. I've had a part of my anatomy inside a part of hers, so I don't think her sleeping in my bed is a big deal."

"Just making sure, relax."

"Someone's all tense," Derek teased.

"Well, I did just go through an intervention." I refilled my mug from the pitcher and took a long drink. "Do you guys really think Colby likes me?"

Derek and Marshall exchanged quick looks before Derek replied, "Yeah, to be honest. From the limited time I've hung out with the two of you together and from what and *how* you've talked about her, I'd say she likes you."

"Do you like her?" Marshall asked.

"Yeah," I said, "she's pretty great."

"Then ask her out."

"I'm not ready." I took another long drink of beer and polished off my glass before stepping outside to make a phone call.

It had started raining by the time I made it home. My apartment (blessed because) was on the second floor of the building. I really got me a steal when I found it. The rent's decent and I can actually afford it, unlike most of the rent in this city. Colby had dropped by the bar via a taxi. She drove us back to my apartment like the kind soul she was.

"Remember last time I was here?" Colby asked as we stepped in, her hair just delicately damp enough for it shine under the dim light of the apartment.

"Yeah," I replied. "You broke my lamp."

"*You* broke your lamp."

"It was *your* foot." I walked into the kitchen and flicked the light on. "You hungry?"

"Not really. I had mac and cheese before coming to get you." She sat down at the table, looking over her nails. She must have painted them tonight. "I could eat though, if you're wanting to make me something."

"No, I'm not that hungry. I had nachos at the bar." I sat at the table with her and looked at her until she looked up from her nails at me. She smiled softly at me, the kind of smile that makes all your problems go away, the kind of smile that gives you feelings that should only be reserved for when you're falling in love or achieving your life's dream.

"Are you tired?" she asked me.

I shook my head. "Are you?"

She nodded. "I had to get up early to cover someone's shift at work. Not a big deal, but it was earlier than I usually get up, so I'm a little tuckered out tonight."

"Feel free to sleep, I'm not gonna stop you."

"Boo, you're no fun." She pulled a chair in front of her and rested her feet on it. "I was thinking we could do something before we go to sleep. I didn't come here *just* to sleep and then leave in the morning."

"Well, what d'you wanna do?"

She blew a raspberry. "Movie?"

"You know where it is. Go get it set up. I'll get us some snacks," I told her.

"Aye, aye, captain." She stood up, saluted me, and then pranced off to my bedroom. I watched her walk down the hall as she pulled her pants off her legs. She sure makes getting comfortable a priority.

I rifled through my kitchen and settled on a bowl of grapes and some crackers. I guess I should try that whole making healthier decisions thing. Physically, mentally, emotionally, all that crap. I suppose being a little more conscious with life couldn't hurt. I walked into my bedroom to see Colby wrapped in a blanket on the edge of my bed. Her feet were sticking out the bottom of her cocoon and her face was lit up by the screen of the TV and the starting credits of some movie she chose for us.

"Grapes?" Colby questioned as I sat next to her.
"What?" I said. "You don't like grapes?"
"I do. Just didn't think you did."
"Well, I'm trying to be healthier."
She smiled. "Well, you can never go wrong with grapes." She took a handful and popped one in her mouth.

This might be the least depressed I've been since Fiona passed. It's something about Colby. She's just a calming presence. She slows everything down and makes everything that isn't the moment she's in simply not matter as much. She drowns out the bad and replaces it with a bright smile and a joyful laugh. Even when her eyes are fixated on an animated movie about squirrels, she still has me in a trance at how a human can be so seemingly flawless. She gives me the same feeling as a starry night sky does; namely that I'm so pathetically worthless in the presence of something so fucking ridiculously beautiful and transcendent.

After forty minutes, she fell asleep on my lap. Once the movie was over, I laid her down in the bed and pulled her onto my chest and we just slept. It was the most innocent I've felt in a long time. I felt at peace with myself. And at least for one night, it was nice to feel that again. Even when the colours betwixt were cold and uncoordinated, it was nice to feel a spark.

Part 3
Chapter 6

The Party

Dressed up and ready for one last romp in the bedroom of someone I barely know. Derek had picked us up and offered to be the designated driver for the evening, because he's a cool dude like that (or he just wanted to babysit me).

"Don't get too drunk, okay?" Derek said as we got out of the car.

I nodded. "Yes, I get it. You lectured me the entire way here. Relax. I get it. I won't overdo it."

"You say that now."

"Let me live. In a week or so, all those high school kids are gonna be free from school and going to parties all summer and ruining the mood with their petty who-likes-who bullshit, so just let me have one more good night."

Derek sighed. "Whatever."

"I'll keep an eye on him," Marshall stated.

"Sure you will." Derek looked us over. "Okay, well, I'm gonna go get something to eat and I'll be right back. Call me if you dusters need me to pick you up before then. Have fun."

Marshall and I waved Derek off as we turned to head over to the house party that was a-raging already. I checked my phone, no messages. "Okay, Marsh, let's go have ourselves a night."

And
    the
        night
            wore
                on.

Derek made his way back to us in the party, sipping on a peach green tea drink, non-alcoholic of course. I was only a little drunk when he got back. Marshall, however, was off the deep end already. He pounded back one too many shots and was running around the party dancing and just having a genuinely good time.

"You could have brough' me some food," I said as Derek and I took a seat on a sofa.

He shrugged. "I figured you would eat some snacks here or something."

"I raided their cupboards and found pita crackers, but I don't have any dip." I handed the package of crackers to him. "You, uh, can you hold those for me?"

"Yeah, sure." He shook his head. "Well, at least you're not wasted, that's a good sign."

I rested my finger on his nose and smiled. "The night is still young, my sweet bender."

"You're a fucking bender, hoser."

"Rude." I leaned back on the couch and scoped the party

over. People were drunk. People were stoned. People were enjoying themselves, so I was enjoying myself. I like seeing people happy and having fun.

"What've you been doing all night?"

"Drinking, dancing, chatting up random people," I told him. "You know, the usual shit."

"I see a lack of flute at your side," Derek noted. "Are you having an off night?"

I scoffed. "The Edwinner doesn't have off nights."

"Whatever you say." Derek got up and stretched a little. "I'm gonna go find Marshall and try to get him to eat some of these crackers. Alcohol and empty stomachs don't mix."

"I'll be somewhere if you need me."

He shook his head. "You're an idiot. I'll text you."

My eyes followed him as he walked into the kitchen and out to the backyard. In the kitchen, however, something (or rather *someone*) caught my eye. A rather pretty blonde girl with an undercut and some weird design shaved into it. And hello, what a wonderful backside on her. She was having trouble with the keg. Well, I suppose that's my signal. I got up and walked over to her. "Hey." I opened the fridge once she looked over. "Bottle service for the lady?" I pulled a bottle of beer out and handed it to her.

"Thanks," she said, grabbing the bottle. "The keg was being a little shit."

"Yeah, it's been like that all night." I grabbed myself a beer and closed the fridge.

"Well, you're my hero, thank you." She smiled a bright smile, not Colby-esque, but still beautiful. "And does my hero have a name?"

"Edwin." I outstretched my hand.

"I'm Lou," she said as she raised her hand.

I took her hand in mine, raised it, and kissed it (cliché). "Nice to meet you, Lou."

"Likewise." She looked around and then back at me. "Um, okay, so I don't know who else to ask. I'm not from around

here, but um, do you know a place where we can spark up?"
I nodded. "Follow *moi*." I turned and walked down a hallway. Derek was walking the opposite way and gave me a slight nod. I noticed he was carrying a bottle of whisky that he no doubt pried away from Marshall. I looked down and cocked an eyebrow. As we passed each other, I swapped my unopened beer for the whisky. I walked with Lou upstairs to one of the "guest" rooms. I closed the door and locked it (because you don't want people just barging in). I cracked the window and pulled a table and two small stools over to it. "Voila!"

"I don't think we need the table," Lou noted as she took a seat on one of the stools. "You get high?"

"That's my secret, Lou," I said, beginning to make an *Avengers* reference. "I'm always high."

She laughed. "Do you want some, for real?"

"Yeah." I sat down next to her as she doled out a joint for both of us. "So you mentioned that you aren't from around here. Where are you from, then?"

"Port Perry," Lou replied. "I'm on a road trip with my dearest friend Jude. Thought it would be cool to stop at a party and blow off some steam."

"That's pretty cool. It's a long way off, Port Perry."

"I know some people in some places."

I smiled as she handed me a lighter. "Thanks."

"You're staring."

"You're just really attractive. Sorry." I put the joint to my lips and lit it.

She blushed and hid a smile. "Thanks, man. You're very sweet."

"I don't know what to say next." We exchanged a nervous laugh as we both took a pull from our joints.

"What're you doing at this party? You know why I'm here, but why are you here?" Lou asked me, grabbing the whisky from beside me and opening it.

"Well, I wanted one last party before I focus on making better choices for myself, I guess." I sighed and took another pull. "I just have a bad way of coping and parties don't help me, they enable me, they make me worse. So this is my last one for a while."

"Making good life decisions is something I've never been good at." Lou sighed. "Sorry. This is probably gonna get heavy, huh?"

I chuckled and nodded. "Seems that way."

"Okay, well, after tonight, neither of us are likely to see each other, so let's just... let's just get it all out and vent to each other, man. We'll feel better about it," she stated. "Well, probably."

"You go first."

"That's some lame-sauce, bro." She huffed and sighed. "But fine, ladies first or whatever." She took a long pull and began. "I don't know what to say."

I pouted in thought. "What do you wanna be when you grow up?"

"I'm twenty-two," she deadpanned.

"Answer my question."

Lou sighed. "A baker. I wanna be a baker. What do you wanna be?"

"A painter," I replied.

"Why?"

I shrugged. "I just really love colours, I guess. There's just something so wonderful about colours and how they can change the feel of a room or how they bring up certain feelings. I love them."

"That's cool," Lou said. "I guess I never really looked at it in depth. Anyway, we were getting to venting, I believe?"

I nodded. "Right. So, what's your favourite colour?"

"What does that matter?"

I shrugged. "I just like colours. I always like knowing someone's favourite colour. It helps me relate to them, I guess."

"Magenta," Lou replied. "My favourite colour is magenta."

"What's your biggest fear?"

"Becoming, or I guess staying, a low-life pothead." She ran her hand through her hair, pushing it off her undercut side. "I guess I'd be scared of getting picked up. I don't wanna end up in jail."

"Then quit the pot. Chase your dream of being a baker. You can do it, and you know how I know?" I asked. She didn't reply. "Because you're the only one who can. You gotta do it for yourself, right?"

She nodded. "Right. It's just hard, I guess. I need the pot to get away from the stress and then it itself makes me stressed. Ironic. And sometimes I feel like I live in the shadow of my friend—Jude. She's amazing and I just feel like I'm sometimes not, I guess. I dunno."

I hushed her. "You're fine. Don't doubt yourself, ever. You're amazing in your own way, that I can promise you."

She smiled at me. "Thanks."

I smiled back at her. "Okay, so what's your biggest priority in life, Lou?" I asked, taking a pull from the joint that I was still holding. It was almost done now, but not quite… not quite.

She shrugged. "I dunno, man. I guess just making sure you're happy at the end of the day, you know?"

"Well, are you happy?"

She mustered up a half-assed smile. "I dunno."

"What's your biggest accomplishment so far in this life?"

"I graduated with honours in my business course at college." She smiled. "Totally nailed it, to be honest."

"See, you're smart. You have a brain. You're never gonna be a dumb pothead, alright? Just don't give up on yourself."

"Thanks." She took the joint out of my hand. She clamped her fingers right down on the cherry and snuffed it out without so much as a whimper or a wince. "Were you trying to burn the whole thing down to ash, or…?"

"I was gonna put it down," I told her. "You know, when it started to burn my fingers."

"Mm-hmm." She inhaled the rest of her joint and blew

smoke at me. "Okay, your turn. What's in your vaults, Edwin?"

"Well, to start, my girlfriend died a just over a year ago and—"

"Whoa, what the fuck? Heavy, bro. I wasn't ready." Lou scooted her chair a little closer to mine and grabbed my hand. "You don't have to say anymore if you don't want to."

"No, venting is good," I stated. "I want to tell you. It'll be nice to get an outside opinion."

"Right. Then continue."

"So she passed away because of a car accident one snowy night, and ever since then, I've felt empty. Just numb and grey beyond all hope," I said. "A couple months ago, my friends had me get back out there and I did. I met a girl named Colby and we had sex. Then I started a spiral and began fucking all the girls I could and drinking all the booze I could until just last week when I slept with a friend's girlfriend. 'Not cool, bro.' I know. I've had that lecture. So now I have to just figure out how to cope, how to be a person again."

"How to feel?" Lou questioned.

I nodded. "Yeah, something like that."

"So who's Colby?"

"Some girl."

"Some girl you mentioned by name in your little story," Lou noted. "Who is she? Do you like her or something?"

"I don't know. Honestly, we've just fucked a few times. It's not serious, she's just the first girl after my ex," I said. "I doubt she's anything special." *Oh, Edwin, you fucking liar. Colby is an amazing human being and you should be begging at her feet for a chance to love her for even a single moment.*

"If you want her, you gotta go get her. I'm sure she's great, so don't let her go just because you feel like you're not ready to move on. Sometimes you have to do something that terrifies you," Lou told me. "That's the fun of it."

"Not tonight. Tonight I am a free man. I don't wanna think about feelings and shit."

"I don't blame you."

I smiled a little. "Gimme this." I grabbed the whisky from her and downed a good-sized gulp. "That hits the spot."

"Yeah. I'm feeling it right now."

"So," I said, looking around the room, "what now?"

Lou shrugged. "Beats me. We could go back to the party, or we could get higher, if you want?" She pulled out a small baggy and laid it on the table.

And so we did just that. We got higher and higher, man. Like a couple of kites in the breeze, not a care in the world except for the fall. We laughed, we talked, we joked, we smoked, we kissed, we made sure the door was locked. We had easily peeled two hours of our lives away from one another and then went our separate ways, because the colours betwixt were starting to sober up again.

Part 3
Chapter 7

The Green Tea

I knocked obnoxiously on Derek's door until he answered it. He looked me over and sighed before returning inside to go and get dressed. It was eleven in the morning and Derek didn't have work today, so I suppose I ruined his peaceful morning. After a few moments, Derek emerged much more wide-eyed in a T-shirt and shorts.

"Where are we going?" Derek asked.

"I'm amazed that you know that we're going somewhere," I said. "Come on, I'll drive."

"You didn't answer my question," he grumbled, following me nonetheless.

I got in the car and turned to him as he got in his side. "We're going out for brokefast."

"What?"

"It's like breakfast, but for people that are broke."

He nose exhaled. "You right. So where are we going?"

"I was thinking we could just go get some green tea and bagels somewhere. Any ideas?"

Derek blew a raspberry as he thought. "Lattedale, perhaps?"

"Always a good choice," I said, mentally setting a GPS for the nearest Lattedale shop.

"It's far too early for this," Derek muttered.

I shrugged. "I don't think so. I love waking up early. It makes me feel like I've accomplished something before I've even put pants on, and I like that feeling."

"That's a fair point, I guess. But you know what else is a great feeling?" he asked. "Sleeping in on your day off."

"It's not your day off if you have plans," I quipped.

"I'd still like to have slept in."

"Well, getting up early is a healthy choice."

Derek sighed. "How so?"

"It energizes you or some crap. I dunno."

"No."

"Regardless, here we are." I pulled into the parking lot and found us a spot. "Am I paying or are you?"

"You're paying," Derek said as he got out of the car.

"I kinda figured as much."

Derek and I copped a window table, because I enjoy looking out windows. I bought both of us a green tea and a bagel. Green teas are healthy, but I've heard some negative things about bagels lately, but they're good, so I don't give a shit.

"This tastes weird," Derek said, sipping his tea.

"You've never had a green tea before, have you?" I asked, taking a sip of mine. "It tastes perfectly normal to me. Like a good way to start your day."

"How do you know what normal green tea tastes like?" Derek grumbled. "It tastes pretty bad."

"Fiona used to make me drink it sometimes." I shrugged. "I dunno, I like it. I guess it's just not for everyone though. But yeah, she loved it."

"Oh, I didn't know she liked green tea."

"Because why the fuck would she have invited *you* of all people over for green tea?" I asked. "She knew you wouldn't like it. You barely liked black tea."

"Yeah, I'm gonna go buy a coffee." Derek pushed the tea towards me. "But by all means, you finish it off for me."

"Duster," I scoffed to him.

He smirked and shook his head as he walked back over to the counter to place his new order. I sat and ate my bagel while I waited for him to walk back over.

"Hey, so look who I found." I looked up to see Derek standing next to Colby.

"Hi," she said, smiling down at me. Wow, she looks beautiful in this light, or any light, or just in general.

I smiled softly at her. "Hi."

"What're you doing out this early?" she asked as the two of them sat down across from me.

"I'm not entirely sure. I just wanted to come get some tea and breakfast with my dear friend Derek."

"Tea is gross," Derek muttered. I feel like he may not like green tea, but he loves black tea. It just reminds him too much of Fiona. Derek was also grieving about her still, whether he knew it or not. I remember how hyped he got to drink tea with her and I and Marshall back in the day.

Colby rolled her eyes a little. "I'm just on my way to work, stopped in to grab a coffee and saw Derek in line, so I thought that maybe you were here as well, and it turns out I was right."

"How long do you have till you have to get to work?" I asked her.

"I dunno, twenty minutes or so, I guess," she replied. "Why?"

"'Cause you could stay here and have your coffee with us. If you want to, that is."

Colby smiled at me and then Derek. "You guys sure? I don't wanna interrupt your little bro-date."

"He's sure," Derek said, his eyebrows raised at me. "Right?"

I nodded. "I'm pretty sure I'm sure."

"Cool." She smiled and took a sip of her coffee. "Still really hot."

"So what are you two kids doing later?" Derek asked.

I shrugged. "Sleeping, probably."

"Same, probably," Colby told him. "Why? What are *you* doing later?"

"That's not why I was asking. I have plans later. I don't need to hang out with you two, but I was asking because I think you two should go on a date."

"I dunno, nah." I shrugged.

"Rude," Colby barked. "You can cum on my face, but you can't take me out to dinner?"

"TMI," Derek muttered.

She shushed him. "Edwin, do you wanna go on a date with cute little me?"

"I dunno," I replied. "I don't think I'm ready."

"Of course not," Derek groaned. "When will you be ready though, Edwin? How long is it gonna be before you wake up and realize that life is passing you by because you're not ready to *move on*?"

I shrugged. "Couple years, tops."

"Edwin."

"What?" I whined, taking a drink of tea.

"Go on a date with Colby."

I turned to Colby and looked her over. She smiled at me and I kept looking her over. *Yes,* my mind shouted. "I dunno," my mouth spoke.

"I need an answer," Colby replied. "If you're gonna reject me, then just say you don't wanna go on a date. I won't be offended or anything. I get it, some people move on slower than other people do. There's no shame in that."

"Yes, there is," Derek barked. "Stop enabling him."

"Be nice to him or he's never gonna move on because he'll be too busy repressing memories of you," Colby quipped. It was kind of fun to watch them have a little back and forth, almost reminds me of the same thing Derek and Fiona would do. They bickered back and forth for a few moments, but I tuned them out and sipped on my tea.

I took a quiet breath and turned to Colby. "So, where do you wanna go?"

She turned and cocked one of her eyebrows. "Huh? What do you mean?"

"For our date," I said, "where do you wanna go?"

"Oh." She was flustered slightly. She fixed her blonde hair and smiled at me. "What did you have in mind?" Her eyes were lit up and her face showed traces of a blush starting to rise. It's nice to see that I'm not the only one of us that's nervous.

"Twisters in Toronto?" I asked.

"Toronto's a two-hour drive?" Derek interjected.

Colby smiled at him and then looked at me. "That sounds good to me. Meet me there Thursday at eight?"

"Yeah, sounds perfect." I smiled at her. "I'll see you then."

"Cool. I should be off to work now." Colby got up and smiled at Derek and I. "Have a good rest of your days." I watched her as she walked off, because how could I not watch as her petite frame and bubble butt, bubble bubble bubble butt walked away from me.

I turned to Derek once she was out of view. "Am I making a mistake?"

"Nope," Derek said quickly, as if he were waiting on me to ask that very question. "You're doing just fine, hoser. The mistake is going to Toronto for dinner."

"Well, there's no Twisters here and I like Twisters," I told him. "And I just feel bad, like I'm doing wrong by Fiona or something." I sighed and took a sip of tea. "I dunno, I'm just… confused, I guess."

"You're not," Derek stated. "She would want you to be happy. No matter what, your happiness meant more to her than anything else in the world. Even if she were still here, she would rather you be with Colby than her if it meant that you would be happier. That's just the kind of girl she was, Edwin, and you know that better than anyone. The only person you're doing wrong by not moving on is yourself."

"I guess you're right."

"And besides, Colby's fucking great. What was that line she chirped you with? The cumming on her face thing? That was brilliant. She's great, so do us both a favour and keep her around."

I chuckled softly. "No promises." I've developed a tendency to fuck things up recently, so I really can't make a promise. There's no telling if Colby and I will work out, and to give credit to Derek for something, there's no telling we won't work out either.

"How's that green tea?" Derek chirped.

I scoffed. "Better for me than that coffee." I groaned. "But I want coffee so badly."

"Go get one."

"I've already had two green teas and a bagel. I don't wanna spend any more money."

Derek shrugged. "Well, that sounds likes a *you* problem."

"Fuck off."

"So, I've meant to ask you, but where is your new job at?"

"Oh, at a hotel. I'm a humble housekeeping attendant now," I told him. "My last few jobs sucked ass. I'm sick of my body feeling tired all the time."

"Was it because of the jobs or the partying? I wonder," Derek taunted. "No, but if you like this new job, then good for you. I'm glad, buddy."

"Should be. It pays better than any of the old jobs."

"Yeah?"

"Yeah, nineteen an hour, man."

"That's dope."

I nodded. "It pays bills. I like being on top of shit for once. I might even be able to pay off my credit card in full soon, so like, that's pretty fucking stellar if I do say so myself."

"Well, don't jinx it," Derek said. "You guys hiring at all?"

"I'll keep my eye out and put in a good word."

"Thanks. I can only cook pizza for so long before I go insane."

"You cook good pizza, to be fair."

He scoffed. "Yeah, thanks, but I still don't wanna work there any longer than I have to."

"Speaking of work, I wonder what it is that Colby does." Hmm, I wonder. Probably a retail job from what she's mentioned so far to me. She was wearing a black collared shirt and white jeans, so maybe she works someplace fancy. Either way, she looked so beautiful in her outfit today. *Swoon.*

"Golf course."

"How'd you figure that out?" I asked.

"The logo on her sleeve was for a golf course."

"Oh, I guess I wasn't paying attention to that."

"Which is good," Derek stated. "I want you to get lost in her eyes. Fall in love, asshole."

"I'll get right on that." I took the last sip of my green tea and looked into the cup. The colours betwixt were diluted and pale, almost like looking in the mirror lately.

Part 3
Chapter 8

The Date

My apartment was quiet, quieter than I think it's ever been. I stared at myself in the mirror, water dripping from my chin and into the sink. I was careful not to get anything on my white dress shirt or pants, even though the pants are black and water isn't gonna show up on them. The bathroom stunk of cologne musk. There was trimmed facial hair in the sink, a razor I had dropped was there as well.

"Come on, Edwin," I mumbled to myself. "Stop being nervous. You literally had sex with her already. Come on." I took a few deep breaths and tried to stop my palms from getting clammier than they already were. I haven't even left my apartment and yet I'm nervous as all hell. I suck at dating, but you can't blame me. I've been on exactly one proper first date before, and that was with Fiona. And I can't just wish away the nerves because, for the most part, if I'm nervous, it means I'm doing something right. You have to step out of your comfort zone and feel anxious and nervous and scared once in a while, it's part of the human experience, it's a part of growing as a person.

I tidied up the sink and put everything away. See, I might live on my own, but I still enjoy a clean place to live. I'm not trying to further the myth that all men are messy and live like pre-electricity era savages. I clicked the bathroom light off and walked to the kitchen. My apartment was a nice open-concept type place. Kitchen and living room were all connected and then down a small little hallway was the bedroom, bathroom, and a small walk-in closet. The view from the living room was nice; a nearly all-glass wall gave me a nice view out into the world.

I poured myself a glass of water and looked out the window at the sky. Blue as ever. But I really love the sky so much. I love how many colours it can be. Blue, pink, purple, red, orange, yellow. All so beautiful. I finished my water and then headed downstairs. I double-checked the lock on my door to make sure it was locked. I wasn't paranoid, just liked to be on the safe side. I headed downstairs and got in my car. Time to head off to Twisters for a date with a very, very beautiful girl.

Waiting is always the worst part. It was only 7:03 PM, but she said she wanted to be here at 7:00 sharp, so maybe I'm getting nervous for nothing, but maybe I have reason to be nervous. Maybe she's standing me up. I stood out front of Twisters like an idiot, watching the cars pulling into the parking lot and hoping that one of them would be driven by a blonde goddess, but none were, though one was driven by a very old woman who seemed to be straining to live. I hope I never get that old, *sigh*.

Perhaps suggesting a place that was in Toronto rather than

Belleville was stupid. It's a two-hour drive, but I do *love* Twisters. And I mean, I can just hotel it for the night. I also love Toronto, I like the feeling of the city, all the bright lights and colours and the people. It makes me feel like I'm a part of something bigger than just suburban and small-city life.

I checked the time. 7:22.

I'm being stood up.

7:31. I'm being stood up.

7:38. I am being stood up.

7:46. Why the fuck am I still waiting around the front of Twisters like an idiot? I got stood up. I should just go home. But yet, I wait.

7:59. She stood me up. I waited an hour for her and she's not here. I knew this date wasn't going to go well. I sighed and put my phone back in my pocket, walking down the stretch of concrete towards where I parked my car. Then a small blue car rolled into a parking spot in front of me. Colby stepped out and walked up to me. It was hard for me to be mad at someone who looks so gorgeous. Her bright eyes and golden hair in the dim evening light. Her porcelain skin, taught and smooth under a form-fitting one-armed dress getup. Everything about her screamed stunner. I've never seen a girl look so elegant, so magnificent. She looked so make-me-fall-in-love-and-forget-how-to-say-words beautiful. Colby is the kind of girl you write love songs about just based on how fucking beautiful she looks when she walks into a room or smiles or just exists at all.

"Hi," she said, a wide smile plastered on her face. "You look ravishing this evening."

"Where were you? I've been waiting for an hour."

She smiled and then laughed a little. She noticed my expression didn't change and so she dropped her smile. "Oh, you've seriously been waiting for an hour?"

"Yeah," I said, unamused.

"We were supposed to meet at eight. I'm right on time." She showed me her phone. "See, it's eight now."

I thought for a moment and groaned. "I knew I should

have written down what time you said to meet here."
"Well, I shoulda reminded you. My bad." Colby smiled.
"Well, let's go get some dinner, huh? I'm starved."
"Yeah, a two-hour drive'll do that to you." I walked to the door and opened it for her.
"Oh, I got a hotel room for myself for the night," Colby said. "You're more than welcome to join me after dinner."
"Smart."
"Well, if you have to drive two-hours for dinner, you might as well enjoy the city for a night."
"See, that's why I drive two hours for Twisters."
Colby giggled. "You're an idiot."
I smiled at her and turned to the reception/waitress lady person. "Table for two, please." Come to think of it, I don't know what this job position is called. Are you a receptionist? I mean, you receive people at the door, right? Are you a seater because you seat the customers?

I did a quick web search on the way to our table and found out that they're called hosts/hostesses.

Within seconds of us sitting down, a waitress appeared at the side of our table, smiling down at us with a notepad in hand. "Hello, my name's Shay. I'll be your server for the evening. Can I get you guys something to drink to start off?"

"I'll just have water," Colby replied.

I turned to the waitress. "I'll take a cola, or a root beer. Surprise me."

The waitress, Shay, smiled and nodded. "Gotcha, surprise it is. I'll be back in just a moment with the drinks." She bounced off into the mass of tables and other servers. She was quite the beautiful girl herself. Blonde, sea green eyes (the really noticeable feature on her), and freckles on her cheeks and nose. But I guess there's this notion that only "pretty" girls can be waitresses, so of course she was going to be a pretty girl.

I looked at Colby. She was sitting looking at me and looking beautiful doing it. I smiled. "So what was that dinky-ass car you were driving?" We both started looking over our menus.

"Don't you dare disrespect my baby!" she barked. "It's a 1972 Honda N600 and she's beautiful and I love her."

"Sorry, sorry."

"You better be, Edwin *Flowers*," she teased. "Speaking of, what's your favourite kind?"

I shrugged. "I love all flowers."

"I like sunflowers."

"Is your favourite colour yellow?"

She nodded. "Duh. Yellow is the colour of happy. And I enjoy being happy."

"That's good."

Shay popped back up before Colby and I could continue our talk. "Here's are your drinks. Now," she said, taking a breath, "have we decided on starters?"

"Garlic toast and spinach dip with those pita bread things," I said. Colby gave me a look like she was angry for me ordering a starter.

Shay smiled. "I'll get that to you ASAP."

"Spinach dip?" Colby protested. "What if I don't like spinach dip?"

"Have you ever had it?"

She pouted a little. "No."

"Then give it a try."

She sighed. "Okay." She looked around a little and then focused back on me. "So what's your life story, Edwin? Where are you from? I wanna get to know you a little more beyond the small talk."

"Um, I dunno. I'm from Belleville, born and raised. Nothing special." I blew a raspberry as I thought about it. "Yeah, I guess that's it. Where are you from?"

"Sweden," she replied.

I cocked an eyebrow. "Sweden?"

She nodded. "Yep."

"Well... Care to explain?"

"Okay, so I was born in this little town called Kiruna in north Sweden. My mom, who's from Belleville originally, worked as a tourist guide and a hiking guide. My dad, from Sweden, was an accountant for some company. They met, fell in love, gave birth to me—" she daintily cupped her face in her hands and smiled "—and then after a few years they moved to Canada to be closer to my mom's family. I don't have an accent or anything because, well, I was raised here for the most part. And much to my father's dismay, I never had much interest in learning the Swedish language."

"Wow, a Swedish girl. That's pretty cool."

"Yeah, so that's where I'm from."

"Much cooler than my story." I sighed. "All well."

"Okay, what about the story behind your colourful geometric owl tattoo?" Colby asked. "You never gave me a meaning to it."

I shrugged. "It doesn't really have a meaning. I dunno. I just like colours and geometric tattoos. I guess I chose an owl because it's a cool bird of the night and the nighttime is calm and I like calm things. I dunno."

She nodded. "Cool. Tattoos don't all need deep meanings. Sometimes it's just because they look cool. That's why I got the bird silhouettes on my ribs. They look cool."

"What about your other tattoos?" I pointed to her forearm. "Like that arrow. What's that one for?"

"A reminder that when life pulls me down, it's gonna launch me forward." She smiled. "Hopeful thinking. I like to try to think positively."

"What about the fox tattoo on your calf?"

"Oh, the one that's in the *same* place as your owl tattoo?" she asked. "Yeah, that's because I love foxes, adore them, and because foxes are cute and quick and sly and clever, and I am also those things."

"Foxes are pretty great."

She smirked. "Duh. Also, it should be stated outright: I don't like chocolate. Never have, never will."

"You don't like chocolate?!"

She shook her head. "Not even a little bit."

"Who the fuck are you as a person?" I was astonished, offended to my bones, to the very *core* of my soul. "How don't you like chocolate?"

"I dunno. I'm just not too hot about it. I don't mind chocolate milkshakes every now and then, but chocolate itself? Can't do it."

"Weird," I teased.

"So, what do you do for fun?" Colby asked. "Like, what are you passionate about?"

Give me a month and it'd be you, I thought to myself. I shrugged. "Painting, I guess. I've always painted, as long as I can remember I've wanted to be a painter, but there' s not really a job market for that kind of thing."

"That's why I asked what you're passionate about, not what you wanna be when you grow up or what you do for work now. I don't care about jobs. Jobs are jobs," she mused, "but not everyone has something that they're passionate about. Some people give up on their passions because they feel like it doesn't fit in with life, but that's the stupidest thing to think. Passions are important, Edwin."

"I know they are." I took a sip of my drink (it was a root beer, surprise). "So what are you passionate about?"

"People."

"People?"

She nodded. "I love people. I love how different we all are. We all know things that other people don't. Every person has a different, but still totally valid, story of life. I love that. I love that so many different stories are all unfolding at once, together as part of a bigger narrative. There's a word for it, but I can't remember it right now."

"People suck," I said with a small laugh, laughing at myself mostly.

She shrugged. "Depends on your perspectives, I suppose."

Shay popped around with our starters and smiled at us. "So, do you guys know what you want for your main course? I can take the order now."

"I'll take a deluxe burger, the works," I told her.

Colby blew a raspberry and looked the menu over once more. "I'll have a six-piece chicken meal. Curly fries with that. Thanks."

Shay smiled (again, I know, servers smile a lot). "Sure thing. Enjoy the starters, you two. I'll keep an eye on your table and have the mains around."

The view from the eighteenth floor of this hotel was quite remarkable. The city seemed so much quieter from up here, so much more dim as well. The lights of the street weren't harsh, but rather, they were just rivers of light flooding the building-banks below.

"If you look hard enough, I'm sure you'll find Waldo," Colby said from behind me. I wheeled around and she handed me a glass of whisky. "Drink up. I didn't pay for a bottle to not drink it." She stepped up beside me and looked out the window. "I love the city sometimes. Not to be down in the noise, but above it, where things are a little quieter and not so harsh."

"Yeah," I said, turning and looking out the window again. I took a sip of whisky and smiled a little. "I like watching the cars drive on the streets and watching the lights change from red to green to yellow to red to green and so on and so on."

"You didn't comment about my galaxy nails." Colby placed her hand against the window. "Look at them. They're dark purple and sparkly."

"They're very pretty, Colby."

She smiled. "Thank you."

"I have work tomorrow at nine."

"Sucks to suck." Colby turned and walked over to the bed and sat down on it. "Wanna get some sleep, then?"

"I could call in sick."

"Oh?"

"I have my co-worker's number. I could see if he wants to

cover my shift. He's part-time and always whining about needing more hours."

Colby smirked. "I'm not stopping you."

I pulled my phone out and smiled as I texted the aforementioned co-worker and then my boss to let him know I wouldn't be able to make it because I was stuck in Toronto due to "car troubles." So what if I fibbed, everybody lies to their bosses once in a while. Even my boss has lied to their boss before, so relax. It's human nature for someone to lie to get out of work so that they can stay in a hotel with a beautiful girl and then have sex and get drunk with that girl all night and then sleep in until ten minutes before their checkout time.

I set the glass of whisky down and walked to the window again, taking one last look at the colours betwixt the buildings, all a soft yellow, a calm nighttime. I smiled and turned back to Colby, my mind on one thing and one thing only.

PART FOUR
The Colours

Part 4
Chapter 1

The Colours of a Journal

There's nothing quite like doing some spring cleaning on a Friday night in the middle of summer. See the joke there is that I'm bad at cleaning. The bigger joke is that I'm bad at unpacking. There's still a stack of boxes in my closet despite me having moved in months ago at this point. I just have to go through everything and see what needs to be unpacked or not. And now that I'm back from Toronto and all my friends have plans, I figured tonight was as good a time as any to get through the rest of my boxes.

A pile of boxes now rested on the floor of my living room. Some were full of clothes, some full of unpacked dishes. I had pushed my coffee table to the side so I could sit on my couch while perusing the contents of all these boxes. I'd wager I could throw out or donate half the things in these boxes. Always donate what you can, by the way. Just because you have no use for something doesn't mean that the something in question is useless.

I sorted through a bunch of boxes, saving the heaviest one for last. It was the box with photo albums and journals, Fiona's photo albums and journals at that. I sighed and pulled the flaps of the box open and peered inside. Memories upon memories, bound in books that Fiona will never get to flip through or read. I pulled out the secret journal, the one she kept at her little cabin in the woods. The key was in the box somewhere. I dug around under the photo albums and other journals until I found it. Maybe I should look at it. Enough time has passed, and surely this time I won't be able to stop my curiosity from coming back to this journal every day. It's going to win eventually, so why not just let it win now?

I pushed the key into the little lock and twisted it. The journal hadn't been opened in so long I damn near thought I heard a creak when I pushed the cover open to the very first page. It was dated just over four years ago.

Oh, Journal,
    Today was a good day. I bought my very first locked journal: you! You're the journal that will house all my deepest secrets. I'll write more soon. I'm going on a date with Edwin tonight and I have to get ready. Edwin is my boyfriend. He's amazing. I love him. You'll hear about him, Journal. Don't worry.

I smiled as I read the small opening paragraph. "I love you too," I whispered, half-hoping that perhaps this journal could be used to communicate with Fiona in the great beyond. She didn't answer, of course.

I flipped through a couple pages and found a sudden gap between entries, a gap of a couple months, which I hadn't seen. She had been writing weekly throughout the journal for the most part up to this entry. It was dated a little over a year before she passed.

Oh, Journal,

I've decided you need a new home. Edwin's been coming over lots lately and as we get older, no doubt we'll be spending more and more time together, therefore making it riskier to keep you in this house, Journal.

I know a place though. There's a small cabin north of the city that I can store you. And it'll be a great place for me to escape the real world for a while! So it's good for both you and me. I'll have to get a lock on the cabin though.

Hmm.

I'll write again when I get everything set up! I'm so excited to have a little getaway cabin. Nobody ever goes up there. It's mine for the taking. Can't wait.

She emblazoned the bottom of the entry with a drawing of herself holding a journal near a small house surrounded by trees. I smiled again. She must have been so calm and peaceful out there, reading and writing in her journals, drawing and eating snacks. I wish she had shared it with me, but I suppose I was part of the "real world" that she wanted escape from occasionally. And that's okay, I never expected for her to want to spend every waking moment with me.

I flipped through the journal some more, reading little snippets every few pages. It wasn't anything I didn't know. She told me most things. Sure, there were some thoughts I didn't know, sexual fantasies she never asked me to carry out with her, and things she didn't like about me written down, but I sort of expected that kind of stuff. It wasn't until I got to the last entry when it started to hurt. It was dated the morning of her death, the morning before we left to go to the cottage, the last morning she ever woke up.

Dear Edwin,

I love you. Let's start there. Let's start with the fact that you're a beautiful shining sun and nothing in my life has ever come close to the happiness you give me. There's nothing I love more in this world than you and all you are. You're so much more than just my boyfriend, you're my soulmate, my world, and I love you. Let's also start with the fact that I'm sorry to have to write this letter in the first place, but let's remember that I love you so much, Edwin.

And that's what makes this letter so hard to write, is because I love you so much, but I've decided on something, decided on something serious, something permanent.

I know what I'm about to tell you isn't fair of me. But if you've made it to this point where you're reading this, perhaps you won't be mad. Perhaps you understand already the things I'm going to tell you. And if you're reading this, I guess you know what this letter is.

Over the past few months, more so the past few weeks, I haven't been feeling like myself. I never have really felt happy, only fleeting moments of it. It got really bad in these last few weeks though. My blue skies have all gone grey, Edwin. All I feel anymore is anger and sadness and hopelessness. I can't be expected to live like this, can I? Would you want to live if all you felt in every one of your waking seconds was an inescapable, intangible, unfixable, omnipresent dark cloud hovering over you wherever you went, and a cloud that wouldn't clear, no matter how much it rained or how hard the sun shined behind it?

I guess that's just it. You can't expect someone to /want/ to live a life that way. I hope you'll learn to forgive me... assuming you ever read this.

And Edwin. If you are reading this, I don't need to tell you what I've done. You already know. You should have known that I would never have driven the snowy roads, you know I'm smarter than that, I always have been. I wouldn't drive in unsafe conditions. So if you're reading this, I apologize for leaving so abruptly. I apologize for whatever may befall you in the wreckage.

I love you, Edwin. I love you so much. You are my light, my stars, my fresh pot of coffee. I love you.

Yours always,
        Fiona   xoxo

There it was, in her writing. A letter addressed to me, dated the morning of her death, and clearly telling me that her death wasn't an accident. I should have known, to be honest. I closed the journal and took a breath. I needed a moment to really process it.

She had planned her last words. They were written down and she spoke them to me. She meant for her last words to be this, so of one thing I'm certain: She did love me.

The journal lay on my lap. I looked at it and put it back in its box, the key too. I didn't want to read any more of it. I didn't want to think any more of it. I just wished Fiona was back. That's all. I wished she had spoken up. I wished that she had talked to me, or to her mom, or to anyone at all that she was feeling that way. She wasn't alone, never. Nobody would have turned her down. There was help all around for her if only she had asked, or if only she had wanted the help to begin with. Maybe Fiona was just of the mindset that if she couldn't get better by herself, then she didn't deserve to get better. In the end, that line of thinking might have been her undoing.

I folded the flaps of the box in on themselves and stuffed it under my bed for safe keeping. I put some other boxes there too, to make the Fiona box not so noticeably important. Now I need to go somewhere, see someone, take my mind off things. But where do I go on a Friday night? My friends are probably already drunk or on their way to get drunk, or they're asleep because they had work today.

And then my mind smirked at me. My physical brain smirked and that's when I had an idea. I grabbed my keys and wallet and got outside to my car as quick as I could. I hopped in, started it up, and off I went.

I didn't have to buzz in because I texted ahead of time. I walked over and took the stairs up to the top floor, which is the third floor of this particular building. I was looking for room

C9. Shouldn't be too hard to find, there are only ten units per floor. I got to the door and texted her. I had explicit instructions not to knock on the door, lest I disturb the roommates.

The door opened. "I wasn't expecting company." Colby smirked at me. "Come in and be quiet. Take off your shoes, carry them with you." She was wearing a loose-fitting shirt and plaid-patterned pyjama pants. Her hair was done up in a messy bun and her face was clean of any makeup. She still looked so gorgeous. I could get used to seeing her walk around *my* apartment like this.

I nodded and took my shoes off in the hall and she hurried me into her apartment. I guess she didn't want her roommates making a big deal of me being here which they probably would if they saw me, so this was just easier, I guess. I don't mind. Whatever gets me out of having to make small talk with people I won't hang out with often is fine by me. (It's not because I'm awkwardly shy, by the way.)

"So why'd you wanna come over?" Colby asked, closing her door tight. She flicked her light on and I looked around her room. It was messy, clothes and makeup everywhere, and wires from game controllers and charging cables criss-crossing on her carpet.

I shrugged. "I just didn't wanna be alone right now. I'm having a bad night."

"Well, you're always welcome at *Le Château d'Moi*." She walked over to her bed and sat down. It was a bunk bed, but the bottom was a futon, and she had it set up to be her couch, because obviously you would do that with a bunk bed that has a futon.

I sat down next to her. "Thanks for letting me come over. I wasn't intruding on anything, was I?"

She shrugged. "I was gonna masturbate a little later maybe. But other than that, nope."

"Whoops, sorry."

"No, you're not." She blew a soft raspberry and looked at me. "So, do I get the story?"

"Story?"

"Yeah, of why you came to me and not one of your bros," she said. "And if you're up for telling me, I'd like to know *why* you're having a rough night."

"They're all probably busy. I didn't wanna bother them."

"Oh, so I wasn't your *first* choice," Colby teased. "It's fine. I get it. I'd want my best friends over someone I've only known a couple months too."

I nodded. "Right. And as for the story, you remember the night we met and I told you my girlfriend and I had a rough end to things."

"Right, and?" Colby questioned. "Did she come by your house or something? Want me to kick her ass? I'm trained in jujutsu."

"Really?" I asked.

She nodded. "Black belt."

"That is so cool." I landed me a badass. "Anyway, no, you can't kick her ass."

"Why not?"

"Because she's dead, has been for a year and half."

"Oh," Colby said, dropping her tone, "so that's what you meant when you said you guys also had a messy end to things."

I nodded. "Yeah. I found out today that it was on purpose."

"Oh." It went silent for a few seconds and then Colby's arms were wrapped around me, cradling me in a certain kind of warmth I don't think I've ever really felt before. "I'm so sorry."

"You don't have to apologize," I said, wrapping an arm around her midriff. "It's not like you caused her to die or caused her to *want* to die."

"What was her name?"

"Fiona."

"Tell me about her."

"I don't want to. I hate remembering her. It just reminds me that she's not here anymore."

Colby tightened her grip on me. "That's okay. Just know you're not alone in this, okay?"

I nodded. "You know, I'm as old now as she was when she passed." I laughed, to myself mostly, and a little to Fiona. *I'm older than you now, babe,* I thought. I could picture myself saying that to her and her laughing and then I would laugh and we would both be smiling, happy. But that's just a fever dream, it's not real life, it can't be. So I shut my eyes. I shut them tight, tight enough that the colours betwixt began to drown themselves in a swirling array of fleeting patterns.

Part 4
Chapter 2

The Colour of the Moon

Colby turned her light off and opened the blinds of her window. The moon outside was bright, brighter than it usually is. She shrugged. "I like the moon."

"I like it too," I said as I pulled myself down from the bed to the ground and cleared a space for her beside me. I looked out the window and could only see a piece of the moon, the window frame blocked most of it out of my view. After my eyes adjusted to the new dimness, I could see pretty well. And Colby sat down next to me and rested her hand on my thigh. Her hand was warm and soft; incredibly warm and extremely soft, even through my pants, the warmth radiated. It was nice; calming and relaxing.

"So, um, you're welcome to stay the night if you want. I'd rather you stay here than go home anyway, you know, since

you're having a rough night and all."
"I smiled. "Thanks. I think I will."
"Stay?"
"Yeah." I nodded. "I'll stay for the night."
"Are you hungry?"
"No, not right now. Thanks though."
"Yeah, no problem." She smiled softly. "If you need anything, don't hesitate to ask. It's no big deal to make us food or something to drink if you want it."
"Maybe a tea later."
She nodded. "So… whatcha thinking about?"
I shrugged. "I don't really know. A whole lot of stuff, I guess. My mind can't quite focus on one certain thing."
"I hate when that happens," Colby mumbled. "Sometimes it's good to just focus on other things though."
"I can focus on you."
Colby turned to me. "Okay, what colour are my eyes?"
I rotated my body to face hers and stared at her face, though I could only really see outlines, I couldn't see any discernible colours. "Hazel, but I knew that already. I can't see the colour in them right now."
"Your eyes are brown," she stated. "They're not dark, but they're not bright. They're perfectly in the middle, but I knew that already. I can't see the colour in them right now either." She smiled softly at me and cupped my cheek in her hand. "I *can*, however, see that you're kinda cute."
"Thanks." I'm glad we can't see colour in the dim light, otherwise she might have seen some red rise to my cheeks.
"You feeling any better?" Colby asked.
I nodded. "Yeah. I feel more relaxed."
"Okay." She smiled. "That's good. Anything on your mind right now that you wanna talk about? I'm all ears."
"No, I dunno." I sighed. "I guess I'm just tired."
"Tired, huh? Do you wanna sleep?"
"No," I replied. "I'm tired of the weight."
"Weight?" Colby questioned. "Edwin, you're in really

good shape. Like, 'let me hop on it right now' good. Is it me? My weight?" She looked down at herself. "I'm pretty slim, so I guess not."

"The weight of her," I stated, cracking a small smile at Colby's rambling. "It's a metaphorical weight. You know, like a heavy heart?"

"Oh. Wanna talk about it?"

"I don't, I wanna get rid of it."

"Edwin," her voice was soft, "you're never gonna get rid of the weight. You'll just get stronger, better at carrying it."

"I don't wanna carry it. I'm sick of being so broken."

"Hey now, even broken crayons can still colour." Colby smiled reassuringly at me. "You have to break sometimes so you know what you're made of, right? You just have to piece yourself together, but you don't have to do that alone."

"Yeah, but it's still there and I have to live with it. It just drags me down."

"So let it. Nobody ever got anywhere by not going to their depths." Colby sighed and looked off out the window. "People are always so concerned with the sky and climbing mountains, it's like they forget that *up* isn't the only way to go. Sometimes going down helps. It's all about perspective, I guess. I went down, I faced my depths. I'd like to think I'm a better person for it. I didn't let my weights anchor me, I anchored them. You get it?"

"Yeah. Let it hurt and then move on. Carry the weights with you and then move on."

"Good."

"You sound like Derek."

"Is he the skinny one?"

I nodded. "That's the one."

"Yeah, he's cool. I'll take that as a compliment." Colby shifted her weight and leaned on me. "This is nice, right? Just looking out the window at the moon?"

"Yeah. It's nice."

We sat there for a couple minutes in silence before Colby

suddenly jumped up. "Hey! Do you like cats?"

Her sudden jump had startled me, so all I muster up was a half-assed, "Yes, I do, why?"

"I have one! Oh, how didn't I show her to you already?" Colby stood up and made for the door. "You stay right here, I'm gonna go find her."

I waited on the floor of Colby's room, in the dim moonlight that was trickling through her window. I got bored and found myself staring at the window itself, not through it. It was dusty, dirty. She had drawn on it when the window fogged up, I could see the marks left by her fingertips. They were just happy faces, mostly. A flower too.

Colby opened the door behind me, shut it, and flicked her light on. "This is my sweet little angel." She was holding the fluffiest white-furred cat in her arms. The cat mewed softly as Colby sat down next me. "Her name is Red Velvet."

"Why Red Velvet?" I asked, taking the cat from her arms and putting it into my lap.

"Because it reminds me of cream cheese frosting, but I can't name a cat that, so I named her Red Velvet instead. Kinda cute, right?"

I nodded as I pet Red Velvet. She was the softest cat I've ever felt in my entire life. "Where'd you get her?"

"A friend's cat had kittens a couple years ago and I volunteered myself to take care of one until they found an owner, but then my mom decided to just let me keep it because I took such good care of it. I paid for her litter and food by myself."

"How old?" I asked, scratching Red Velvet's ears.

"She'll be five soon." Colby reached behind her and dug out a small pack of cat treats. "Here, give her a treat."

And so I did give her a treat. And then she walked three feet in front of us and plopped on the ground and just laid there. "She's pretty cute."

"She's my rock," Colby stated. "All the shitty things I've gone through since I've got her, she was always there to cuddle me. I know she's a cat and all, but like, she's still my best bud."

"She's pretty great."

"She is." Colby stretched out her legs and Red Velvet mimicked her. They both spread their toes and yawned. Two peas the same pod, I suppose. "Do you want a tea?"

I nodded. "That'd be nice. Thanks."

"Cool. Keep her company." Colby stood up and walked out the room, shutting the door behind her.

I reached over and gave Red Velvet a couple pats before focusing back to the moon outside for a minute or two. It was marvellously bright tonight. I looked around Colby's room some more, trying to find some semblance of personality in the dim mess of it. I couldn't. My eyes didn't want to register what I was looking at. It was firing things to my brain, but not keeping a grasp of the information. Eventually the doorknob shuffled and Colby came in with a cup of tea. She placed it down on the floor beside me before going back out of the room to get her tea.

"Hope you don't mind, but I'm dropping the pants," she said, laying the cup down next to the other cup. "Can't be doing this leg prison shit."

She pulled her pyjama pants down, balled them up, and tossed them onto the futon. The way she was facing allowed all the light in the room to land on her pale bottom. It was beautiful. I had never thought a pair of cotton panties on a booty could look so beautiful in my life, but here I was being proved wrong by the most beautiful bum that had ever graced my sights.

"I don't mind at all." I smiled at her as she sat down and crossed her legs.

Colby pushed a tea towards me. "I made this one for you."

"Thank you."

"So what should we do for the rest of the night?"

I shrugged. "Dunno."

"Well, if I have you to myself for a whole night, I wanna do something."

"Well, let's just sit here and talk."

"Or we could watch a movie?" Colby suggested. "I have a Netflix account after all."

"Do you wanna watch a movie or *watch a movie?*"

"I want to actually watch a movie." She pulled a laptop from under her futon and opened it. "Do you want funny, sad, romantic, action? I'm up for suggestions."

"Nah, you decide."

"Okay." She flicked through a couple categories and put on an animated movie about a rabbit. "Come here." She demanded that I move over to her so we could sit against the futon and watch a movie on the laptop that was perched atop her gorgeous bare legs. She's gonna get laptop burn if she doesn't at least put a blanket over her legs, but I doubt she cares much about getting a slight burn. She wrapped an arm around me and pulled me in. I wrapped my arm around her and we exchanged soft smiles as she played the movie. The colours betwixt the pixels flashed bright colours and for once, the brightness of it all wasn't overbearing.

Part 4
Chapter 3

The Colour of Safety

The air is stale. That's the only thing I can think about. It's stale, unmoving, and fucking stale. It's not humid, not hot, but it's still warm enough to be uncomfortable. I'm on a bed. I shake my head a little and sit up. Looking around, it feels so familiar, but yet it's all so distant. The world is bright, but I feel so dark. It's too bright to see anything at first, actually. I just sit here, dazed and confused waiting for my eyes to work like eyes should. My eyes do eventually adjust to the brightness of the room I'm in and I see now that everything is in a shade of white. The bed, the blankets, the pillow, the curtains of the windows, the frame of the open glass door that leads out to a large, half-moon shaped, glass balcony.

Where am I? I think to myself. Though am I really thinking at all? I stand and look around. White flowers in white vases on white tables. White chairs tucked into white tables with white plates and white cutlery set beside them. White walls and white doors. White curtains and white floors. I looked down at my feet; I was even wearing all white. My shoes were white. I was wearing a suit that was white. I grabbed a mirror, half-expecting for my hair to be white as well, but it wasn't. It was regular old brown hair, longer on top and shorter on the sides.

I walked around, sluggishly might I add. The apartment... or condo—whatever this place is—was completely empty. There's nobody here but me. But I don't feel alone here. I walk back to the room I woke up in, the large room with a king-sized bed and a glass door to the half-moon balcony. I walk and step outside. The glass is crystal clear, clearer than I'd ever imagined anything that wasn't air could be.

Everything here is silent. Even my feet barely make thuds as they fall on the floor with their every step. The highrises make no sound of whistling winds. Noise from cars is nonexistent. There's nothing. I train my ears on the silence around me, but all I hear is more of the nothingness. There are no birds chirping, no people moving about. There is only silence, a silence so empty that my ears have to ring to fill the void.

The air is still stale and unmoving. I exhale and dare for the wind to exhale back at me, but it does nothing, it just sits. I walk to the edge of the balcony, to the glass "railing" at the edge There's a thin gold bar along the tops of the glass panelling. The building I'm currently in is seemingly the tallest of many other tall, all-white, sleek building that are jutting up into the sky. They all create a massive skyline of white and glass, reflecting a harsh light.

I squint and let my eyes adjust to this new brightness. When they do, I take in the view. The buildings seem to go on for miles and miles, never ending so it seems.

I lean on the railing. I expect it to break right out from under me and for me to end up toppling downward for however far down until I hit the ground. But it doesn't break. I don't fall. I just remain there, leaning and looking.

"How did I get here?" I ask myself aloud. I begin to pace the balcony, trying not to look down at the endless sheets of glass and white stone below my feet. "How far down do you think it is?" I'm not talking to anybody, just to myself, trying to vocalize things as if that'll make me come up with the answer. I can't see the end of the building though. Perhaps it has no end.

Maybe if I jump off, I'll just fall forever. That's a theory I don't want to test. I'll see if there's an elevator first.

"Hello," a feminine voice says, floating through the air as if carried by something tangible. The voice sounds familiar but yet so distant in my memory.

My ears perk and so do I. I'm not alone after all. "Hello?"

"Edwin?" she calls out.

I walk back toward the apartment. "I'm here. Hello?"

"There you are." Fiona walks into my view. "I was looking for you. I didn't know you'd be waking up so soon. You only just fell asleep."

"I did?" I ask her. My body feels like it had been sleeping for days at a time. It's sore in places it's never been sore before.

She walks over to me and cups my face in her hand, looking at me with a tenderness in her eyes that I've never seen before. "Were you thinking about jumping off again?"

"Not entirely," I spoke. "I just got curious of what lies below."

"The dark," Fiona replies. "You know this, honey. Please stay off the balcony. I can't keep babysitting you like this."

"You don't have to."

"But I do."

"No. You don't. I'm a grown man." My voice has a flare to it, a certain edge I never get with Fiona, the kind reserved for when someone cuts you off in traffic. "I'm just so sick of living in this empty white kingdom. There's no place for colour in the betwixt, and I want colour. Where the fuck is it all?"

"There's no colour at the bottom," Fiona states. "Only darkness."

"But isn't the darkness better than just an abyss of empty white?"

"No," she says, "because this empty white is what keeps us sane."

"There's no air, no wind. Are there even other people?"

Fiona smiles and shakes her head. "The only people here are us." She then walks to the glass railing and looks over. "Perhaps you're right. Perhaps there's not enough room for even the two of us in this betwixt." She takes off the white slippers that she had been wearing and she lays them down next to her feet. And then, she pulls herself over the railing. No hesitation, no resistance, she just pulls herself over and begins her fall. I'm left entirely speechless for a second.

I rush to the railing and watch as she disappears into the distance below, a never-ending hole of white and glass. I watch her grow smaller and smaller in the distance. *"Fiona!"* I shout, though the voice is not mine, but it is, but I didn't shout it. Something else in me shouted, something instinctual.

"Yes?" her voice says.

I turn heel and look behind me. "But I watched you fall?"

Her eyes gloss over and she steps forwards. "You did. But now it's your turn. You want to know so much what it's like to see colour again, then go, fall. Fall for the dark. Fall for the coal."

I step back. She steps forward, her face twisted into a sinister smirk. Her teeth appear to be razor-sharp, shaped like the teeth of a shark. I step back until I can't anymore, my hands clasped to the gold railing perched on the top of the glass panels. "Fiona, stop."

"Fall for her, the coal darkness. She's all you've ever wanted deep down anyway, isn't she?"

"Fiona," I mutter, but it's useless. *Her hands are on my shoulders, pushing me backwards. I can't fight back, she's too strong or I'm too weak or maybe both, regardless of what it is, I'm now falling. I watch the glass balcony grow smaller, I watch as her silhouette walks back into the apartment. I pivot and turn and get myself facing towards the ground, or to the way I'm falling, if you can even claim there to be ground at the bottom. I see nothing new, nothing more than white buildings all around me and their glass shimmering from a should-be-blocked-by-the-buildings light source. I fall, but still no air rushes around me. I still breathe the same staleness as if I wasn't moving at all.*

I begin to feel a current of air after a few moments of falling. It's refreshing, cooling even. I look at the distance below and see a small black dot appear—and it's getting bigger. This is the coal darkness Fiona mentioned, it has to be. I try to keep myself calm, but it's human nature to fear falling, especially now that I know that there is an end in sight. The black dot is painstakingly small still, but it grows larger with every minute I fall. Who even knows how long I've been falling for, for that matter? It could be seconds, minutes, hours, shit, it could even have been a full day by this point. I don't know. Time doesn't exist here. At least not in the way I used to know it.

The black dot grows larger, forming a small circle in the empty whiteness below. It's not a shadow. Shadows don't seem to exist in this place either. It's something definitely black, a pond or a hole perhaps. It stops growing in my vision for a few seconds. Then it grows larger quickly, beginning to take up more than half of what I see when I look directly below. It looks like a liquid, a thick one at that, but it's dark as coal. It doesn't reflect any light, though there is more than enough light around to be reflected, the pond of coal stays dark. It's bigger than I thought at first. It's massive, it encompasses the whole of my vision when I look down. I look around me and see that the buildings are floating above this black ocean of coal tar. The buildings thin into a singular point, and then all that is below me, all that I can see around me, is black liquid.

The coal darkness. How much further? *I question. It seems so imminent but yet so far, there's no telling how far. The ground below is just a swath of sloshing tar. I crane my neck to look up. I watch the buildings fade into the sky behind me. I must be falling awfully fast. I look back down. This ocean, though liquid, has no waves. It is only flat and still, unmoving and dark. It waits. And so do I.*

And what waits beyond the darkness? Is it better than where I am now? Is it worse? Will I even be able to tell the difference? Why do I ache to go where I cannot return from? Why was I so willing to jump for something with no promises? How can I be sure that there even is something on the other side? I can't be, that's how. There's no way to know. Maybe I should have stayed on the balcony. Maybe I should have just listened to her and stepped back into the apartment. It's too late to change my mind, of course. There's nothing between me and the ground now. No buildings, no cars, no people, no sounds, no colours.

The ground grows closer.
       Closer.
     Closer.
   Closer.
Closer.

My hands are clammy with nervousness. I've been falling too long. I blink for the first time in what feels like years. Had I not been blinking the whole time? My eyes are raw, aching, burning from the fresh moisture. And then I feel a heat suddenly overtake my body. A warm and humid heat, the tar is closing in. The "air" is almost boiling. I feel sweat dripping from my face and my sweat pools in the palms of my hands. The heat is unbearably hot, but somehow I can bear it for much longer than I ever thought I could.

I finally hit the ocean. Everything gets dark, endlessly so. My skin feels like it's on fire. I grit my teeth, because if I were to open my mouth in pain, I would swallow this tar, and that's the last thing I want to do right now. Then a noise, a soft hum at first, but it grows. The noise grows to a loud, alien language being shouted at me. The ocean shakes, or maybe it's an "underwater" whirlpool.

My eyes shot open and I tried to catch my breath. My body was soaked in a cold sweat. I looked around. I was still on the futon in Colby's room. The room was still dark, only lit by the moonlight. I turned to see Colby sitting up next to me with a worried sort of look on her face.

"What's wrong?" I asked.

"You were having a nightmare."

I sighed. "Yeah. I was."

"Do you wanna talk about it?" Colby asked. "Sometimes talking about it helps me. I promise not to judge you on whatever it is. I know sometimes how dreams just make you feel all anxious and stuff and, like, it's not a conscious thing. You can tell me. I'm here."

My eyes refused to focus on anything, I felt lightheaded, and my skin was crawling, little pins and needles prickling me under the skin. I just sat there silently. Colby smiled softly and wrapped her arms around me, pulling me closer to her. She ran a hand through my hair and kissed my forehead. I let myself fade away into her arms.

Fiona was in my dream again. I thought I was doing so well. It had been a couple days at least since the last dream I had of her. It all felt so real, it always does. Every dream with Fiona feels real, no matter how absurd they are. Even that place, though, with its bizarre floating buildings and endless tar ocean felt real. Even now, it still does.

I turned and smiled at Colby. "Would you be so kind as to hold me until I fall asleep again?"

She nodded. "Of course." I lied down and rolled over, facing away from her. She shuffled around a bit, but then her hand and arm snaked over me. She snuggled into me and gave me a squeeze. "Goodnight, Edwin."

I smiled softly as I shut my eyes. "Goodnight, Colby."

And the colours betwixt went back to sleep.

Part 4
Chapter 4

The Colour of Comfort

I rolled over and kept rolling. There was no Colby in the bed. I sat up and looked around the room. The sunlight shone in through the window, making everything in the room glow with a sunny orange. Red Velvet was fast asleep on the floor, curled up on a pile of clothes. I swung my legs over the edge of the futon and sat up. I reached for my shirt that was just on the floor by my feet and slipped it over my head. I yawned and looked out the window at the bright blue sky.

I stretched out and stood up. I walked over to the window and looked down at the street. So many brightly coloured people walking around. Oranges, blues, pinks, greens. That's how you know it's a nice day: people only wear bright colours on nice days. That's why winters are so grey and black and white and boring.

I walked over to Red Velvet and pat her a few times. She perked up slightly and purred, but as soon as I moved my hand away from here, she just curled back up and kept sleeping. I wish I was a cat. They can sleep for up to 18 hours a day and only move when they need food (or when they see a moth on the wall or something).

I found my socks and put them on. I walked out of Colby's room and into the rest of her apartment. It was a nice little apartment with hardwood flooring in the hallway and kitchen. The rest of the rooms (minus the bathroom) were carpeted with a weird grey-green colour. I walked to the kitchen and saw Colby in front of the stove. She was in the same baggy shirt she fell asleep in and the same bare legs too. The kitchen had an L-shaped island that separated it from the living room/dining room. Only the kitchen light was on, so the rest of the room was dimly lit from the light that was forcing itself through their curtains. Colby's phone was on the counters, softly playing a sleepy-sounding song as she sang along perhaps just as sleepily and as softly.

I snuck up behind her and wrapped my arms around her, kissing her neck softly. "Good morning, Colby."

She stretched her neck a little and smiled. "Good morning, Edwin. Sleep well?"

"I did. Minus the nightmare," I replied, pulling a stool out from the island counter and sitting down. "Did you?"

"I did," she stated. "Minus the nightmare." She turned around and grinned. "I made us breakfast." She pulled the pan over from the stove and rolled what looked like weird little burritos onto two plates that already had slices of bananas and cut up strawberries on them. She carried the two plates from the counter and sat next to me. "Cinnamon French toast rolls with chocolate spread inside." She smiled. "Hope you like them."

I smiled at her and watch her put a piece of strawberry in her mouth. Her hair was a mess, a right proper mess at that, but even in spite of looking like a mess, she looked stunning, a true goddess.

"Are you gonna eat?" she asked, cutting a piece of roll off.

"You just look really beautiful right now."

She smiled and began to blush a little. "Stop that. Eat."

I couldn't take my eyes off her though. We ate in silence, just the clicking of forks and knives on the plates as we cut the rolls and stabbed the banana and strawberries. Everything felt diluted but in the best way possible. Things felt softer and less abrasive for once. The colours were soft and warm. The silence was inviting and comfortable. The food was tasty and fresh. When we finished up, Colby stuffed the dishes into the dishwasher and then that was that.

"So," she said, leaning against the counter, "did you like it?"

"I did. It was great." I walked over and kissed her cheek. "Thanks for making breakfast, Colby. You didn't have to though, really."

"Ah, hush. You're a guest in this house, I'm just being a nice host." She turned around and opened a cupboard and pulled out two mugs. "Coffee?" she asked. I nodded and she pulled the coffee maker over and flicked it on. "I figured you'd want a coffee."

"So where are your roommates?"

"Well, they're still students, so they're all at work today."

"Oh."

"So, whaddaya wanna do today, Edwinner?" Colby asked as she put some sugar into each of our mugs.

I shrugged. "Beats me, dude. What do you wanna do?"

She blew a raspberry and went back to making coffee. Not really an answer, but I guess it'll have to do. I watched her as she poured steaming coffee into our cups. A dark green mug and a pale red mug—not pink, pale red. She went into the fridge and got the cream and poured some into each mug. She put the cream away and mixed our coffees. She handed me a mug. "I think I'd like to watch more movies. Maybe go and get something to eat. You're welcome to hang out with me if you'd like." She smiled. "I'd hate to have to go out to lunch all by my lonesome."

"Are you asking me to lunch?"

She nodded. "I was thinking Greek."

"I'm down." I took a sip of coffee and winced. "Hot. It's too hot. Ouch. My tongue. Ow."

"No shit, I *just* made it. Come on. Let's go watch ourselves a movie, maybe fuck, and then go get lunch," Colby said as she started for her room. "I also would like a shower before we head out. I feel dirty."

"Well, I also need a shower. Two birds, one stone."

"We could also do the love-making in the shower," she said with a smirk. "Three birds."

"I like the way you think." I followed her into her room and she set her mug down on the floor. I sat down next to it as she got our movie ready. She actually buys DVD copies of movies she likes. What a fucking dork.

Colby wrapped her hair in a white towel and handed me a towel from the shelf. For someone I met fairly recently, Colby is (and I guess always has been) very open about her body with me. Her bare breasts out in the air, nipples erect because, well, things get cold when wet and cold nipples get hard. Her skin was nearly as pale as the white tiles on the floor. A real-life, porcelain goddess.

"My eyes are up here," she barked jokingly at me.

"Sorry," I said, smiling at her. "When I see a pretty naked girl, I gots to look."

She scoffed. "Yeah, yeah. I'm gonna clean up and do my makeup, so if you just wanna get dressed and go watch some TV, you're more than welcome to do that. Or you can stay and watch me. Your call." She flicked the fan on to remove the moisture from the air. She took a small towel and wiped the condensation off of the fogged up mirror.

I walked back to her room and shut the door. I got dressed

and looked out the window. The sun was well in the sky and the city was still full of brightly coloured people. I smiled. I love the world when it's colourful like this. I walked back to the bathroom and sat on the toilet, watching Colby as she tediously applied eyeliner to her eyes, trying to get the wings just right. I made no sounds. I was just here to observe a goddess in her natural habitat.

Colby let out a frustrated groan. "I fucking hate this. I get one eye perfect and the other eye looks like it was drawn on by a monkey with Parkinson's for fuck's sake."

"Turn around." I got up and grabbed the eyeliner from her and drew on her little flick wings for her.

She gave me the *dirtiest* glare as she turned around. "Thank you," she muttered, looking over the wing I had drawn on. "It matches the other side. You're a wizard."

"No, I just have eyes and a working hand-eye coordination." I sat back down on the toilet and smiled at her. "But wizard works too, I guess."

"Shut up." She ruffled her hair and then tossed the towel at me. "I need to get dressed." She walked out of the room and came back a minute later with panties on and a bra that was on backwards as she did up the hooks. She spun it around and fixed her boobs into their cups. "Okay, get out. I gotta pee."

"Does your bra have little ghosts on them?" I asked as I stood up from the toilet.

She nodded. "They're *boo*-bies." She smiled. "Okay, now get out."

I nose exhaled and left the room. "*Boo*-bies," I murmured to myself as I closed the door behind me. I walked to the kitchen and sat at the island, waiting and scrolling through memes on my phone.

After a few more minutes, Colby came out to the kitchen in jean shorts and a pink tank top. She had the ghost bra underneath, but it had black straps so it somehow just *matched* the straps of pink.

Also, I wonder if she ever tans. I see her show skin a lot,

but she never seems to get tanner. She's as pale as ever, even in the middle of summer. Maybe she gets even paler (if that's possible) in the winter. Maybe she becomes translucent. That'd be pretty cool, to be honest. She had a small black purse at her side, resting easily on her hip. Such a simple elegance with this girl, an elegance that I've never seen before (or noticed, I guess (I'm sure a lot of girls have an elegance like that though (whoa, brackets in brackets)).

Colby smiled at me, breaking me from my thoughts. "Ready to head out?"

"Yeah, I've been ready for an hour."

She scoffed. "I didn't take an hour to get ready." She slipped her bare feet into bright pink flip-flop sandals.

"Did you decide where we're going for lunch?"

"Nah. Let's just go and see what we feel like."

"Okay, works for me." I opened the door for her as I slipped my shoes on. "Are we taking your car or mine?"

"Mine," she replied. "It's cuter than yours."

"That little blue clown car, yeah, sure, *cuter* is for sure the word I'd use to describe it."

"Don't make fun of my car."

"Oops," I said, "I just did."

She glared at me and locked the door to her apartment. "I'm watching you, Flowers. Now let's get out of here. I'm hungry."

"Wouldn't be so hungry if you didn't take so long to get ready."

She scoffed and walked ahead of me, lifting her hand up and raising a middle finger to me. I just smiled and followed her down the hallway. I don't know how, but I've been blessed to have a friend like Colby in my life. The colours betwixt this hallway, though strange as they may be, made things feel comfortable, safe, and warm, all things I could get used to someday.

Part 4
Chapter 5

The Colour of Benefits

Colby came over to my apartment tonight because her roommates were being boring. Her words, not mine. She wanted to hang out with someone that wasn't busy sticking their head in a textbook, ergo me, the Edwinner, whom is now done school. Though, with a degree in journalism (a field with few jobs and a lot of competitiveness) I'll end up back in the revolving door that is the North American post-secondary education system.

"I feel like you don't have any colour in this place," Colby said as she rested her feet atop my coffee table. They were a little dirty from her flip-flops, but I wasn't a real stickler about it. I don't eat at the coffee table and nobody else does either. I don't have that many visitors outside of Colby.

"What do you mean?" I asked as I walked over with a large pitcher of lemonade and a bag of chips. I set them down and flicked on the TV.

"You're a painter and you love colour, but your apartment is just chock-full of the dulcet tones of grey and navy blues." Colby looked around. "It's weird for your personality, that's all."

"Not everything needs colour, I guess. Besides, greys and navies can be really nice too." I sat down and put on the pre-hockey game coverage show.

Colby sighed. "You're lame."

"Um, nope, that would be you." I grabbed one of the cups that Colby had brought to the table and poured some lemonade into it. The ice in the glass cracked as the liquid hit it and then it clinked against the sides of the glass when the liquid swooshed.

"So... Edwin, my dear boy, I've been meaning to ask something."

"Oh, fuck," I groaned. "This is it, isn't it? The relationship so?" Every relationship at the beginning has someone ask that long "so." And it's awkward if both of those people want different things from the relationship. Very awkward.

She sighed. "Well, I mean, I would like us to know what we both want out of this, that's all."

"I don't love you," I told her, "if that's what you were trying to ask me about."

"God, no. It's far too soon for the L-word." Colby grabbed my glass of lemonade and took a drink. "I just want some clarification on what we are. Like, are we friends? Friends with benefits? Friends with exclusive rights to each other's bodies? Dating? Boyfriend and girlfriend? Wife and husband? Divorcees?"

"Well, we'd have to be married for those last two."

"Day's still young, Edwin."

"I like that 'friends with exclusive rights to each other's bodies' idea you had," I told her. "I could do that. I don't know if I wanna be in a relationship with you, but I do know that I like hanging out with you and that I like sex, so..."

"I'm okay with this." Colby snickered a little to herself.

"What?"

"Well, you want exclusivity but not a relationship. It strikes me as odd."

"I just don't love you," I told her. *Yet.*

"Yeah, I know. I don't love you either. It's just odd."

"All well." I grabbed my cup of lemonade back from her and took a drink. "Got any cool stories from your past to tell me to kill some time until Derek and Marshall get here?"

"Well, to kick off story time, I've done porn."

I nearly choked on my drink. I stifled a few coughs. "Um, wait, what? Excuse me?"

"I've done porn," Colby repeated as nonchalantly as she had said it the first time.

"Would you like to explain a little more?" I asked. "Do you still do porn?"

"Nah. I stopped a while ago. I didn't do it long." She blew a raspberry. "I think I did, like, eight solo videos and maybe eleven or twelve videos with a partner, all lesbian stuff. I didn't like the idea of being crammed with dicks all day."

"Does anyone else know you did porn?"

She shrugged. "Like, yeah. I don't *tell* people. I was with a boyfriend at the time, so he didn't know. I didn't tell him. I didn't tell my parents or *any* of my family for that matter. I just needed some extra cash to help me out in college. It was my little secret, and now it's your little secret too."

"So why are you telling me this now?" I asked.

"You deserve to know. I can tell you're cool," she answered. "Besides, I'm not ashamed of it or anything."

"What kind of porn did you do, then?"

"Submissive-dominance stuff, mostly. I wanted something less mainstream so people I know wouldn't be able to find me as easily. I was usually the dominant one, so that was cool. I got to be bitchy and get my toes sucked, aww, go Colby. I tried being the submissive, but I'm not into girls, so it's a lot harder for me to enjoy *giving* to a girl as opposed to receiving from one."

"Well, that's a pretty cool story from your past, I guess."

"I think everyone should try doing porn a little. It really helps you discover who you are sexually. I, for instance, found out that I quite enjoy people worshipping my feet. It makes me feel more confident."

"I'm not a foot guy, sorry," I said.

She smiled. "See, and that's okay. We all have different interests and shit, sex is no different. But if you do have any weird sex kinks, just let me know. This is a judgement-free zone."

"None here, really, I'm pretty straightforward and vanilla, I guess." I shrugged. "I'm open to things though, I suppose."

"Good, be open about everything in life, Edwin." She reached over for the bag of chips and ripped them open. "So do you have any cool stories for me?"

"No, but I have a question."

"Shoot."

"What was your porn name?"

"What, do you wanna look me up? You've literally fucked me, isn't that better than porn of me?" She sighed a little. "It was Caroline Foxxx, with three X's."

"Why?"

"I like foxes and Caroline is my middle name."

"Oh."

"You're cute."

"How so?" I asked.

"You have no idea how to process this information, and watching your eyes gloss over as you try to is cute." She smiled. "Sorry if it's a lot to take in, but we're friends with a possible romantic future ahead of us, so it's better you find out now rather than later. I don't want this to be a possible issue for us down the road."

"Sorry. I've just never met or known anyone who's done porn."

"Yeah, you have. I guarantee some of your college friends

have at least made homemade porn and uploaded it to some site for the sexual thrill. You just can't find it because it's one shittily made video in a sea of millions of just as shitty videos."

"You're probably right." I grimaced at the thought of Derek or Marshall making porn for the world to see. "Now let's stop talking about my friends doing porn before I throw up."

Colby smiled and shook her head a little. "You're cute, Edwin."

"You're cute."

"Am I?" She turned to me and eyed me down. "How do you think of me based on physical attractiveness? Be honest, not matter how romantic or brutal it is."

"I find you beautiful."

"How beautiful?"

"More beautiful than words could ever do justice."

She smiled. "Really?"

I nodded. "You told me to be honest, so I was."

"Hmm. Where would you rank me all-time in your beautiful girls list?"

"What?"

"Everybody has one," Colby stated. "I have a hottest guys list. Right now you're sitting quite comfortably in first."

"I guess you'd be in first too."

"Even more beautiful than... *her?*" she asked, nearly whispering the last word.

My heart panged. It was a good question. Did I find Colby more beautiful than the most beautiful person I had ever seen? The short of it was: yes. And I hated myself for it. Fiona was supposed to be my *be all, end all.* I nodded softly. "Yeah," I spoke softly, "more than her."

"Well... I wasn't expecting that."

"I wasn't either." I took a sip of lemonade. "Let's just forget I said it. You're gorgeous, Colby, and that's that."

Colby smiled at me and kicked my leg with her foot. "I'll bet you ten bucks Toronto loses by three tonight."

I laughed. "Deal." I reached my hand over and she shook it. "You just lost yourself ten bucks."

Derek and Marshall did eventually show up to watch the game, though they got there after the first period was over. I'd be mad that they were late, but they brought pizza and wings, so Colby and I were a little easier on them for it.

"...and so that's when Edwin fell out the window," Derek said, finishing the story he must have been telling to Colby as I walked back into the room from going to take a piss. Derek looked over at me and smiled. "Just telling your new lady friend the tale of when you almost died."

"Which time?" I asked, probably more cynically than I meant it to come off.

"When we pranked you and you thought the house was on fire and you ended up panicking and falling out the second floor window at Fiona's cabin," Derek stated. "Good times."

"Yeah, not for me." I laughed a little. "It hurt, for one, and I had cuts all over for weeks it felt like."

"Anyway," Colby said, interrupting Derek as he was about to say something, "these two think we make a cute couple. I've been trying to tell them we're not, but they're not biting."

"We're not a couple," I stated as I sat down on the couch and in between Derek and Colby.

"Oh, please," Marshall said, "the *friends with benefits* thing you two have right now, that's just a precursor to easing the two of you into a relationship."

"I'm just a friend trying to help a friend get over a relationship," Colby said with a smile, raising a hand and patting my back a little. "No romance, just sex and hanging out."

"What she said. She had a bad relationship and just wants to have a little fun," I said with a smile of my own. "No romance, just sex and hanging out."

"Right, so when's she moving in to your apartment?" Marshall asked.

"Yeah, do you guys need help with moving her stuff in?"

Derek added, then taking a sip from his beer while eyeing the two of us down.

"I'm not moving in," Colby replied.

"Yeah. She has roommates that she likes and would never wanna leave," I stated. "She's also got quite a nice setup at her place."

"You guys are so cute," Derek teased.

"Shut up," Colby barked. She then let out a loud burp. "I'm anything but cute."

"Yeah, you're a fucking goddess," I muttered under my breath.

She smirked and nudged my leg with her knee and then mouthed the words, "Thank you."

I sat back and looked at the three people sitting next to me on my couch. I looked to the TV as the puck dropped to begin the second period. I let myself soak in the unfamiliar familiarity of the four of us sitting and watching a hockey game. This felt no different than when Fiona was the girl next to me. Colby wrapped her index finger around mine and she smiled softly when I gave hers a subtle squeeze. The colours betwixt were so much more beautiful than I would have lead myself to believe, more beautiful than my eyes could ever see, more beautiful than words could ever describe.

Part 4
Chapter 6

The Colour of a Spark

Colby sat across from me, looking as gorgeous as she ever has. Her beautiful pink lips tucked up in the corners because she's always at least smiling a little bit. Her eyes were flickering back and forth on the menu in front of her. She bit and chewed at her lip a little as she thought about what she wanted to get for dinner. I smiled softly at the sight of it. She's so breathtakingly beautiful sometimes and she doesn't even have to try, she just has to exist.

She pushed her platinum-blonde hair off her face and then looked up. "I would like the Swiss cheese and mushroom burger," Colby said, setting the menu down. The waiter scribbled the order down. "I'll have the thick-cut fries with that too, please." She smiled and handed the menu to the waiter. And then the waiter was off. I had already ordered an 8-ounce steak sided with a loaded baked potato for myself. Colby turned to me. "You were staring at me again."

"No, I wasn't," I lied.

"You were." She smiled as she took a sip of her water, leaving a slight reddish-pink mark on the tip of the straw from her lipstick. "But it's kind of cute."

"Shut up. I wasn't staring."

"You were."

"Was not."

"You were," she said flatly. "Anyway, how about that waiter?"

"What about him?"

"He thinks we're on a *date* date."

"Because we're two young adults, dressed up and at a restaurant," I stated. "Not all that weird for people to think we're on a date."

"But he called us a *cute* couple," Colby noted. "Said he hasn't seen a couple look so entranced by each other in a long time." Colby smiled widely. "I think I agree with him, to be honest."

"Because I was staring at you?"

"Ha!" she whisper-shouted. "So you admit it?!"

"Sure." I might as well humour her. "But do you admit that you think we're a cute couple?"

Her smiled dropped a little. I could tell we were into serious waters now. She sighed. "I mean, like, yeah. I guess so. We're both attractive, we both love spending time together. You make me happy, Ed. You make me feel like myself, or rather, like I can *just be* myself. There's no pressure with you. All these smiles you give me—they're real."

"I don't love you though, you know?"

Colby nodded, ducking her head down to avoid unnecessary awkward eye contact with me. "I know, Edwin. I know what we are. I'm not trying to profess my love to you or anything like that. I'm just saying, I like having you around."

"You're a healthy distraction," I stated. "You're a really

wonderful girl and I'm glad I got to meet you. I don't regret any of the time that I spend in your presence. I just can't love you. It'd make me feel guilty... and I guess I just don't know how to get rid of that anchor."

Colby smiled, reaching her hand across and laying it in mine. "I know. It's not even something I'm asking you to do. The future is open, Edwin, and that's the important thing. You're young, and you have a whole life to figure out how to pick up the anchor and set sail again."

I nodded. "You're right."

"Just don't deny yourself happiness because of it. Promise?"

"I promise."

"You promise what?"

I sighed and rolled my eyes. "I promise I won't let the weight of it all or the anchor in my soul deny me of happiness."

"Okay, good." She shuffled her silverware around and got an empty place on the table ready for her food. "So... I'm thinking we should do something fun."

"What'd you have in mind?" I asked.

She shrugged. "I'm sure something will come to mind in a bit. I just wanna *do* something tonight." She looked around at the restaurant, paying particular attention to tables that had food. "Man, I would kill to work at a place like this to cook the food."

"Oh, yeah?" I asked.

She nodded. "I took a culinary program in college. I've always wanted to be a chef. I love food and food loves me."

"So why don't you try to get a job here?"

Colby shrugged. "Dunno. I have a good job right now, so I don't wanna fuck that up unless it's for my dream job."

"Which is?" I asked.

"To run my own kitchen," she replied. "Whether that's here or at a small diner in a small little roadstop town, doesn't matter. I just wanna be the one in charge."

"Don't give up on that dream."

"I won't."

"Promise me."

She smiled at me. "I promise."

"You promise what?"

"I promise you I won't give up my dream of being a head chef."

I gave her a triumphant smile. "Good."

"You're such a dork, Ed."

"I've been told." I smiled softly and watched as she spun the ice in her cup around with her straw. She took a sip, leaving more red on the edge of the straw. Her hazel eyes darted around before falling on mine and then she smiled, softly at first, but a little wider the longer she looked at me. My insides felt warm, tingly, a nervousness that didn't make me nervous at all. I felt a butterfly float inside my stomach.

"You're staring," she noted.

It took me a few seconds to notice she had spoken, but I replied, "So are you."

"Shut up." She lowered her face to break eye contact. I could see the blush rising in her cheeks, because when you're as pale as she is, it's pretty hard to hide any sort of blushing. She pushed her hair out of her face, then she looked over to me and smiled softly. "Okay. I think I know what to do for our little adventure tonight."

The minutes passed by. I stood by the hood of Colby's old, blue hatchback. She had taken me to her parents' house because we needed to collect bikes and her mom's SUV, which was big enough for us to stick the bikes into. I have no idea what she's planning to do with the bikes, but I'm just going along with it.

The night wasn't too cold or dark, the moon and stars were all so bright in the sky. I guess it's bike-riding weather. I looked at the front door of the house and waited for Colby to come back out. It must have been ten minutes or more since she went inside. I would have been fine with meeting her parents if it meant having something to do other than waiting around in the dark looking like a stalker.

The garage door rustled and started opening, with a loud creaking sound, might I add. I looked over and saw Colby ducking out under the half-opened door. "Psst, come here."

I walked over to her and helped her get the door up a little higher. "What are you doing?"

"Getting the bikes out, dumbass." She walked back into the garage and pulled something out from behind a box, it made a lot of racket, like she was knocking things over. She groaned and grunted as she pulled. Finally, it was free and she rolled the bike over to me. "Put it in the SUV." She reached into her pocket and handed me a key fob.

I took the bike and clicked the unlock button on the key fob. The SUV lights blinked and the horn beeped a short burst of sound. I walked over and stuck the bike in the back. Colby came out from the garage shortly after.

"Go close the garage door." She grabbed the keys from me. I sighed and walked back over to the garage and pulled the door down. It was pretty stiff, but I gave it a few good pushes and it eventually closed fully. I walked back to the SUV and Colby started it up as I hopped in the passenger side. She looked over at me and smirked. "We're going on an adventure, Ed. Smile. You look so glum. I want my adventuring partner to be happy with me."

"You haven't told me where we're going. I'm a little skeptical of this adventure so far."

"Ed, shut up. I'll let you touch my boob later if you behave yourself," Colby said as she pulled the SUV out of the driveway. It's so bizarre seeing Colby drive a normal-sized vehicle. The size difference from her little hatchback to this SUV was a pretty big one.

I decided to just let her drive. I figured any protests I have about our adventure would go unheeded by Colby. She's very set in her ways about our adventure, so it would seem. I just kept my mouth shut and stared out the window.

I watched the houses flicker by, the light from the streetlamps shine and then dissipate as we passed by them. I listened to the soft hum of the tires on the asphalt, the revving of the engine, the soft music of the radio playing as a distant soundtrack to our night.

"You haven't pried about where we're going," Colby noted. "I'm proud of you, Ed."

"Edwin," I corrected her. I wasn't too keen on being called *Ed*. Just never liked the sound of it, I guess. I know most people love to have their names shortened, but I was not like one of those people. I just never really took notice about her calling me Ed before.

"Yeah, look, the bigger a deal you make this, the more often I'm gonna call you Ed," she stated. "That's how this works."

I sighed. "You suck."

"Shut up, Ed."

"Stop that," I barked. "It's Edwin."

"This is something you can't Ed-*win*, Ed." She smiled at her own stupid joke. I smiled too, because when Colby smiles, you have to smile. She has a smile more contagious than anyone else I know. She's my manic pixie dream girl. *I think I'm starting to love you, Colby. I really do. You're something else.*

"Hmm?" She cocked an eyebrow at me.

Did she hear my thoughts? I thought to myself, but then asked her, "What?"

"Did you say something?" She glanced over at me. "Coulda swore I heard you say something."

"Nope," I replied quickly. I wasn't even sure if I had said anything. It's entirely possible I just spoke my thoughts aloud, albeit a whisper, but still loud enough for her to maybe have heard what I said, or thought. I've got myself confused.

Colby gave me a small smile. "I got my ears on you, Flowers."

"That's better," I muttered.

"I got my ears on you, *Ed*," she said, correcting herself, much to my displeasure.

I rolled my eyes and ignored her attempt at irritating me.

"So," I said, "where are we going, Colby?"

"It's weird when you say my name." She grimaced a little. "Can't you just call me bae, or babe, or pumpkin, or baby girl. Ooh, call me baby girl. I'll melt. Do it once. Do it."

"Um, okay." I was suddenly getting a little tongue-tied for words. "Where are we going, *baby girl?*" I nearly couldn't spit out those last two words. It felt weird to say them because they were forced, not natural.

"Fuck, Edwin. If I weren't driving, I'd be dropping these panties." She bit her lip and grumbled a little bit. "Yeah, but anyway, we're going to the racetrack. And before you ask, I'll tell you when we get there." She turned to me and smirked. "You only asked where we were *going* instead of *what* we were going there to do. And I'm only granting you that one answer." Colby grinned and turned the radio up. "I love this song." And then the SUV was overtaken by the sounds of some indie band I don't know the name of. She smiled and lip-sang along with the song playing. And the next song. And the one after that. And I watched her as she sang and smiled and tapped her fingers on the steering wheel.

The colours betwixt were warm from the heat of the SUV, loud from the speakers playing Colby's favourite songs, and yet still vibrant enough for me to feel it in my bones. The colours don't make sense, but then again, neither does anything else when you're falling in love.

Part 4
Chapter 7

The Colour of Racing Hearts

Colby parked the SUV in a very dark parking lot just outside the racetrack, and not even at the main entrance. It was around the back, where the trucks and cars would enter for the race, not the public entrance. I didn't even bother to ask what we were doing here until Colby shut off the SUV. Once the darkness settled in around us, that's when I got really curious.

"What are we doing here, Colby?" I asked. She ignored me, like very obviously ignored. I sighed. "What are we doing here, *baby girl?*"

"Oh, we're going on an adventure." Colby opened the door and walked to the back of the SUV. "Come help," she called over to me. She started tugging one of the bikes out, so I got out and went and helped her.

"What are we doing?" I asked again.

"We're gonna go in and ride bikes around the track."

"Why?"

She shrugged. "Why not?"

"Is this legal?"

She smirked. "It's not illegal, if that's what you're *really* asking."

"What isn't illegal?"

"Breaking into this racetrack." She grinned as she rolled the bike a few feet and kicked down the kickstand. "It's not illegal if we don't get caught."

"Excuse me? That's still illegal."

"Not if we don't get caught."

"And if we do?"

"Simple misunderstanding. We leave. We maybe get a fine for trespassing," Colby stated. "All we're doing is riding bikes around the track at night. It's not like we're stealing anything or breaking anything or interrupting any events. Relax and have a little fun, Edwin."

"We're entering," I noted. "That's half the crime of breaking and entering. I'd say that this is still very illegal."

"What's life without a night or two in jail, Edwin?" she asked, grabbing the second bike from the SUV. She raised her eyebrows at me. "Well?" I had no answer to give her. She grinned at me. "Exactly. If you keep living with anchors and living in fear of a trespassing fine, you're gonna miss out on some fun memories. We're not hurting anyone by riding bikes around a racetrack. So have a little fun, will ya?" She pushed the bike towards me. She grabbed a backpack from inside the SUV and then closed up the SUV and locked it. "Now let's get a move on, shall we?"

I followed her as she rolled her bike over to a large gate This is where the racers all enter the track. Colby swung the backpack onto her back and then began to pull the gate open. For whatever reason, the gate wasn't locked up. We walked in and she closed the gate over. She hopped on her bike and started pedalling, so I too hopped on my bike and began pedalling after her. We biked until we ended up in the middle of the racetrack.

Colby turned to me. "Follow me." She began pedalling again. I knew where we were heading—the finish line. I pulled to a stop next to her. She turned to me amd smiled as she tossed her bag onto the patch of grass to our left. "Okay, it's simple: one lap, whoever gets back here first, wins. Wins what, you might ask? Just wins. Are you ready?"

"Yeah," I said.

"Okay. We'll count down from three and then we'll say go and then we'll go." She readied herself on the bike and smiled. "Okay. Count with me, Edwin."

"One," we said. "Two." I readied myself. "Three." We both got ready to haul ass. "GO!" we shouted. Our feet both began circling around and around as we pushed the pedals. We picked up speed and took off down the track. We were pretty evenly matched right from the start, but (I'll be honest with you) I started slowing down a little to let Colby take the lead. I know how big she'd smile if she beat me in a race. So I let her lead, and I followed.

She's the lighthouse and I'm the ship lost at sea.

The track seemed to go on forever, or maybe it just felt like that because it was dark out. We winded around the turns and pedalled harder and harder, or so we tried. My legs began to ache and burn, remembering all those times Fiona would make us go bike riding.

But I pedalled on and on.

I pushed my legs harder.

And harder.

I was outrunning a memory.

And then it swamped my mind.

Fiona and I.

And our bikes.

The sky opened up as we reached the top of the hill. My legs had turned into a vibrating ocean of gelatin. Fiona wouldn't let me just walk the bike up the hill. We had to ride the bikes up it. My legs were in so much pain. I'm active and I'm fit, but that doesn't stop the burn.

"There it is," Fiona said, smiling at me. "We can take a break for a minute before we go any further." She got off her bike and sat down on the curb of the street. I sat down without putting down my kickstand, I just let the bike collapse to the ground (because the bike was just as tired as I was, probably maybe).

"Why'd we have to bike all the way across town for some ice cream," I whined. It was sweltering out today and this little shit wanted us to go on a long-ass bike ride.

Fiona pulled out a bottle of water, pushing her wavy brown hair out of her face. She tossed a bottle of water to me and then took a drink out of hers. "Come on, Edwin. You're not gonna give up on me now, are you? The rest of the way is pretty much all downhill. And I'll let you walk your bike up the hills on the way back. Deal?"

I was panting but caught my breath long enough to say, "Deal."

Colby slammed the brakes and jumped off her bike and raised her arms high up in the air and started cheering and spinning in circles, celebrating her momentous victory over me, the Edwinner.

"Are you done yet?" I asked as she turned to me with the widest possible grin (in hindsight, this might have been the minute I fell in love with Colby for real, seeing her so happy and smiling so wide).

"I win." She ran up and jumped at me, bumping off my chest. "I beat you! I beat the Edwinner! I'm the Colbwinner, and Edwin is the Edloser. HA!" She kept on grinning. I felt the butterflies swarm in my stomach and grow restless, that comfortable nervousness pounding in my veins, and all I could do was smile back at her as she danced around in the moonlight. I could watch her twirl her hips around and move her feet in a non-rhythmic pattern all night. She was a beautiful sight to behold, and so I was beholding it as much as I could.

Colby eventually did stop celebrating. She walked over to me and smiled. "Shall we take a seat?" She walked over and picked up her backpack from the grass. As she walked back over to me, she pulled out a throw blanket and threw it on the ground at our feet. She sat down and pulled out a can of stacked chips. "I'm pretty tired. My legs need a break."

I sat down next to her and grabbed the chips from her, pulling the lid off and taking a few chips. "Yeah. I haven't felt my legs burn like that in a long time." I sighed and ate a chip. "So why'd we come here of all places?"

Colby shrugged. "I've always wanted to race around a racetrack."

"So you wanted to do it at midnight and on bikes?"

She smiled and took a chip from my hand. "No, but I don't get caught up with the details. I got to race around the track, and that's what matters to me."

"I guess you're right." I took some more chips from the can and handed the can to her. I stuffed a couple in my face and looked up at the sky. It was so beautiful and open tonight, like someone finally decided to clean the atmosphere of dirt. The stars shone brighter than I had ever remembered they could. "So now what?"

She shrugged. "We just sit here, I suppose." She lied down on the blanket and looked up at the sky, inhaling deeply. I watched her stomach rise and fall, rise and fall, rise and fall.

I smiled to myself and lied down next to her. The sky was beautiful tonight. The girl next to me was beautiful tonight. Perhaps, even, the colours were beautiful tonight. I rested my hand down at my side and felt Colby's slide over to mine. Her fingers laced between mine and she gave me a little squeeze. I wrapped my fingers closer to her hand and smiled. *This is nice,* I thought.

"Edwin," Colby said suddenly. "You're holding my hand."

"Yeah?" I looked over to her. "You were the one who grabbed my hand. I just went with it."

"Yeah, I just wanted to say thanks for not rejecting my hand holding. I know holding hands is a romantic thing to do, and I would have understood if you pushed it away, but thanks. Rejection hurts even when it is your best friend rejecting you." That said, she moved her hand behind her head.

"Your best friend, huh?"

"Well, best *dude* friend," Colby said, smiling softly. "My best friend is Tara. She lives across town."

You know, I think I really might be falling for this girl, I thought to myself. I sat up and looked at her. Her pale skin in the moonlight, her pink lips pursed ever so slightly. She had a hand on her stomach and her other arm behind her head. She was beautiful. She closed her eyes and exhaled a deep breath for what seemed like forever, she started to grin softly. She turned to me and opened her eyes. "You were staring?"

I laughed a little. "I was, yeah. You just look beautiful right now."

"Because it's dark and you can barely see me?"

No, because even in the dark you're all *that I can see,* I thought. I turned and lied back down. "Yeah. Little bit."

My words and my thoughts paint two separate pictures of how my life should be. In my heart, Colby and I throw away all labels and fall in love. There's no barriers, no obstacle to overcome, no anchor to pull back to the ship. It's just bright and happy and warm and comfortable and safe and secure. My heart sees things through rose-tinted glasses, like there can be no wrong done by letting Colby drown me in a sea of emotion, swelling over my riverbanks and soaking into my soils. But there is, there's always a wrong to be done. Love is a gamble.

My head never lets me forget that.

Remember how Fiona died? It would say. Of course I remembered. Fiona was the love of my life, but maybe we were never meant to have just one soulmate. But my mind didn't care about that thought. Every future I could ever envision with Colby was already dystopian. In every future, she dies or I die or Fiona comes back or I stay too distant to ever be loved. In every future, something goes wrong.

My words just play keep-up with the world around me. I don't wanna give away my heart's intents and I can't give away my mind's either. I don't want either my mind or heart to lose this fight, but I don't want either one to win either. Thinking about loving someone else after Fiona is a challenge for me, actually loving someone else would be impossible. I'm a wreck, surely Colby knew that already. I wondered how much longer would it take for Colby to get sick of waiting for me to get better.

It'll happen eventually. She'll get so sick of playing the side chick to a dead girl. And even if she is just a friend, how long until she meets a guy and has to cut me out because, let's fucking face it, it's weird for people to hang out with other people they've fucked once in a new relationship. It's just unnecessary drama and awkwardness, really (but that's a rant for another day).

But Colby, she'll grow cold on me. She'll become scarcer and scarcer, until she's eventually gone from my life completely. I've seen it happen. People just start to not reply to messages and then they stop asking you to hang out and then they stop talking to you altogether. Sometimes they just stop all at once and there is no gradual ease into the falling out. It's called ghosting, and it's the shittiest feeling to get ghosted. Colby will no doubt do the same when this arrangement of ours gets too stale for her.

Colby deserves better anyway. She deserves someone not so fucked up like me. She deserves someone that will *actually* fall in love with her. Sooner or later, she might end up falling in love with me, and I'm scared of that, because I really don't think I'll be able to give her the same love back.

"Ed, come here," Colby said, snapping me out of my thoughts. She climbed over and hugged me. "Whatever it is that you're thinking about that made you have such a sad look on your face, it's okay. If you wanna talk, I'm here for you."

I smiled into her neck, breathing in the smell of her perfume (a vanilla fragrance). The colours betwixt are warm and soft; the colours of Colby were too.

Part 4
Chapter 8

The Colour of Beating Hearts

Colby pulled the garage door closed. We had dropped the bikes and SUV off in favour of her little blue hatchback. We didn't need the bikes anymore, so there was no sense driving around the SUV. We both got in her car and she clicked her tongue and then pressed it against the inside of her cheek in thought. She finally started the car and started backing up.

"So what now?" I asked. "My place or yours?"

"Pfft. You think this night is over?" she asked. "Come on now. Where's your rebel spirit? We need to go do something to really get your heart pumping. I wanna see you feel alive."

"Not sure I like where this is going."

"One more adventure. A big one. Something more dangerous." Colby twisted her lips into a devious smile. "Something that will get that heart of yours pounding in your chest."

"Can we just go back to my place and fuck?" I groaned.

"Yeah, obviously," she replied. "Just later. We're gonna go get into some actual trouble first."

"What are we gonna do?"

"We're gonna go break in to this other place I know of." She smiled. "Just trust me, it'll be good. We'll have fun. Just relax. How are your legs feeling?"

"My legs?"

"Yeah, do you think you could run a mile if you had to?"

"I-I guess so. Why?"

"Well, we might have to run. That's all." Colby swung a hard left turn and I wasn't ready, so I was pushed against the door. "If someone finds us, we have to run, or we *will* go to jail."

"Where are we going, Colby?"

"Back to college."

"Why?" I groaned.

"We're gonna break in to the library," Colby stated. "It's one of my favourite places, to be honest. I used to go in at night all the time and when a security guard would find me, I would just say that I had been studying and lost track of time."

"You just go into the library past hours and...? What do you do?"

"Read, masturbate, eat food." She shrugged. "Whatever I feel like doing."

"Okay, so then why are we going now?"

"To read or masturbate or eat food." She shrugged again. "Whatever we feel like doing."

I sighed. "Okay, fuck it. Let's do it."

"Yes! There's that can-do attitude I knew you had in ya." Colby smiled widely. "This is gonna be fun. Just remember to relax and have fun. Save the worry for when we're running away from security, because there will be running."

"Good thing I put on my good shoes tonight, huh?"

Colby laughed. "You don't have good shoes. You're a dude. You have like two pairs of shoes. Everyday shoes and wedding-funeral shoes."

"You right," I muttered.

She smiled as she blew through a red light. I guess I can give her a pass on that since there's nobody around and since we're about to go commit a bigger crime anyway.

The car pulled to a stop on a very quiet and quite sleepy side street just nearby the college. There was a small alleyway that led from the street to the college grounds. Colby put the car in park and took a deep breath. I cocked an eyebrow at her and she just grinned.

Colby popped the door open. "Let's go see what kind of trouble we can get ourselves into, shall we?"

I got out and followed her to towards the library. The lights were still on, but they always were at the college. They never turn the lights off. We walked to the back of the library and Colby pulled open a door. "They never lock this one," she said, shrugging. "It's a convenience thing."

"For them or for you?" I asked, walking past her into the library.

She laughed a little as she closed the door behind us. "Why can't it be both?" She walked in front of me and looked down the halls. "Okay, well, I think we're clear down here. Let's go up to the top floor. The security doesn't go there very often."

"Okay, lead the way."

Colby turned left and started walking. The lighting was dim here in the hallways. The actual books part of the library was still lit up though. I wonder why that was. These access halls are used more by security at night than the actual library space was. Colby led me to the large concrete stairwell and we walked up the highest floor. Though it was only a four-story building.

The fourth floor was empty and dimly lit, but then again, I don't know what else I would have been expecting. The whole library was empty. If there were any security guards in here, they would have to be the quietest guards in history, and they must like walking around in the dark, because there were no beams of light anywhere.

Colby walked over to one of the large glass panels that comprised the wall. This side of the library overlooked a large courtyard. On the other side of the courtyard was the main college building with the classrooms and lecture halls. She turned to me and raised her arm, motioning with her hand for me to come over. "It's beautiful tonight." She took my hand in hers and placed her other one on the glass.

I looked over and saw the reflection of her face in the glass. She had a small smile formed on her lips. Her eyes were bright even in the dimness. She was as beautiful as ever. "Yeah," I said. "It's beautiful tonight." Of course I meant her though. And I think she knew that, because she smiled softly and squeezed my hand gently.

"I love how quiet it is here," Colby spoke softly. "It's nice to take a few moments and retract from the world. Real life is so stressful sometimes, that's why people get lost in movies or music or books, to escape. But some of us just like this, this quietness. I like this quietness." She smiled again, looking over to me. "Do you like the quiet? What's your stress relief? Where do you go to escape?"

"Colours," I replied. "That's my escape. I paint or do something with colours." I turned to her and smiled. "Colours are my happy place, but I haven't really been happy since Fiona passed away."

"I understand." Colby turned back to look out over the college. "Man, it feels like just yesterday I was a freshman here."

"Yeah."

"Time moves too quickly for my liking." She pouted softly and furrowed her brows ever so slightly. "Life just doesn't wanna slow down, huh?"

"It certainly doesn't." I laughed a little.

"What?"

"This is your way of telling me to move on before I get left behind, isn't it?"

Colby half-frowned and nodded. "In a way, I guess. I just mean that life moves so fast. Just a few years ago I was in high school with no idea how to live or how to be my own person, and now I know *exactly* who I am. I know what I want. I know how to live. I live on my own, well, with roommates, but the point is that I've moved out. I have my own car. I work a full-time job. I've graduated high school and college. Just a couple years ago, I had nothing. Now I have a life. It's just crazy how fast it all moved. So yeah, I just don't wanna see you get left behind because you anchored yourself to a—"

"To a dead girl," I finished the sentence for her. "I know. I'm just not ready to move on yet. Maybe someday, but just not *yet*."

"Sorry."

"It's not a big deal," I stated. "It's the truth, isn't it? I'm anchored to a dead girl."

"I didn't mean it in a bad way."

"I didn't either. I'm not mad at you," I told her. "It's the truth."

She sighed. "Let's just change the subject. I feel like an asshole now."

I nodded. "Mm, okay, so you know who you kind of look like?"

"Who?" Colby asked.

"Jennifer Lawrence in *Passengers*."

"Oh, I guess so." She looked at her reflection in the glass. "Mm, my nose is a little perkier, like upturned at the tip. And I have darker eyebrows. But I see what you mean."

"Your nose is so adorable." I smiled softly at her. "I also feel like your face isn't as round as hers."

Colby shrugged. "A face is a face is a face."

"I guess, but you have a very nice one."

She blushed a little. "Thanks."

"Wanna hear a joke?"

"Is it my life?" She forlornly looked out the window as she sighed. "What's the joke?"

"What kind of bed do fruits sleep on?"

"I dunno. What?"

I snickered a little and she rolled her eyes at me as I answered, "Apri-*cots*."

Colby smiled at me. "Well, *orange* you cute." She smirked. "See, I got puns too."

"I can see that," I said, looking back and blatantly checking out her ass. "And nice puns by the look of it."

"Keep it in your pants, buddy. It's not the time or place for that." Colby looked around the library. "We're in a library. Maybe we should look at some books."

"I agree." I looked around at the little genre signs. "Looks like a lot of general and young adult fiction in front of us."

"Perfect." Colby walked down on of the aisles. "Young adults is what we are, and I love a good relatable tale of young people falling in love."

"I'm gonna pick a book at random and then you should read it." I placed my hand down on a shelf without looking.

"What book do you got?"

I pulled the book out and looked the cover over. "*Umbrellas*," I told her. I read over the back of it and put it back. "Might be your kind of thing."

"I'll look into it."

"What's your favourite book of all time?" I asked her.

She shrugged. "*Before I Go to Sleep*, maybe. I liked that one."

"I'll also look into it."

Colby suddenly perked up. "Hey, did you hear that?"

"Hear what?"

She shushed me quickly and we trained our ears for distant sounds. "That," she said as a door opened. "Someone else is in here."

"Yeah, the fucking security guard we're supposed to be not getting caught by."

"Get down, dickhead." Colby grabs me and pulls me down to the floor. We're both on our hands and knees, watching for any movement in the distance. "Try not to breathe if you can," she whispered to me.

I lightly scoffed. "I'll get right on it."

"I don't see him," Colby stated.

"No, but I can see you," a voice said from behind us in the aisle.

Without hesitation, Colby grabbed my arm and we began running down through the library. Colby was smiling widely and when we reached the end of a bookshelf, she turned around and started pushing the shelf over, hard too, harder than a girl her size should have strength for. Without thinking, I helped her. And we watched in awe as they began to domino down the length of the library floor. No doubt, the security guard was now on the floor, crawling under a bookshelf as they all tipped over and fell on top of one another.

"That was fucking cool," Colby whispered as we listened to the triumphant thuds. She turned to me and nodded towards the door. "We should probably get out of here now."

I opened the door for her and we began running down the stairs. We took off the same way we came in, passing by a security guard on the first floor as we did. As we ran across the field back towards Colby's car, we heard the footsteps and frantic key clattering of the security guard hauling ass to catch us. He couldn't of course. Colby and I were two young adults in peak physical form. The security guard probably hadn't done any fitness training in years.

Colby slid across the hood of her car and we hopped in our seats as she fired the engine up. The tires squealed as we peeled the fuck out of there. "You feel that thumping in your chest, Edwin?" she shouted. "That's what feeling alive feels like."

The colours betwixt thudded in my chest, a beating heart for an unscathed return to the safety of her car. I felt alive, more alive than I had felt in a year and a half.

Part 4
Chapter 9

The Colour of 61 BPM

The barista handed me the two cups, a large double-double and a caramel macchiato. I walked back over to the table Colby had sat down at. The world outside was dark, illuminated by the lights of passing cars and the streetlights. I stopped beside where she was sitting and slid the double-double in front of her and she looked over at me and smiled sweetly.

"Thirty-four," she stated.

"Pardon?" I asked as I pulled my chair out from the table and took my seat across from her.

"You can see thirty-four streetlights from this table."

I turned and looked out the wall (seriously, what is it with every place having walls of glass) and counted up the streetlights. "Thirty-five." I smirked at her. "You can see thirty-five streetlights from this table."

"Same thing." She took the lid off her coffee and blew the steam towards me. She blew a little harder and then took a sip. "It's perfect."

Yes, you are.

"You are staring again," she said, rolling her head and looked up at me. "Why do you keep staring at me? Am I really *that* attractive?"

I nodded. "Mm-hmm."

"You're cute." She stirred her coffee with her pinky. She didn't even flinch about the coffee being literally still boiling hot. "So when we were running away," she said, pulling her now-pink finger from her coffee, "you had this huge smile on your cute little face."

"What do you mean?"

"I mean that you looked happy. It was nice, you looked carefree, like you were actually enjoying this whole *being alive* thing."

"Yeah, being alive does suck for me lately."

"Exactly." She eyed my drink. "Maybe if you stopped drinking fancy $7 coffees it would be better for you."

"I like being pretentious, thank you."

She laughed. "Yeah, me too sometimes."

"Let me dye your hair."

"What? No, fuck you. Dye *your* hair." Colby scowled at me. "I love my blonde hair the way it is, thank you very much. You so much as lay a colourful finger on it and I'll body your ass all the way back to last week."

"You're smaller than me. I would love to see you try to body me at all."

Colby glared deep at me, deep into my soul. "Watch it, Flowers. I know jujutsu, remember."

"I'm not scared of you," I told her. "I was in hockey for years. I can hockey fight like nobody's business."

"I can break your dick. I've done it before."

"Pause," I said. "You've broken a dick before?"

She nodded. "High school boyfriend slipped out and I kept

going down. *Snap.*" Her eyes looked down at the general area of my groin. "So be careful."

"Still not scared of you."

Colby rolled her eyes and took a sip of her coffee. "So what do you wanna do for the rest of the night?"

"I wanna go and sleep," I groaned. "I'm getting pretty tired."

"Weak, Edwin." She sighed. "But I'm getting tired too. You wanna go to my place or yours?"

"My place. My car is already at my place and I don't want you to have to drive me home," I told her. I took a sip of my macchiato and swirled it around my mouth. "If you're not doing anything tomorrow, you can stay and hang out with me, you know, like, if you want to, maybe?"

"Probably. Either that or I go home and do laundry." She placed a hand over her mouth as she started to yawn. Her nose crinkled and she let out the cutest yawn my eyes and ears have ever seen and heard. "I don't really wanna do laundry, so I'll just hang out with you."

"Because you don't wanna do laundry? Wow. I'm feeling the love."

"Shush." Colby looked over to the menu and squinted as she read over what they offered here.

"They probably don't have half of this stuff made at this hour, you know," I told her. "It's too late."

She shushed me. "I'm sure they have something. I'll make a mental list of the stuff I want and then order." She got up from the table and blew a raspberry. "Do you want anything?"

"Just get me whatever you're getting."

She nodded and walked back over to the counter. I watched as she pushed some hair out of her face and start speaking to make the order. She smiled, she laughed a little. She ordered three things that they didn't have before finally getting to something that they did have: cream of broccoli soup with cheddar cheese.

Colby smiled as she carried two little white containers of

soup over to our table. "Cream of broccoli." She sat down and slid one of the soups to me. She pulled some plastic-wrapped spoons from her pocket and handed me one.

"Thanks," I said, taking the spoon.

My eyes caught hers and for a moment here, time seemed to stop. The world outside shuddered and became a blur. The bright light of the coffee shop illuminated Colby's face and she smiled at me. Her eyes were bright and I swear they even sparkled.

"You," she began.

"Are staring," I finished for her. "I know. I can't help it sometimes."

"Eat up. I wanna go home."

"You wanna go home?"

"To your apartment." Colby sighed. "You know what I meant. Eat up. I get cold when I'm tired and you don't wanna see me when I get cold because I get whiny as fuck, and neither of us wanna deal with that blow to my image."

"Your image?" I popped the lid off my soup. "What image is that? A cute blonde girl who sometimes sucks her thumb in her sleep?" I looked at her as she scowled at me. "Because you do that sometimes."

"I do not!" she shouted. "You're lying!"

"You suck your thumb when you sleep. When you passed out the other night, I walked in and you were curled up with my blanket and you had your thumb in your mouth." I scooped some soup into my mouth, trying not to wince at the sudden heat.

Colby pouted at me. "Keep it a secret. I can't have that getting out to the masses."

"Colby, everyone knows you as this cute eccentric girl, not as a badass. Sucking your thumb fits your persona just fine, in my opinion."

"But I'm a grown-ass woman! Grown-ass women do *not* suck their thumbs!"

"This one does." I smiled at her. "And there's nothing

wrong with that. "Now eat up before you get cold and whiny."
"Will you cuddle me for warmth?"
"Nah, you can sleep on the couch tonight."
"Rude."

I smirked and continued to eat my soup. Of course Colby can cuddle me for warmth. She knew that I wasn't about to turn her down, not tonight or ever (probably). I wonder if she realizes just how under her spell I really am. I don't even love her, I just love being around her and talking to her and looking at her (not in a creepy way though).

The door was stuck, so I gave it a little check and it unwedged itself. Colby stifled a laugh as she walked into the apartment hallway after me.
"Does the door really always do that?" she asked.
"Only when it's late and I'm tired." I led the way up to my apartment and let her in. I closed the door and locked it after us. We slipped our shoes off and before she even took another step, Colby had begun ripping her clothes off. "What are you doing?"
"Getting ready for bed," she replied, pulling her legs out of her pants. "There's no one else in the apartment with us, is there? Like, you don't have Derek shacking up with you for the week or anything?"
"No."
"Then what's it matter if I undress here or in your room?" She scoffed. "I've been wearing pants and a bra all day, so cut me a little slack if I wanna undress right away. I'm *un*comfortable."
"Yeah, yeah." I walked to the kitchen and pulled a cup out of the cupboard. "You want anything to drink?"
"Nah, I'm alright." Colby walked into the kitchen after me. Her shirt, bra, socks, and pants were all balled up and stuffed under her arm. "Just tired. And cold."

"And whiny." I turned and smiled to her as I filled my glass with water. I downed the water and set the cup on the counter. "Wanna go get ready for bed?"

Colby nodded and headed to the bathroom to clean off her makeup and brush her teeth (yes, she keeps a toothbrush at my place because that's what *friends* do). When she was finished, I brushed my teeth and cleaned up my face a bit. It's nice to go to bed feeling A1 instead of A-none.

I walked into my room and crawled into my bed. Colby was already fast asleep by the time I got there though. She was curled up, thumb in her mouth, snoring as softly as anyone probably could. I smiled and wrapped my arms around her, pulling her in and then I wrapped us up in a blanket. I kissed her forehead, pulled her closer, and I then listened to the sounds of her heart beating next to mine.

Thump. Thump. Thump. Until I, too, fell asleep.

It's been a long night and the colours betwixt are still coming back from the adrenaline highs and serenity lows.

Part 4
Chapter 10

The Colour of Questions

Colby smiled and gave a small wave as she backed out of the parking spot she was in. I didn't kick her out, she was just leaving because she did have to do laundry at some point. I watched as she pulled out onto the street and then she was gone. I heard the rattle of her little car for a few more seconds as she drove off down the street.

Once she was gone, I pulled my phone out and called Derek. "Where are you?"

"Um, at home, why?" Derek replied. "Is something wrong?"

"Nothing's wrong. Can you meet up with me?"

"Want me to collect Marshall?"

"That'd be nice of you," I told him. "Meet me at the superstore. I gotta pick up some stuff."

"You're taking us shopping with you?" Derek mused. "How thoughtful of you. I'll go get him and we'll meet you by the garden centre entrance."

"Cool. See you there." We hung up the call. I walked over and hopped into my car. The superstore was closer to Derek, and Marshall's place was in between Derek's and the superstore, so we should get there around the same time, or that's the plan at least.

Derek and Marshall were off in the distance, walking towards me at a snail's pace. They didn't get a very good parking spot, so the walk was long, but at least it was sort of sunny and warm today. Derek was busy looking down at his phone. It's a miracle he didn't get pegged by a passing car or that he didn't trip up the curb.

"Took you guys long enough," I chirped them as they got within earshot.

Derek scoffed. "Pretty boy here needed to do his hair."

"I was on the shitter," Marshall chimed, walking over and bumping the fist I had raised for them.

"So, what's going on with the Edwinner lately?" Derek asked. "You haven't filled us in on any of your dubious conquests lately. Have you stopped being such a slut?"

"Yes, I have," I stated as we walked into the store. "But I didn't wanna talk to you about my lack of flutes lately." I grabbed a basket so I could hold stuff without holding as much stuff.

"Then what is it?" Derek said, picking up a chocolate bar from a display. "I'm allowed to buy my own snacks, don't give me that look."

"It's Colby," I told them.

"Ooh, Colby," Marshall said. "I like her. What's going on

with you two lately?"

"Oh, quick sidebar, remember how you guys drove to *Toronto* to go to Twisters?" Derek asked. "Well, guess what they're opening here rather soonly."

"Wow, that's unlucky for my mileage." I scoffed. They would open a Twisters here now after all this time. Finally.

"Anyway, back to Marshall's question," Derek said, putting his phone into his pocket. "What's going on with you and Colby lately?"

"We've been fine," I replied.

"Then what's with the needing to talk to us?" Derek asked.

I shrugged. "I dunno. It's about Colby, I guess. I kind of think I wanna be with her."

"Like, with her or *with* her?" Marshall asked as we turned down the soaps and shampoos aisle.

"What's the difference?"

"Well," Derek said, "do you wanna be with her sexually or with her romantically?"

"Both," I replied, "I guess. I dunno. I just wanna be with her."

"So be with her," Derek said.

I stopped and grabbed a bar of soap and tossed it into the basket. "Well, I just don't wanna be with her either. I'm too emotionally detached for a relationship."

"You're just fucking stubborn," Marshall noted. "You'll grow out of it."

"No, he's not stubborn, he's stupid," Derek *corrected* him. "And unfortunately for us, his stupidity is terminal."

"Which shower gel do you think smells better?" I asked, holding up two different scents of shower gel from the same company.

"Are you asking us what Colby would rather your balls smell like?" Derek asked. "The black ice one."

"Thank you." I eyed him down and tossed the black label gel into the basket. "I need shampoo."

"Are you at any time going to ask Colby to be your girlfriend?" Marshall asked as we moved down the aisle to the shampoos."

I shrugged. "That's what I'm thinking about doing. I need you guys to talk me into it."

"We don't need to talk you into it," Derek stated.

"Yeah, you clearly have feelings for her," Marshall added. "If you didn't, you wouldn't even be asking about asking her to be your girlfriend. I thought you guys were doing the whole friends with bennies deal."

"We were," I told them.

"But," Derek added.

"But," I said, "I've realized how awesome she actually is. It just makes sense for us to be together. We love being around each other, we make each other laugh and smile, we get along better than I've ever gotten along with anybody."

"Thanks, bro," Marshall and Derek said in unison.

"Well, it's true. We have our fights."

"But you still love us more, right?" Derek asked, pouting out his lip a bit. "I don't want some dumb girl to come between us. I love you, Edwin."

"Shut up." I pushed him a little. I grabbed two different scents of shampoo. Derek and Marshall both rolled their eyes at me. "Okay, okay," I said, putting one of the shampoos into my basket. I didn't really care. Except, like, what if Colby liked the other scent better? What if she doesn't even like either scents? What kind of stuff does Colby like to smell, anyway?

"Where to next?" Marshall asked.

"Um. I need some food things." I thought about what else I needed. "Yeah, food. I can get that later. Um, paper towels though. I need those."

"You came here for paper towels and shower supplies?" Derek asked. "I'm really glad I came out for this."

"Shut up. I missed your ugly face, you duster."

"I missed yours too, you soggy cockbite." Derek sighed as we walked down the aisle towards the section that housed the paper towels. "Anyway, I think you *need* to make Colby your girlfriend before she realizes that she's too good for you and leaves your ass for good."

"Seconded," Marshall said.

"She *is* too good for me," I stated. "There's no arguing that. That's a fact. But, in your guys's expert opinions, do you think I'm ready to move on to a new relationship?"

"I would hope you'd be able to move on from Fiona by now, dude." Derek tossed a bundle of paper towel into my basket.

"Why's that?"

Derek sighed. "Okay, look, I'm gonna say something, not because I want to, but because I think you need to hear it." He took a breath and then exhaled sharply. "You need to ask out Colby. She's an amazing girl, literally a wonderland inside a human body. We like her, your parents like her, everybody likes her. You *love*, or are falling in love, with her. As for Fiona, she's gone, Edwin. And no amount of pushing off potential partners is gonna bring her back. You're only damaging yourself by refusing to let go of her. She wouldn't be mad. She would have wanted you to move on, probably a lot quicker than you decided. You're young, and you have so much ahead of you, but you have so much *right here* and right *now* that's just waiting for you to say yes to. Don't let this wonderful girl slip through the cracks because of Fiona. Don't. You *will* regret it. I promise you that, Edwin."

"So… should I go put back the black ice and get the blue thunder shower gel?" I asked him, completely disregarding what he had said in an attempt to divert the conversation, because let's be honest, I don't wanna talk about the way Colby makes me feel or how I feel guilty for feeling the way I feel. If Fiona hadn't died, I wouldn't even know Colby. I'd be happily with Fiona, probably even thinking about marriage at this point in our lives. *Maybe* even warming up to idea of one day having kids with her. Maybe. Kids are a lot more work than I think I'm cut out for, to be honest.

The two of us, Fiona and I, we just clicked, on a spiritual level too. We didn't just come together and end up staying together because no one else wanted us or that we were scared to be alone. We stayed together because we wanted to, we really did. We loved each other, more than I'll ever love anybody else in my entire life. To have that kind of love so young is one thing (a fucking *great* thing), but then to have that same endless love ripped from you, that's a whole other thing. There's no words to be able to adequately describe the kind of damage something like that can do to a person's mind and soul, really.

I've lived my life since Fiona's death with an almost PTSD-like post-love disorder of sorts. I have nightmares nearly nightly about her. Most are recurring, the same handful of dreams repeating behind my eyelids when I fall asleep each night. I've been better at not waking up in cold sweats, but I still do a lot of the time. It's fucking hell.

And sure, Colby's fucking great, but she deserves someone who will be fully and entirely hers. And I never will be. A part of me, my love, my heart, it died on the same stretch of road that Fiona did. It wouldn't be fair to have Colby give up a real chance at finding love (because she no doubt would, she's beautiful and smart and funny and kind) for trying to love me, or trying to fix me. Fixing me might even break her, and that's something I definitely do not want to happen.

"Oh, Edwin," Marshall said, sighing a little as he rested a hand on my back. "When will you ever learn?"

"I'm not gonna yell at you because we're in a store right now, but you're gonna get a stern talking to, young lady," Derek barked at me.

"Okay, *Dad*," I said, humouring him a little to make whatever lecture that was coming down the pipes a little less harsh. Derek loves getting harsh with me. He knows what I *need* to hear. He doesn't usually sugar coat it either, and yes, there's usually a fair bit of screaming, but also a lot of hugging and brotherly love. I don't know what I'd do without Derek sometimes. Marshall's cool too, I guess.

"Can we just go pay for this shit so I can give you a 15-slide presentation on why Colby is a prime choice for being your new soulmate?" Derek groaned.

I nodded. "Sure. I got all I need for now I guess."

"We could have just went to the pharmacy up the road for this stuff," Marshall muttered.

"Too bad," I told him. "I thought I would maybe want more stuff, so I came here. Deal with it."

"You're paying for lunch, then, Mr. Big Guy With A Fancy Job," Derek ribbed me.

"It's a housekeeping job, it ain't fancy." I walked up to the nearest cashier and began piling the few items I had onto the little conveyor belt. I stacked the basket with the other empty ones and got my debit card ready. And after that, the three of us went across the plaza to a sushi place for lunch. And that was the day. All of it. I got a good lecture about how Fiona's dead and gone and I'll be dead and gone before *I'm* ready to move on. He said I have to just take the plunge, that nobody likes cold water at first. You know? Like, the water starts off cold but then our bodies adjust and the water warms a little and all that shit. I dunno. I stopped listening halfway through the lecture if we're being honest.

I suppose he's right about most of that shit though. But it doesn't stop the colours betwixt from questioning everything and making me doubt myself and my emotional well-being at every turn.

Part 4
Chapter 11

The Colour of a Canvas

Ding. Dong. My apartment buzzer doesn't actually make that noise. I wish it did. Instead it sounded more like this: *bzbzbbbzbbzeezzzz*. I walked over and hit the talk button, "Hello?"

"It's me," Colby's cheerful tones rang through the crackly intercom. "Let me in, pwease?" I bet she's doing the pouty lip thing.

"How about I come down?"

"Oh. That's even better. I was gonna ask you to come over after raiding your kitchen for food, but okay. I'll wait out front in my car. Hurry your ass up." I heard her hang up the intercom and then I sighed a little. *Oh, Colby.*

I walked around my apartment, trying to find clean clothes and a pair of socks that didn't have holes in them. Must have taken me quite long because I got an angry text from Colby as I was heading out the door. I locked up and headed downstairs to meet her out front. It was cloudy and rainy today. She was sitting in her car, staring in at the lobby as I came outside. She had a scowl on her face but lightened up when I flashed her a quick smile before walking to the passenger side and getting in. I don't get why she's all salty at me. She didn't tell me she was coming over for fuck's sake.

"You took entirely too long," she berated me. "Be quicker next time or you get to walk."

"Well, you gave me no notice," I told her. "And I have a car, so I would have just driven to your place if you wanted to hang out."

She shrugged as we pulled out of the parking lot. "Visitor parking for my place is a bitch."

"Visitor parking anywhere is a bitch."

"True."

"So what's the special occasion?"

She shrugged. "I missed you a little. I wanted to see your face. Friends can miss friends and wanna hang out. Why does there need to be a special occasion?"

"I dunno. You don't usually come pick me up randomly. I usually get some sort of warning."

"Not today. I wanted to surprise you and I knew you were home today because you don't work weekends, ever."

"True. But being that it's Saturday, maybe I was going to be busy with errands."

Colby laughed, more like a mockingly cynical laugh than a friendly laugh. "You don't run errands, Ed. They run"—she sniffled a little—"they run you. Sorry. I might have a little bit of a cold. I dunno how. It's still summer."

"Don't get me sick. Thanks."

"I won't. It's just a little tickle in my throat and a little snot in my nose. I'm fine."

"Why do you have an easel in your trunk?" I asked, noticing the wooden abomination in her back seat. It was composed of light-coloured wood. I hated light-coloured easels. I like them to be dark colours, less distracting for me. Kinda weird, I know.

"Um, I just thought maybe you wanted to paint some stuff," Colby said. "That's all. I picked it up the other day and haven't brought it into my place yet. I just thought it would make a nice little gift for you."

"It's perfect," I said, smiling at her. And just like that, I liked light-coloured wooden easels.

It's amazing, isn't it? How that works? How you can go your whole life not liking something and then when someone you like and care for gets you that thing, you suddenly like it, regardless of how long you spent not liking it. Maybe it's just a *me* thing.

"How much do you usually sell paintings for?"

I shrugged. "I dunno. I usually don't."

"Oh," she mouthed. She stayed quiet for a moment. "Okay, how much can I buy a painting for? Ten bucks?"

"That's insulting," I deadpanned.

She blew a raspberry. "Shut up. Name your price."

"Buy all the supplies and make me a coffee or two and I'll paint whatever you want," I told her. "Do you know what you want me to paint?"

"Nah. I'll think about it and let you know when we get to my place. I just wanted to make sure it was cool with you to do a painting first. I didn't wanna get my hopes up or anything just to have them crushed."

"No promises that it'll be good. I haven't painted in a while."

"But I've seen your paintings," Colby stated. "That kind of talent doesn't just disappear because it goes unused for a few months. You were born with a gift to be good at painting and then you did it so much you became great, because really any art form is half natural talent and half worked-for talent. I know that much."

"Well, thanks for the vote of confidence."

She smiled. "Yeah, anytime, dude. Also, I bought lasagna for us to have for dinner."

"I love la-zawg-na."

She snickered a bit. "Good. I bought a big one, so there'll be leftovers for you to take home if you want them."

Colby's apartment was eerily quiet. It always is though. I never see her roommates. I think that's her goal though. Don't let the FWB meet the people she lives with. Keeps the two worlds a little more separate. Or her roommates are just always either at work or doing school things or visiting family. I know one of them is taking summer courses to graduate earlier. The other one might be home with family for the summer.

"There's a canvas in the closet," Colby stated as we walked into her house. She nodded down the hall towards a small little closet. Sidebar, why does every hallway have one of these? Every house or apartment has this little closet. I've never seen a purpose for it, really.

"Did you buy the canvas too?" I asked as I walked to the closet. I opened it and feasted my eyes upon several canvases and paints of all colours. "You bought all of this for me?"

"Yeah," Colby replied, popping up behind me without making a sound. "Perks of not having a boyfriend to spoil. I get to spoil my best dude instead." She smiled and kissed me cheek. "Now, let's go figure out what I want you to paint."

"You want me to paint you, don't you?"

She turned back and smiled at me. "I might."

I rolled my eyes a little as I followed her into her bedroom. "Where do you want me?"

She pulled a stool out from behind her open door and carried it to her window. She peeled the curtains back so the visible glass formed a trapezoid-like shape. "I'm gonna sit here in the window, and I wanted you to maybe paint my silhouette, but like, do it colourful like your other paintings."

"Okay, and then food?"

She nodded. "Yes, then food."

I sighed and helped Colby get into position. She stripped out of her pants and replaced her shirt with a baggy sweater. Aesthetic, I guess. And then I put in earphones (I always keep a pair of earphones in my pocket) and I tuned the world out as I began to paint the image before me.

Colby was a stellar subject, she barely moved at all. The only thing she really did was stretch her toes and roll her ankles. I guess that's to alleviate the fact that she didn't want to move her head or neck at all. When we were done, she applauded my painting and then I forced her to go make food while the painting dried. And I refused to let her see it until it was dry. She might ruin it in excitement.

It feels good to once again make colourful images appear where blankness was. I always loved that feeling of turning something empty into something full of life, something beautiful. It's like the blue sky fading to a starry night. I was a star-painter, painting colour where there was nothing. But even in the midst of all the colours, I still felt so empty. A blank white canvas, or so that's how I feel. I lost my painter. I lost the machinery to colour. I lost the colours into the void. My empty white, never to be filled again. But in a way, I suppose love will do that.

It fills you with colour and all the bright things. Flowers, rainbows, butterflies, the shit that covers every toy marketed towards little girls. It makes life feel like every indie movie with a dusty rose filter. It makes you feel like every morning is as carefree as the morning of a holiday. It makes you strong. It fills you, enamours you, completely eclipses you.

And then it's gone, whittled out like a flame dying. Sparks and embers burning slower and slower until it all fades away. The colours go black and white. All those bright things don't last. The flowers wilt, rainbows replaced by heavy showers again, and the butterflies die.

But when Colby made me paint her, something ignited in

me. A fire, maybe, but more like a spreading of colours all over my blank canvases.

Something about her had made a flower start to grow somewhere in the cracks of my soul. Deep down, the clouds are peeling back, the rain letting up. The caterpillars are forming cocoons. It's filling me. Enamouring me, vehemently swamping the cracks with colour.

It's there that I realize that the colours betwixt her and I are calling out. For what? Well, I've yet to learn to listen for that.

Part 4
Chapter 12

The Colour of a Chimera

Even my eyes are sweating. That's what it feels like anyway. Everything is hot again. My hands are clammy. I'm in the white city of floating buildings again. I run to the balcony and glare down through its glass floor. Deep down below is an endlessly vast tar ocean.

"Why am I here?" I ask, looking up to the sky, as if the sky will answer me. It doesn't, it can't, it's an empty white sky. The buildings are all empty, white-stone buildings. How did I get here again? Where even is here *for that matter?*

I step back inside. Last time, I jumped. This time, what do I do this time? Do I wait for Fiona to show up? Do I jump? I decide not to. I walk to the front door and put my hand on the knob. The metal is cool to the touch, which is nice since the air is so hot. I don't remember it being this hot before.

"Edwin!" Fiona's voice shouted out. I spun around and the ceiling gave way. A car came crashing down. Fiona's car, her little red sedan. It *lay upside down on the ground, Fiona inside, hanging there in her seat. Her eyes were lifeless. Her mouth was slightly agape. She didn't move. And neither did I. I just stared and she stared and neither of us moved.*

The world went cold and I blinked once and was on a dark road, snow covered the ground. I turned and in the distance saw a set of taillights, one on top of the other. The car was on its side.

So I ran.

Maybe this is God's way of giving me a chance to save her. To save her and he can take me.

I run, and I run, and I run.

My lungs are heaving to take air in this cold. I'm only in a white T-shirt and thin white pants, but I run. My white-socked feet slapping the ground and losing grip in the snow. But I press on. I run and run. I reach the car and began to push it back on its four wheels. I open the door and take Fiona out of the car.

She looks as beautiful as she ever did. I lay her down in the snow. It melts around her, for whatever reason. I don't have the sense to question it. I look back to the car and see that Fiona is still in the driver seat. I look back at Fiona and Fiona is still lying at my feet, albeit slightly transparent. This is her soul. I killed her. It's my fault. I took her.

I get in the car, sit in the passenger seat, and I wait. The radio crackles and Fiona speaks, "Close your eyes, Edwin. Focus on what you feel, focus."

Suddenly things are warm again, not hot, but warm. They're comfortable. Cozy even. I open my eyes and see that I'm in Colby's room. The painting I had painted for her just earlier in the night was hung on the wall. I turned beside me and Colby was lying there, softly snoring in my ear, even drooling a tad on my chest.

There's a banging outside the room. Not of her roommates, it's something worse. Something sinister is in the room just outside this one. Beyond a few inches of wood, lies something feral. I can feel it. My blood crawls at the thought. I get out of bed and walk to the door. The metal is again cold to the touch, like it's been outside for a long winter.

The door creaks open and I step through it. Behind me, the door slams shut. I snap my gaze to the kitchen where I see a figure atop the counter. It cranes its neck at me and twists its mouth to a smile. It's wearing a white dress. It steps forward and I realize that it's Fiona.

"Her?" she hisses at me "Some little wannabe of a Scandinavian princess fairy tale?" Fiona seems to glitch in her movements as she walks towards me. Her breath prickling the hairs on my neck as she looks me over. "You don't deserve her."

"I know," I whisper.

"YOU DON'T DESERVE ANYONE!" she shouts in my ear. "You let me die that night, didn't you? DIDN'T YOU?" Her breath is sickly warm, almost tangibly so.

"No! I didn't!"

"YOU DID!" She threw me against the wall and pinned me there, shoving her face close to mine. Her skin was grey, her teeth were sharp, and her eyes were dark and dead. "You let me die so you could fuck some little blonde whore, didn't you? Was I not good enough?" She bit her lip a little, which cause a small trickle of blood, and tried to give me flirty eyes. "Come on, Edwin. Tell me I'm pretty. Tell me I'm the only one you love."

"No!" I shout, pushing her off. "I don't love you, I love Fiona, the Fiona I knew."

"She's dead! And it's YOUR FAULT!"

"NO! I found your journal! I read the last thing you wrote in it. You killed yourself, Fiona! You knew the GPS would pick that road from the coffee shop! You planned all of this out. You just didn't plan on me making it through the crash, that was your mistake!"

"Edwin?!" Colby's voice yells out from the room.

"Better check on that little bitch." Fiona's neck twisted nearly 180 degrees around as she looked toward the door. Her movements were staggered and shaky as she ran into the room. I heard a scream and ran in after this monster that was Fiona.

"Edwin," Colby says as I enter. "Don't let her hurt me, please. Do whatever she wants."

Fiona lets out a loud screech as she slams Colby into the nearby TV face first. She picks Colby up and holds her up.

"Edwin," Colby says, blood creeping down her face. "I love you, Edwin. I love you. You are my light, my stars, my fresh pot of coffee. I love you."

Fiona gave me a twisted smile and in a fluid motion, turned Colby's neck further than any neck can reasonably turn. A sickening crack sounded out through the room. I fell to my knees and shut my eyes as tight as I *could, listening as Colby's body hit the ground with a* THUD.

My eyes darted open and I grabbed the person on top of me, throwing them off the bed to the floor. I was ready to throw a punch when I saw that it was Colby. She had her arms up and her head to the side, waiting for me to throw said punch.

"What happened?" I asked.

"You had another nightmare," she asked, sounding distraught.

"Are you crying?" I dropped down to the ground and helped her sit upright.

She nodded and wiped her face. "I thought you were about to fucking deck me one, man. I got scared."

"I'm sorry." I grabbed her and pulled her into a hug. "I'm so sorry."

Her tears soaked into my bare skin and she wrapped her arms around me. "Fuck, Edwin, you literally tossed me to the floor like I weighed two pounds. It's just scary coming from a dude as gentle as you."

"Just… a *bad* dream," I told her, holding her as close I could. I could feel her shaky hands even though she was hugging me tightly. "I'm so fucking sorry, Colby. I didn't mean to scare you. I'm sorry. Fuck. Are you sure you're okay?"

"It's fine," she said, sniffling. "It's not like you could control something like that. I shouldn't have been so forceful in waking you, but you were shout-mumbling and sweating and I just knew you were in the middle of a nightmare."

"Well, thank you for getting me out of it."

She shrugged. "It's what I do."

"Are you okay?"

"I will be. You just did me a good startle. Nothing I can't shake myself out of." She gave me a weak smile. "Okay."

I exhaled sharply. "I need to go."

"What? Where are you going?"

"I just have to go."

"Okay." She smiled. "Call me tomorrow."

"I will," I replied as I stood up. I helped her up and onto her bed again. I tucked her in, kissed her forehead, and then took off.

I was heading far out of town. It was still the middle of the night, so that gave me lots of space and freedom to let my car fly down these roads at 150 per hour (kilometres per hour, by the way). Speed lets the colours betwixt turn into a blur, which is nice, because the blurrier it gets, the less I have to focus.

Part 4
Chapter 13

The Colour of Silence

Before I left, I had further told Colby via a long text message that I needed some for myself. I told her I just needed some space and some time to clear my head, and she understood that because she's a really awesome and cool human being. And then I said goodnight so she could sleep peacefully knowing that I was okay (even if I wasn't).

Before I got to where I was going, I stopped at the last coffee shop Fiona had ever been to and got myself a large coffee. It wasn't that cold out tonight, but the warmth of the cup in my hands would still feel nice and comforting. Always has felt like that and it always will.

My car made a turn onto a road. The last road Fiona ever turned on. I drove for a little while until I got to the bend at the end of the hill. I pulled the car to the side of the road and put it in park. I got out and held my coffee in one hand as I pocketed my keys. I doubted that anyone would come all the way out here at this hour of night, but I also didn't want a bear or moose stealing my car and taking it for a joy ride.

I took a deep breath in the air. It was cold, but not cold enough for me to need anything more than the sweater I kept in the back seat. The coffee cup in my hand was causing warm tingles in my fingers. A feeling that's delightfully comforting for some odd reason. It's just a nice kind of tingle. I always had enjoyed that kinda warmth. I remember nights on the porch with Fiona in the fall when it would be cold and she'd wrap her fingers around mine and mine were around a hot cup of cocoa and we'd take turns sipping and eating the marshmallows that we'd stack on top.

I walked over to the other side of the road, the side where Fiona's car had ended up on its side. I pulled my phone out and turned on the flashlight, lighting up the gravel road beneath my feet.

They couldn't even sweep the broken glass to the forest floor five feet away. The sparkling glints that dotted the ground below made me angry. It was a reminder, a reminder I didn't want to see. I wanted to come here and see nothing out of the ordinary. That maybe it was all a dream, that Fiona never did crash the car. Or maybe I was in a coma back at the hospital, deluding myself into believing that this whole path I've begun with Colby is in any way real life.

I kneeled down and dusted over the glass, rolling it in the dirt and stones. Maybe they didn't want to erase it. This was a makeshift memorial of sorts. The last spot where Fiona Grier drew breath. The last spot she ever got to see. Out of everything in the entire universe, of all the places she could have died, she died right here, right in the place where I stand now. And where I stand now is the same place she should be standing with me. *"Remember that time…"* she'd start saying.

It all feels so faded, like a distant memory of a film I watched as I child. It didn't feel like something real that had actually happened to me. It felt further from my mind than that. Something I could picture as someone watching the events unfold before their eyes rather than someone who lived through them.

I exhale sharply and try to hold back any tears that might poke their way up and through my eyes. The world around me is painfully silent. The moon hangs by a thread in the sky and the stars sprinkle the darkness around it. It feels like any moment now the whole thing's gonna come collapsing down to suffocate me.

I drink my coffee and sit on the edge of my car's hood. There's nothing else I could have done here, so I sat and watched the empty road, the empty sky, the empty forest around me. And sometimes it felt like all this emptiness was looking back at me, watching to see what I would do next. It even felt like the silence was listening to me, to my heart beating under my sweater, to the sound of my breaths falling on deaf oaks.

I get back in my car and I placed the empty coffee cup in the cup holder. I was too tired to drive all the way back to the city. I also didn't want to spend money on a motel room that I didn't really need.

I leaned my seat back and decided that sleeping here would be as good as any place. It would certainly let me sleep as close as I ever could again to Fiona. Somehow that thought eased me to sleep in the middle of nowhere on a road that cuts through a forest. The world was painfully quiet. The only sound was my heartbeat and breathing. And I fell asleep.

The world is bright. I let my eyes adjust to the sudden whiteness of it all. I stand alone in a long hallway. There are white doors with windows every dozen feet or so. I walk to the nearest one and peer inside. I'm at a hospital. Inside the room is a person I don't know in a bed, hooked up to machines, and a nurse is inside caring to the person's wounds. I reach for the doorknob.

I pull the door open and instantly the scene inside changes. It becomes a snapshot of a car crash. An SUV rolled over in a ditch. A sports car with a smashed-up frontend. I close the door quickly and step back. The scene in the window returns. The nurse continues to care for the patient like nothing had happened.

I walk down the hallway, peering into the windows, looking at people in various states of injury and recovery. The nurse is always the same nurse, and then I recognize her. She's the nurse that I woke up to in the hospital after my crash. She was my nurse.

The hallway seems to go on forever. There's no end in sight, just a hazy white in the distance. I stop and look back the way I came. It's the same. A white haze and an endless distance. It's imposing a strong sense of being lost, but I don't give a fuck. This hallway only goes two ways, so if I keep walking, I'll get somewhere eventually. And so I walk.

My legs begin to ache after a while. I stop to look around and when I try to resume walking in the direction I just was, there's a wall not even ten feet in front of me. That was not there before. I turn around the other way and a wall has appeared there as well. There is only one door in the section of hallway that I found myself now confined to. I look inside and there was nothing, just an empty bed. Is this room for me? *I think. I open the door and step inside.*

I close the door behind me and someone appears on the bed. Fiona. Lying there with casts on her legs and arms. Her head is bandaged and half of her face is covered in dried blood. I walk over and cup her cheek. "Fiona." My voice is barely a whisper, but I can tell she hears me because she smiles softly up at me.

"Edwin." Her voice sounds raspier than I ever though a voice could. I imagine her vocal cords are made of desert twigs and dead grass at this point, or at least, that's how it sounds.

"Fiona," I say, my voice cracking under the strain of this happy sadness I was welled with. "I miss you so much." I kiss her forehead and then press my own forehead against hers to look into her beautiful brown eyes. Oh, how I fucking miss these brown eyes. Looking into them now felt like I was coming home after a long trip away.

There was a light coming from a window that I hadn't even noticed at first, but it was hitting her eyes at just the right angle and making them light up a bright honeyed gold.

"I missed you so much," Fiona speaks, but her voice barely carries to

my ears. *I can barely hear her over the sound of a machine whirring in the background.* "I thought you were never going to come."

"Of course I was going to come," I say, not fully even knowing that I was supposed to come to see her at all. *I smiled at her and brushed some of her exposed hair to the side of her head. She was still so beautiful. I don't care how injured she is, she's still an angel sent to me from God himself.*

I lean into her. I kiss her. I can feel her there against my lips as she kisses me back. I can feel the softness of her lips. The warmth of them. I feel her breathing against me.

She pulls away slowly. "Edwin."

"Yes?"

"Promise me something?"

"Anything," I tell her. "What is it? What do you need?"

"I need you to do something." *She cracks a small smile for me as a tear wells in her eyes and starts to roll down her cheek, cleaning a small trail of blood from her face.* "I need you to move on."

"What?" I ask. "I'm not going to. You're right here, right in front of me. I can see you. I can hear you. I can feel you here. I'm not going anywhere."

"Edwin, you don't have to go anywhere," she says, "but I'm already gone." *And then she was. Her body disappeared and I was leaning on just the mattress and pillow. The bed was completely made, like she hadn't been here at all. I was alone with the empty white room. The machines had stopped whirring and beeping.*

I walk to the window and stare out at the blinding white light. It almost feels like the window is a screen. There's nothing outside but more of the same empty whiteness. Nothing in the distance, nothing to disrupt the purity of the haze.

I smile. I don't know why, but I do. Then I open the window and step outside and begin falling. Falling to where? That I don't know, but hopefully somewhere better than where I've been.

I shudder awake, slamming my knee into the steering wheel. "Fuck," I mutter. That's the last time I fall asleep in the front seat, I never sleep in the front seat, but I got so tired.

I rubbed my kneecap until it felt normal sized again. I

started the car and drove off to the coffee shop to get a coffee and bagel for breakfast.

Something in me felt different today. It's like the colours betwixt had been wiped clean, like someone hit the "CE" button on a calculator. My heart, my colours, all of it was reset.

But my mind was not, not yet at least.

Part 4
Chapter 14

The Colour of Truth

The days go by and I refused to call Colby. She had texted, called, Facebook messaged, and buzzed to my apartment, but I refused to answer any of those things. I didn't need her. Never will. She's just some girl, and she'll never be Fiona. I'm happy with never finding love again. Like the mother from *How I Met Your Mother* put it, "Everybody gets a winning lottery ticket, and I already got mine." And so that's what I told Derek and Marshall.

"Dude," Derek groaned. The two of them gave me a pitiful stare of intolerable disappointment. "Why do you do this to yourself?"

"How long has it been since you last spoke to Colby?" Marshall asked.

"It was Saturday and today's Sunday, so about a week," I

told them. I took a sip of beer and had a coughing fit as the smallest drop when down the wrong pipe (yes, there's two pipes: one for eating and drinking, the other for breathing).

Derek groaned again. "I'm gonna actually kick your ass, Edwin. Why are you pushing her away?"

"Because she'll never be Fiona," I replied, shrugging. "I don't wanna move on."

"Yes, you do."

"Yes," I muttered, "I do."

Derek sighed. "Let's play true-or-false."

"Fine," I mumbled. I hated this game.

"True or false, you have an attraction to Colby sexually," Derek asked.

I nodded. "True."

"True or false, you have an attraction to Colby as a friend," Marshalled chimed.

I grumbled, "True."

"True or false, you have an attraction to Colby romantically as well," Derek asked.

"True."

"True or false," Derek began, "you're really, actually falling for this girl." Both of their eyes narrowed on me, and that was bad for me, because I'm a shit liar when I've got alcohol in my system. This, in hindsight now that I think about it, is probably why they got me booze, so we could play true-or-false and I'd end up being truthful about the things I've been dodging. Fuck, these two are manipulative.

"True," I muttered.

"Hmm?"

"True!" I said louder. "Okay? True. I love her. I fucking do. I love that girl, but I'm too fucked up for her. She doesn't deserve to have someone like me in her life anymore. She deserves so much fucking better than some piece of shit bell boy that has no motivation to do anything more with his life because he can't stop crying over his dead girlfriend. I'll never be able to love her the way she deserves to be loved, so it's better if I just don't love her at all."

Derek and Marshall sat back and stared at me. Derek then spoke, "Okay, so that was more than I was expecting. Feel better?"

I nodded. "A little."

"Well, good. That's good. I feel a little better hearing you say that shit too."

Marshall nodded. "It's good to see you admit your feelings instead of bottling them up. Now are you gonna go get this fucking girl or what?"

"Tomorrow." I raised an empty can of beer and tossed it towards the box of empties. "We're all a little too drunk to be driving anywhere just yet."

"Okay, yeah, that's smart," Derek said, walking over to the can on the floor, (I had missed the box) and he put it in the box. "Try not to get cans all over my floor. Thanks, bud."

I raised my hand and mocked him my flapping my hand mouth open and closed a few times. "Anyway, I'm gonna rock a piss and then we should get some games going." I got up and headed to the bathroom. Mostly just to take a moment and look my dumb face in the face and think about how much Colby means to me and how much I love her, because yes, I'm finally admitting it to myself: I love her. I love Colby Claesson with my whole heart. And the colours betwixt love her too, goddammit.

Part 4
Chapter 15

The Colour of Moving On

I woke up on the couch in Derek's basement and sighed as I sat upright. I looked around and felt a sudden hit of sadness. Wistfulness, perhaps? Either or, I wanted to be waking up next to Colby again. I miss waking up to her smile and her warmth and the smell of her hair because her hair always found its way all over my face.

I just want to wake up to her smile, to know that she is all mine and that I am all hers.

And that's all I want, a simple wish that I want to make come true right now. No more waiting. No more excuses. I want to take the plunge. It's time I move on.

I wasted no time in getting myself presentable. I washed my face, used the mouthwash under the sink, and then headed out. I had slept in because we were up late, so I hope Colby didn't end up taking a shift at work today. I would be pretty defeated to find out that my romantic outburst would have to wait. But yet I drove.

Colby's apartment appears in the distance as I round a turn. In the distance, at the entrance to the parking of her apartment, I watched a small blue car make the turn and pull in. That's her. She's just getting back from wherever she's been. *My timing is impeccable.*

My foot fell a little harder on the gas and I rounded a turn into the second driveway to park in the visitor's parking. I ran around the building, to the front entrance. I ran faster than maybe I've ever run in my life. I stop at the door and there she is. She turned around and smiled at the sight of me.

"I love you, Colby," I stated. Her expression changed, but it wasn't a bad change. "I can't hide that anymore. I love you so much, so goddamn much. You're beautiful and funny and smart and talented at everything you seem to do. I get along with you so well and I find you so attractive, so of course you'll find me staring at you when you're doing everyday tasks because you amaze me every minute of the day. And I'm always gonna be scared that I'm not loving you enough, not loving you the way I loved Fiona, but Colby, I promise to try to. I'll give you all I have to give. I'll love you with every fibre of my being and every shred of my heart. All I know is that I love you and I don't want to lose you, not now, not ever."

Colby stood there for a few seconds and smiled softly, taking a step towards me. "I love you too, Edwin." She handed me a bag of groceries. "If you help me carry these up to the apartment, I'll take that as a declaration of our officiality as a couple."

"That's not a word."

She glared at me. "Edwin." She opened the door to her apartment building and I followed close behind her to her apartment. I set the bag she had given me down on the counter and she just smiled at me. "So you're really gonna be my boyfriend, huh?"

I nodded. "Yeah. I'm gonna try."

"Well, you're not allowed to fuck other girls."

"You're the only girl for me, Colby."

She smiled. "Just thought I'd cover my bases." She walked over and kissed me, leading me with kisses to her bedroom. She tugged her sock off and swung it on the doorknob as we sidestepped our way into the room. She tackled me to the bed like she had numerous times before. But this time, the sex wasn't *just* sex. This time it meant something.

Colby's sweaty body laid down on top of me. She sighed and pushed her hair out of both of our faces. We exchanged smiles and she rested her head down on my chest.

"I can hear your heartbeat," she noted.

"I'd hope so," I replied. "Pretty sure I'm not having any cardiac arrest."

"Yeah, maybe we should take up running together?" she suggested. "Might be a could way to stay in shape."

"I'm in perfectly good shape!" I protested.

She made a purring sound and bite her lip. "Yeah, you is. But I'd like to keep us both in shape. That's all."

"Mm-hmm."

"Hey, get dressed."

"Why?" I asked.

Colby rolled off of me and landed on her hands and knees on the floor. She stood up and stretched out, sending her groinal area right to my eye level. "I wanna go do something tonight," she told me. "In the city."

"The city?" I let out a groan. "Why?"

"Because, Edwin, I wanna go do something fun with *my* man." She smiled and giggled a little. "My man." She noticed

I was giving her a weird stare so she stopped. "Sorry. I'm just excited. I've wanted to be your girlfriend since the night we first met. No lie."

"And you lasted this long without making me think that you wanted to be with me?" I questioned. "I'm not even mad. That's pretty impressive of you. Eleven out of ten, would hide feelings again."

"Well, I just figured that if you didn't end up wanting me romantically, at least I got a bunch of really good fucks from a really hot dude, but like, now I can get that all the time because I'm officially *with* the hot dude." She smiled at me. "Sorry, if me gushing over being your girlfriend is starting to weird you out at all, let me know. I'll stop."

"It's out of character for you."

"I'm just so happy about it."

I smiled. "I am too." I grabbed her and pulled her over to me and planted a kiss on her lips. She smiled through the kiss but kissed me back regardless.

"Now get up," she demanded. She tossed my jeans at me, then my sweater. "We should go by Twisters for dinner and then get into some trouble."

"Trouble is all you wanna get into."

"What do you wanna get into, then?"

"Well, you."

"I set myself up." Colby sighed. "Looks like rain outside tonight." She looked out the window for a moment. "Huh, it's raining right now, actually."

"Oh, look at that, I guess we have to stay in."

"Shut up, get dressed, and let's go." She pulled her pants up and glared at me. "Come on. I'm driving." She walked out of the room, pulling her shirt on with a hand that had a balled up sock in it, using her other free hand to take the sock off the doorknob on her way by.

I sighed and got dressed. Another battle the Edwinner can't win. The colours betwixt have been defeated, but in a good way, because I defeated the betwixt. Happiness isn't passing me by anymore. When you see it, you've gotta seize it. Someone like Colby only comes along twice in a lifetime (apparently).

Part 4
Chapter 16

The Colour of the Streets

Colby's little blue hatchback shook to life. Think about a Chihuahua trying to look tough, that was what her car did when she turned the ignition. I'm surprised it still drives. It's getting older and more beat up by the day. But luckily for both her and I, it made the drive to Toronto with minimal janky noises. So that was good. I would have felt better if we just took my car instead, but Colby loves her little blue car and I didn't wanna insult it as often as I thought about insulting it. But sometimes I really can't help myself.

Colby's hand grabbed mine as we walked out of Twisters. She smiled at me and we headed off to get a few drinks at a bar near a hotel where Colby had booked a room a few days prior. I found it bizarre why she booked a hotel room for no reason.

"So again, why did you get a hotel room for tonight?" I asked.

"I wanted to get out of my apartment and do something. I was sad because you had stopped returning my calls and stuff." She shrugged. "I didn't wanna just sit there all weekend and be bored and worrying what I did that made you suddenly not wanna be around me."

"Right." I circled my ear with a finger, and that earned me a light jab to the ribs from Colby.

"Okay, let's duck in here for drinks." Colby made a sharp turn towards a wooden door. I barely had time to read the sign THE SNUG. The bar, Irish-themed, was quite nice. Lots of wood and black cushions and dim lighting and dark green paint.

I found us a booth and Colby went to get drinks. She was wearing jeans and a loose-fitting pullover sweater tonight. Matches my look. Sweater and jeans. Fall is coming. We were already a week into September and the air was getting cold again.

Colby came over with two tumbler glasses filled with ice and a mix of cola and whisky (I assumed). "You had to pick the booth furthest from the bar, huh?"

"Maybe." I took one of the glasses from her as she slid in the other side of the booth.

She took my glass from me and gave me the other one. "Mine is just Coke. I didn't want a drink because I wanna go for a drive."

"It's nearly midnight though?"

She shrugged. "So what? I wanna go for a drive." She made a drinking motion to me and then took a long drink of her cola.

I sighed and downed a third of the glass in one go. "Why did we even stop in here if you just wanna go?"

"I was still thirsty and I wanted you to have something to drink before we go. You're a little tense sometimes, so I thought the drink would loosen you up enough to have some fun." Well, she's not wrong about any of that.

I downed another third of the drink in front of me as she took another long sip of hers. "Why do you wanna go for a drive?"

"I miss the city lights."

"You miss them? You're literally in a city. You *live* in a city."

"Yeah, but I love the buildings and the brightness of the nighttime in Toronto," she stated "I also like freely whipping around the streets because there's a lot less cars out at this time of night."

"Fair. Okay, let's go." I stood up and downed the last of my drink, placing it on the bar counter on the way out. Colby took another long drink, chugging back what was left of her cola. She let out a belch and put the glass down next to mine. I rolled my eyes a little at her as I offered her my hand. "You're gross."

She scoffed. "Maybe." She took my hand. "Now, onward, my trusty steed."

"I'm not a horse."

"No, but I did ride you earlier," she quipped as we walked back outside. The air felt colder than it did just five minutes ago. Maybe the bar was just a little too warm and I didn't notice.

The car shook to life again and Colby began taking us on a tour of downtown. She turned the music up really loud and smiled at me. "You feel that, Ed?" She closed her eyes as she drove in a straight line. She took a deep breath and exhaled sharply. "That's freedom."

"Freedom, huh?" I shouted over the music. She had some indie power ballad playlist set to play.

"Yep. Go on, stick your head out the window. Feel the rush of the air. Soak in the colours of the nighttime."

"I'm alright, thanks."

She turned and glared at me as we blew through a yellow

light. "Edwin, just do it. Trust me. Let go for a minute and soak it in."

I grumbled and rolled my window down. I stuck my face out and felt the rush of cool air flood over me. The sound of everything else was replaced by the sound of wind rushing through my ears. *Whoosh.* And that was it. A constant fan blowing. My eyes fixated on the blurred lights in the distance, contrasted with the yellow streetlights hanging over every street, every intersection. I shut my eyes and focused on the vibrations of the car from the music that was playing. This was freedom, freedom of thought. I felt at ease, like the world had melted and dripped away beneath me. Things felt simple. And sometimes, you just need *simple* in your life.

And then I felt a sudden downpour. I opened my eyes and watched as rain fell in huge droplets all around us. It had stopped for a while there. I was soaked by the time Colby stopped at a red light and pulled me in and rolled my window up. She smiled at me and we kept driving, singing to the songs we knew, dancing to the ones we didn't. The lights flickered by us. The streets became the world's shallowest rivers. Thunder rocked the ground and flashes of lightning lit up the sky. I love a rainy night, such a beautiful sight.

The hotel room was up pretty high. The forty-first floor. From the glass wall, (modern architecture loves glass walls) you could see a lot of streets. The highway was even visible beyond some nearby buildings. There was a lot to look out at, a lot of light, a lot of movement, a lot of people, a lot of life just beyond the transparency.

"Sure is beautiful," Colby said, handing me a glass filled with another cola and whisky. "This is why I love the city, Edwin. *This.*" She put her free hand against the glass, just like before at the library. She looked out the window and, in the reflection on the glass, I saw her crack a small, happy smile.

Her pale skin reflected so well against the darkness of the night beyond the glass.

"Sure is," I said, looking out the window and actually talking about the view this time. It was pretty remarkable how pretty a city can look from up close. We get to feel small from high up above, but not out of place at all.

"I love the city from behind a pane of glass," Colby mused. "I like how it can be so loud outside, with the sirens and trains and highways and shouting and laughing, but then up here, where we can see so much of it, it's quiet. The world outside, beyond this glass, becomes a dull, distant noise. And I really like that. I love being surrounded by life but not needing to hear it so deafeningly."

"I like it because it's quiet. And I get to see further than the people down there."

"I wonder what that says about you." She smiled. "Maybe you like looking forward to things? Or looking out for others? Who knows? Not I, for I am not a psychologist."

"Yeah, you're a ball wrangler at a golf club."

She scowled at me. "I am a managing associate at a high-end resort that just so happens to have a golf course on the property."

"And I'm a strategic itemologist at an exclusive, five-star hotel." I took a drink. "You wrangle golf balls and I clean sheets. Let's just see ourselves for what we are."

"At least I'm a good ball wrangler." Colby smirked as she took a sip of her drink. "Can we have a real-talk moment for a moment?"

"Yeah?"

"Before you, I pretty much completely lost my will to live."

"You're preaching to the choir, sista."

Colby chuckled. "Yeah, but seriously, thanks for being so cool and hanging out with me and stuff."

"I just thought you were someone that didn't annoy me that I could fuck once in a while." I shrugged. "When I first met you, I wasn't really thinking long-term plans. I was just thinking about the *right now* and moving on physically from Fiona. No offence."

"I knew what you were about, well, when you told me." Colby shrugged. "I still think I knew that I was just a fuck buddy to you even when we first started screwing around. It's no big deal. I'm not hurt by it. I think the whole 'friends with benefits' thing really did help the two of us. It was cathartic in a way."

"Sex is always cathartic, Colby."

"Not if you're in love, Edwin." She looked down and then took a sip of her drink. "Not if you're in love, it's not."

"What's that even mean?"

"Love hurts... or something."

I nose exhaled. "Yeah. That's true."

"Real talk hurts my heart. No more."

I smiled and grabbed her hand, interlocking our fingers. "I love you, Colby."

She smiled. "I love you too, Flowers." She took a long drink and then looked out to the great expanse of concrete and lights. "Just so you know, I'm a little turned on right now."

"You're always turned on."

"Only when you're around." She smiled and walked to the end table of the bed. She placed her glass down on it. There was only ice in the glass now though. "Would you like to have a little fun?"

"Am I drunk enough for this *fun*?" I asked, taking another sip of my drink. We had each had a few drinks since getting back to this hotel room.

"You might be."

"Okay. What do you wanna do?"

She raised hand and a finger to me to tell me to wait a second. She took off her sweater. And then her bra. And then her pants. She was standing there in the open space of our hotel room, with nothing but panties and socks on. "I would very much like it if you would push me against this window and fuck me."

"*Pardon?*" I said (the French form of pardon, by the way, because I'm fancy. But, that's pretty much the extent of my knowledge of the French language).

"I want *you*," she said, turning to me, "to fuck *me*," she pointed to herself, "against this window." She placed a hand against the glass. "Show this city that I'm yours."

I smirked a little and nodded to her. I set my drink down on a nearby table. Perhaps Colby just wanted to have her breasts pushed up against the window for the world to see. Maybe she just wanted to fog the glass up with every desperate, vehement, carnal moaning breath she drew.

So let's just say that I'm glad that the colours betwixt couldn't hear the moans of a passionate love-making. I just hope the colours betwixt were equally as blind.

Part 4
Chapter 17

The Colour of Dirt

Colby ran into her room and dragged me out of the house and then over to the nearest coffee shop faster than I could process it. It was a bleak and rainy September morning and it was barely nine and I was still very tired. Colby sometimes has energy for days and days and days and all I wanted to do was sleep in for once, but I guess not. There are perks of being in a relationship, and being woken up to do stuff is not one of them. Sleeping in was always one of the perks of being a wallflower though.

"Here." Colby slid a cup towards me.

"What is it?" I asked, turning the cup and seeing the string and tag of a teabag hanging out the side.

"White hot chocolate."

"And the teabag?"

"Peppermint tea. Just try it. White hot chocolate and peppermint tea are a match made in heaven."

"Maybe I don't like peppermint."

"Yeah, you do. You always eat *both* of our after-dinner mints from restaurants," Colby stated. "And that's especially true with the mints that have chocolate in them."

"You're right, but this is white chocolate. Maybe mint tastes terrible with it?"

"Mint never tastes bad with chocolate. I just want you to know that. Now trust me and take a sip. You'll like it. I promise."

I sighed and took a small sip, trying not to burn the entirety of my mouth. I swished it around and swallowed. "Okay. This is a game changer."

"Told ya."

"Hey, so I was gonna do something today. I was thinking about it this week and I haven't been to see Fiona in a while."

"Oh. I can take you home so we can get your car and you can go." Colby smiled and rested a hand on mine. "I'd figure you want some alone time with her, right?"

"Yeah, but you can come too. I'm not gonna be all day," I told her. "I'll just go pick up some roses and we can head over there."

"There's a flower shop across the street if you wanna go over there and I'll get the car and meet you," Colby suggested.

I nodded. "Okay, sounds good." I grabbed my white-hot-chocolate-peppermint-tea drink and headed out. I walked across the road (blessed that it wasn't a busy street) and went to the conveniently-placed flower shop. I got a small bouquet of roses with some daffodils for *flair*. I met up with Colby in the parking lot and we drove off to the cemetery in which Fiona was buried.

Fiona's gravestone was off somewhere in the sea of other stones. I turned around to look at the car in the parking lot. I could see very faintly the silhouette of Colby on her phone. I

turned back and walked through the cemetery.
Every one of these stones represents a human life. A life that meant as much to somebody else as Fiona meant to me. Hundreds of stones, hundreds of lost lives, hundreds of painful stories. Too much pain encased in one place. I began looking over the names as I passed by them. JOHN MACTAVISH. ALVIN H. DAVENPORT. JENNY ROMANO. MICHAEL TOWNLEY. MARY READ. JOHN SHEPPARD. FIONA GRIER.

I stopped and took a deep breath, looking over the gravestone. It looked the same, though a bit more weathered now. I sat down in the grass before it and read the etched words on the stone:

IN OUR HEARTS,
FIONA GRIER

EVEN AS THE SUN GOES DOWN,
TO END THE LIGHT OF DAY,
IT'S RISING ON A NEW HORIZON,
SOMEWHERE FAR AWAY.

1995 – 2017

It's a year later, and the fact she only made it to 21 years of age still stings. She was far too young to die, far too young for lying in dirt for the next thousand years. She didn't even get to make it to her next birthday, and she never will. I placed the flowers down horizontally at the base of the stone and felt the engraved letters of her name. It's as close as I'm gonna get to ever feeling her again.

I took a deep breath and spoke, "Hi. I know it's been a while since I came to visit, and I'm so sorry about that." I paused and took a sip of my drink. It was still pretty full. "I met a girl, Fiona." I forced a smile. "She's really great, nothing like you, of course. It'd kill me if she was. But she's pretty great. I think you might have even liked her, actually."

I wiped some tears from my eyes and fought back any more, but it wasn't really working. My eyes became miniature faucets. "Fuck, Fiona, I miss you so much. I just wish you'd come back. I know you're never going to, but fuck if I don't wish every day that you would. I hope you forgive me for moving on, Fiona. I didn't want to, I don't, but you're gone. You're just not here and you can't come back and I need to live and be happy, and I know you'd understand that and I know all you ever wanted was for me to be happy, and so I'm trying to be. I'm trying so hard to be.

"And Colby, she's so amazing, Fiona. She's helped me see colours vibrantly again, the way I used to when you were with me. When you passed on, I saw and felt only the grey of it all, like nothing mattered and everything was stuck in the betwixt. I met her and things began to change for the better. Even Derek and Marshall like her, which says a lot because they didn't like any girl that wasn't you.

"I'm happy again, Fiona." My voice breaks there, finally, and I can't speak anything more.

I wiped my face off again, soaking the ends of my sleeves with tears. I shut my eyes and took a few shaky, ribcage-rattling breaths and then opened my eyes again. The stone stared back at me, as grey and as cold as it ever has.

The silence swallowed me up. Nothing but the sound of wind and distant cars filled the air, and I was more than okay with that. I had nothing else to tell Fiona, nothing else I hadn't already told to the stone or to the sky or to the ceiling in my room or the windows of my car or to the thoughts inside my head late at night or to Derek or Marshall or Colby or to the gnawing weight of guilt in my heart that I had let Fiona take the road that ended up killing her or that I didn't make myself open enough to understand that Fiona was suffering and wanted to kill herself in the first place.

So I let the silence envelop me, because silence is what I deserve now, along with the cold air and the grey stones. I deserve to be buried under six feet of dirt. Fiona is the one who deserves to still be drawing breath, not me. If one of us had to be taken early, regardless of if she wanted to die or not, it still should have been me in the ground. Never her, she was too deserving of life to be buried so young. She was so smart, so funny, so talented, so beautiful. She was the kindest and most amazing human being I had ever met, that anyone could ever hope to meet, and then she strived to be even more than that. She was a happy, smiling, outgoing college student. She was a sister. She was a daughter. She was a lover. She was a friend. She was going to do such great things... but instead, here she lies, just cold bones and dust in a crate in the dirt.

I wish I could dig the casket up, pull it open, and see that it was empty. To find out that she was living somewhere else under a new name. To find out she saw something bad and was put into witness protection or something. I'd even settle for finding my own corpse in the casket and then waking up in the hospital to Fiona holding my hand begging for me to wake up. I'd settle for pretty much anything other than the reality of Fiona actually being dead.

But I have Colby now. A girl who I love, and I *do* love her, but I should have never had to fall in love with her, is the point I'm making. I should still be with Fiona. We should be starting our careers and looking into houses and thinking about when we wanted to have our children. That should have been my life, not this one, not a life where I have to question my own ability to love somebody else.

The world around me faded out of focus and I tried to focus on my breathing instead. The colours betwixt were grey like the sky, grey like the stones, but lifeless like what lay in the dirt.

*Part 4
Chapter 18*

The Colourized Photographs

My apartment was somewhat in need of cleaning again. Two weeks into dating Colby, and I've lost all semblance of tidiness for my own living space because I spend most of my time at her place nowadays. As I was digging through boxes again, I found an old photo album of Fiona and I, a part of my life I would rather not relive.

But perhaps one last album would be something to do.

I grabbed my laptop and opened up every social media site that I knew Fiona had an account on. I went to her profile on each of them and began the long and tedious process of downloading or screenshotting every photo of her, her and I, photos of her and her family. The photos we never printed because they were taken with her phone, not a proper camera. I know that under normal circumstances, this behaviour would be that of a stalker, but it's my own girlfriend (well, sort of) and it was for preservation, not for creepervation. It was cathartic too, in a way. It was nice to look back on all the memories she had made with friends and family and me. I looked like a total dweeb next to her in every picture we took together though.

It took hours to get through it all. There were thousands of pictures. But I eventually got every picture transferred to two separate USB drives I had kicking around. One for me, and one to take to the photo printing place, just in case they lose it or something.

It took me fifteen more minutes to get there and five minutes to have my order processed. I didn't even care about the price. I just put it on my credit card and let it be the end of that. I'll pay off the credit card bill eventually.

I did some shopping and avoided everybody for the day. I turned my phone off and focused on getting new clothes, more groceries, more toiletries, and then by the end of the day, I returned to collect a bundle of photos. Before I left, I bought a few album books and then headed home.

Once I got home, I started placing each photo in the new album books. It took literally all night. I didn't want to bend the corners or scratch the photos or anything, so I took my time. By the time the last photo slipped into its little pocket, the sun had risen again.

I smiled at the albums and put them in the Box of Fiona. The box was full to the brim with journals, photo albums, small little knickknacks, and souvenirs of Fiona's life. I taped the box closed and wrote in marker: FIONA — FRAGILE & IMPORTANT.

I stuck the box in the corner of my closet and shut the closet door. The story's almost over. I'm cleansing Fiona from my system entirely, slowly as it may be. There will be a day when I don't think of her at all. A day when my healing will be finished. A night when I don't have a nightmare of her, or a night when I don't dream of her at all.

Fiona's rainclouds are slowly dissipating, breaking way for Colby's sun. My eyes look at colours the way they should be

again. My hand itches to paint. I feel it coming back, I feel myself coming back. It's slow but it's there, and that's promising.
And I inhale.
Exhale.
Inhale.
Exhale.
Inhale.
Exhale.
And I'm alive.
I'm living.
And somehow, without her, I'm living.
I feel alive again.
For however brief it may be.
And I know that nothing can replace Fiona or the colours betwixt, and that's okay, because I would never try to replace her. She'll always be my little bird, and for now, she can rest her wings while I fly for her instead. She lives on in our memory.
My mind paints one last picture-perfect image of her in my mind. And then I let it fade away with the colours betwixt.

*Part 4
Chapter 19*

The Colours of Phoebe

It was a morning. It was a sleepy morning. Colby was at work and I was left to sleep. She had woken me up long enough to kiss me goodbye and then she was off and I curled back into the sheets. I balled myself up on her side of the bed because her smell still lingered there and it was comforting.

By the time I got up, it was nearly noon. Colby had left already three hours ago. I stumbled out of the bed, rubbing my eyes the entire walk to the kitchen. I checked the coffeemaker. Colby had put fresh grounds in it for me. What a sweetheart. I clicked the on button and then sat down at the island counter and rested my head in my hands as I watched the pot of coffee brew. The apartment was utterly silent except for the aggressive dripping of the coffee. I didn't really mind it though. The coffeemaker is sort of relaxing.

I poured a cup and sat down back at the counter. Then after three seconds I realized I didn't have my phone, so I walked to my room and got that, and then sat back at the counter, for realsies this time.

I scrolled some memes for a while and then I got a phone call. Phoebe. She hadn't talked to me in what must be months. We've fallen apart since Fiona passed. We just couldn't bear to see each other. It hurt too much because Fiona was a glue that held her and I together, and without that, there was this void between us that we felt heavily. Even now, looking at a picture of Phoebe from two years ago on my phone screen as it's ringing, I feel that void coming back.

I answered the phone. "Hello?"

"Edwin," her voice sounded deeper, for whatever reason. "Fuck, it's nice to hear your voice, stranger."

"Likewise. So whatcha calling for?"

"Because I was thinking about you." There was a pause and I could picture her chewing at her lip. Her and Fiona do that when they're hesitating on saying something. "Are you busy right now?"

"Not particularly," I told her, staring at my half-finished coffee. "Why?"

"Do you, like, wanna go for coffee?"

I stared at my coffee. "Yeah. Sure. Give me five minutes and I can leave. Where do you wanna meet?"

"Text me your address. I'll pick you up."

"Sure." I put her on speaker and pulled up the messages. The last text I had sent her was well over five months ago. Shit. Anyway, I typed in my address and hit send. Didn't tell her the apartment because I hate the sound of the buzz.

"So I'll see you in a few," Phoebe said. "I'll, uh, text you when I get there."

"Okay, sounds good to me." She hung up and I set my phone back on the counter and swallowed back the rest of my coffee. I walked into the room and got dressed, but really I just threw on what I wore after work yesterday because a half-day's wear does not a dirty outfit make. And Phoebe wouldn't know. It's not like I'm slobby and spill stuff all over myself. I spritzed myself with cologne and used the deodorant and fixed my messy hair and then it was like I was as good as new.

I went outside and saw Phoebe sitting on the hood of a small blue Civic. She smiled at me and waved.

I walked up to her and opened my arms and she just walked up with a look of longing on her face and wrapped herself around me. I hugged her tightly and she rested her face on my chest and squeezed me just as tightly back.

"You've gotten more muscular," Phoebe noted.

"Sex and alcohol," I deadpanned. "I've missed you."

"I've missed you too." Her breath was warm through my shirt. She smelled like peaches. "God, look at you." She pulled away and stared me over. "You got hot." She smirked. "Don't tell anyone I said that."

"Might mention it to my girlfriend," I said, shrugging. "But also don't tell anyone that I think you got hot also."

"I was always hot," she teased. "Come. Let's get coffee and you can tell me about this girlfriend."

The booth seat was cold on my skin, which felt nice. The waitress settled our coffees down on the table and went off to serve another table.

"It's been *far* too long, Edwin," Phoebe said, staring me down. Her gaze was narrowed right down to me, like she was looking at me through a straw.

I nodded. "I'm sorry. I've been, well, I dunno what I've been, but I've been."

"You okay?"

"Are you?"

She gave me a small smile. "Yeah. Elephant in the room, but yes, I'm okay. It hurts still obviously, but I'm getting better every day. I'm obviously always going to miss her and love her. But I'm okay."

"That's good." I smiled and mixed a creamer into my coffee. "Is that why you wanted to get a coffee, to tell me you're okay?"

"No." Phoebe stirred a creamer into her coffee. "I missed you, Edwin. I miss having you around the house and I miss flirt-punching you and I miss making Fiona and you coffee."

"I'm sorry. It's just so—"

"I know," she said quickly. "I know. It hurts to be in that house. At least you had the option to leave. I had to live there. It fucking sucks."

"I know."

Phoebe sighed. "Okay, this got depressing fast. Tell me about this girlfriend of yours. I'm excited to hear about the girl that got the Edwinner to settle down again."

"Her name is Colby," I started. "She's from Sweden, she moved here when she was young. She has really light blonde hair, like, platinum blonde with the dark roots and eyebrows. Real piece. She's funny and smart and beautiful. She drives a shitty little car. She's your height. She's been in porn. And she ruined my life in all the best ways."

"She was in porn?" Phoebe raised a fist and I bumped it with mine. "How'd you two meet?"

"At a party."

"Of course you did."

I took a sip of coffee and nodded softly. "She was the first girl I slept with after Fiona, actually."

"And then you went on to build a roster of women. Derek let me know." Phoebe dipped her finger in her coffee and swirled it around. "So tell me more."

"What do you wanna know?"

"Is she hotter than Fiona?"

"Weird question, but yeah. I think so."

Phoebe thought for a moment. "Hotter than me?"

"Nobody's hotter than you." I winked and clicked my

tongue at her so she knew it was a joke. See, I would have dated Phoebe, easily, if not for the fact that she was Fiona's fucking sister, dude. Every time I look at her it hurts. I can see Fiona so clearly in Phoebe.

"So," Phoebe said, cocking an eyebrow, "do you love her?"

"I think so."

"If you have to think about it, you don't."

I sighed. "I do, asshole. I love her so much. She's absolutely the most breathtaking and beautiful person in my life."

"Oh yeah?"

"Yeah."

"Go on."

"That's it. She's just amazing in every way I thought a person could never be again."

Phoebe smiled at me. "Edwin, I'm so fucking happy you've found something like this. You deserve love, you know. You do. You've got a lot of it to give."

"Okay, but like what about you?" I asked her.

"What do you mean?"

"Are you seeing anyone?"

She shrugged. "Not really."

I cocked an eyebrow. "Who is he?"

"He is a she, for one. And she's just some girl I've been seeing. We've gone on a few dates. Nothing serious."

"You like girls?"

"And boys. Why limit myself to one or the other? Love is a universal language, Edwin," she said. She laughed a little. "Yeah, but I dunno, we'll see where it goes. She's pretty cool, I like her so far."

"I'm glad."

"Me too." Phoebe looked me over and then dug around her purse. She pulled out a folded piece of paper. "I, uh, I brought this for you, by the way. It's something I wrote. It's directed at Fiona."

"Oh." I took the paper from her. "Did you want me to read it or something?"

She shrugged. "I guess you can if you want. I wrote a copy to keep for myself so I don't really care what you do with that one, but I guess I was hoping you'd keep it with that journal you've been writing in."

"How'd you know about that journal?"

Phoebe cocked her head and gave me a *look*. "Derek tells me things because you stopped returning my calls. I still liked to keep tabs on you. I wanted to make sure you were okay."

"So you knew about Colby already?"

She nodded. "Of course I did."

"Played me again." I shrugged it off though. I'm okay with Derek telling Phoebe things. I should have told Phoebe things. Phoebe is an important person in my life, a person I've neglected. "So you want me to add this letter to that journal?"

She nodded. "Yeah, just like staple it into the back of it or something like that. Your call. I was just gonna bury a copy of the letter with the stuff you buried for her."

"Why don't you do that also?"

"I could."

"I miss her so much."

Phoebe bit her lip and nodded. "Yeah. It just never gets easier than what it is right now. There's always gonna be a void in every place she's supposed to be."

"I hope that whatever comes after death is nice."

"I've heard it's beautiful over there," Phoebe said.

I smiled. "I don't know where there is, but I believe it's somewhere, and I hope it's beautiful."

And Phoebe smiled and the colours betwixt us returned to a semblance of normalcy, like the void was shrinking slowly, still omnipresent, but we could see the chink in the armor.

*Part 4
Chapter 20*

The Colours of Colby

Once again, I was awoken pre-9 AM by Colby, and for what reason? Because today was our celebration of being an official couple for one whole calendar month. I don't see the fuss of "monthiversaries," but she apparently does, enough to wake me up early.

"One month, six months, and a year are the only important ones," Colby stated, mixing sugar into a cup of coffee for me. "Well, and I guess every year afterwards is also important, but so is the first month. It's the first step in a year."

"But I don't see why we have to celebrate it."

"Then why'd you book today off work?"

"Valid," I mumbled, taking the cup of coffee from her. "What'd you wanna do today?"

"Movie and dinner." She took a quick glance my way.

"That's the standard, isn't it?" She went back to making her breakfast. Toast and jam. "There's a bunch of movies I wanna see, so whatever you think looks good, we can see. I'd say we can go to the new Twisters in town they just opened, because we both love Twisters and this one is a lot closer than driving to Toronto."

"You got that right." I took a long sip of coffee, swishing it around my mouth. My teeth should thank me that I brush them regularly enough to undo the damages of swishing coffee. "Do you wanna catch an early dinner and late movie or an afternoon movie and late dinner?"

"Let's do evening movie and late, late dinner." Colby said, coming over and sitting at the table with me. My apartment actually has one of those. Not a stupid island counter like her apartment. "Then we can come home and cuddle and watch Netflix."

"Mine or yours?"

"Let's do my place. My car is there and I work tomorrow."

I groaned. "Yeah, me too. So let's try not to be out till three in the morning, okay?"

Colby smiled, nodded, and took a bite of her toast. "Deal." She slid the plate to me, but I slid it right back. "Well, don't say I didn't offer you some."

"I have coffee."

"Coffee isn't a nutritional breakfast."

"That's where you wrong, kiddo," I said, clicking my tongue twice and pointing finger guns at her.

She smiled at me. "You're such a loser."

"Yeah, but I'm your loser."

She leaned over and kissed me, smushing my cheeks together a little. "I love you, Ed."

"I love you too," I said, trying to smile, but she wasn't moving her hands.

I didn't mind. Her hands felt warm against my skin, and they were soft. They were always soft. Every inch of her was soft and warm and I loved it. Every time she touched me, it sent little warm goosebumps trailing behind her touch.

She smiled at me and my heart skipped. And I smiled at her and I could only hope hers did the same. In this moment, I knew for a fact that me being with Colby was not me settling for someone that wasn't Fiona. I wasn't settling. I was falling, falling in love, in love with Colby Caroline Claesson.

The movie was amazing, truly a cinematic masterpiece. So awesome, in fact, that no movie title comes to mind. Dinner was equally as good. Twisters in Belleville might be better than the one in Toronto, and that's good because I don't wanna drive two hours for Twisters anymore (even though I probably still would, to be honest).

We ended up back at Colby's place around eleven or so. It was dark out, cold and windy too. It had begun to rain when we left the movie, so the pitter-pattering of the rain on the window gave her room a comforting ambience that wasn't just the sounds of her neighbours, cars, or roommates shuffling about and doing life things.

Colby and I made a bed on the floor out of her blankets, sweaters, and pillows. She turned her TV on and began to play a TV show that she loved but I had never seen before. But regardless, I lay with her and we watched. She remarked about Netflix and its auto-play feature. It's a real lifesaver because we don't have to constantly press something to start the next episode.

And it was a lifesaver, because for three episodes at a time, we didn't have to move. We could just lay in each other's silent embrace, glued to the TV, taking in the light and taking in each other. She would laugh sometimes and tense her stomach. I would tickle her a little when she did, and she would laugh even harder. It was a better night than I've had in so many months, all because I love this woman with my whole heart.

And I think that's the important thing, that I *do* love her with my whole heart. I'm not letting anything in the way of me loving this woman anymore. She is for me and I am for her.

This girl is truly one of the most beautiful souls I've ever met, so kind and fun-loving, smart and funny. She's magnificent in every way, and I love her more with every passing day. She's truly something I never wanna let go of, not now, and not ever.

As much as I wished for this to all be a dream so I could wake up to Fiona, I think I'm glad that it's not a dream. And the odds of it being a dream are pretty miniscule. This is reality, but reality isn't so bad anymore. Things get easier. The weights we carry don't have to weigh us down, they can make us stronger instead. We adapt and move on.

I've mentioned it before, but the colours all seemed vibrant to me again. I don't feel like the world is grey and void of happiness. It's all right at my fingertips again. The colours, the painting, the happiness. It's there, more prominent than maybe even before Fiona's death. I see the joy in colours again. I fall in love with the hazel of Colby's eyes, the pink of her lips, the blonde of her hair. I see it all and I feel it in my bones. All of my colours, all of her colours, all flooding into me.

Colby snapped me from my thoughts with a small, quick snore. I looked at her and she was fast asleep. She was curled on my chest with her thumb just at the tip of her lips. I kissed her forehead and she stirred a little bit. "Kitties," she mumbled.

"What?" I asked.

"Kitties."

"What about them?"

She nuzzled into me and smiled. "They're cute."

"They sure are." I smiled and rested my head down on hers, pulling her closer into me. I shut my eyes and listened to the sound of distant cars, the sound of Red Velvet licking her paws, and the sound of the TV being unused but still left on. I could get used to this kind of existence.

Of course I'll always love Fiona, but I'll always love Colby as well. It's apples to oranges. We're not meant to have just one soulmate in life, and that's okay. I lost my first soulmate, but it doesn't mean I lost them all. I realize now that we have to love with vehemence every day, because you just never know when someone won't wake up to see another one. And all that matters to me now is that I love this woman with all I've got for every second we're alive on this Earth together. No longer is it even a question. Her colours and mine, they were made to coalesce.

PART FIVE
The Colours of Edwin

Epilogue

My voice is exhausted as I finish the story. I expect a reaction, but get nothing. Fiona stares back at me, unblinking and vacantly sitting there with no words on her lips. "You don't have to say anything," I tell her, because she can't reply anyway.
She's dead.
Still.
The gravestone that I had recounted my story to cannot reply to me for her. The journal I wrote in about my experience of her, I close it tight and let out a deeply held within sigh.
The gravestone, though weathered from the two years it had been sitting here, still read her name and the epitaph perfectly. I wish she could hear me. I wish she could reply to me. It'd be nice to know she forgives me and that she's happy I've moved on.
Today is the last time I'll see her gravestone for a long time.
Colby and I are moving to a town called Sydney in Nova Scotia. We're moving because Colby found her dream job out there. She's gonna get to run a kitchen at a diner there. I'm so

excited for her. She hasn't shut up about it for days since she found out that she got the job. We're heading out in an hour or so. We're just gonna get some lunch and then we'll be off. I'll be 20 hours or so away from Fiona. The farthest I've ever been from her, actually. Even as kids, we lived in the same city and neither of us vacationed very far from there. And when we vacationed far, we had always gone together.

I heard footsteps in the snow behind me and I crane my neck around to see Colby walking over in a black pea coat. She has a grey beanie on her head, wind gently playing with the strands of exposed hair. She smiles down at me. "I don't mean to rush you, Ed, but we've gotta get going if we wanna hit a decent motel before nightfall."

I nod. "Of course." Colby helps me to my feet and I look down at Fiona's grave one more time. The flowers I had just placed will no doubt freeze up and die in the night, but that's okay.

I walk with Colby back to her car (mine is already at the house in Sydney). She drives us to a diner and we eat. And then we leave Belleville, heading eastward to a new life.

I clutch the journal in my hand the whole way.

Scrawled on the front cover: THE COLOURS BETWIXT

About the Author

D. I. Richardson (Darren Richardson) is, of the time of writing this: a graduated alumnus of Durham College. He enjoys writing, napping, gaming, drinking coffee, staying up late, and learning new things.

When it comes to writing Darren likes to write about teen fiction, teen romance, young adult fiction, general fiction, fantasy, crime, and really anything he feels up for at the time. He finds the most challenging part of writing to be getting the motivation to keep going when you're already halfway through a writing project.

When Darren gets older, he hopes to still be writing and creating things in every facet of media and art that he can. He also wants to own a bakery or a book shop or a café at some point.

His advice for writers, young and old, is to just keep writing. Even when it feels like you're completely tapped out of words, keep trying to get something written. Every word is one step closer to a finished product.

Have a good wander, friend.
—D. I. Richardson

Questions About

The Colours Betwixt

With the Author

The Colours Betwixt
Author Q & A

What is the "grey"?
Put simply, it's depression. It's the bland nature of life following a traumatic event, a loss, or hearing of terrible news. It's the process of grieving as well as a depressive episode. It simply makes the world feel like a blur and makes colours seem not so bright and sounds a little too loud.

Is Edwin actually in a coma from the car accident?
Nope. He 100% is awake and alive and well after the car accident. I guess "well" is stretching it, but he's alive is what I'm trying to say.

Does Edwin die when he slips on the rock?
Perhaps. It's entirely possible that everything else that happened was in drowning-induced dream. It's also possible that he lived on and everything that happened was his real life. That's for you to decide. Either or, that scene is meant to be a nod to the way the character from More Than This meets his death. (That's not a spoiler, the whole book is about the fact he died. And also, go read More Than This, it's truly a wonderful piece of fiction.)

What is the "betwixt"?
The Betwixt, to me, is a place between life and death, a sort of non-religious limbo or purgatory. It appears endlessly large and white to keep true to our real-life stories of people seeing a bright white light when they're dying.

Why is the coal darkness so important in the betwixt?
Right, so Colby's name means "dark," essentially. Coal = Colby. Pretty easy to see where that connection is made. Fiona is a name that means: white, fair. So even in name, Colby and Fiona are quite different. And this means that when Fiona tells him to fall for the coal darkness, she means quite literally to move on and be with Colby.

However, there's more to that scene in the betwixt. See, as I mentioned, the betwixt is a sort of limbo between life and death, so Fiona is really talking to Edwin, but both of them cannot actually understand the other as they mean to be understood. To Edwin, Fiona is unhinged and crazy and it's all a dream, but to Fiona, from Fiona's perspective, Edwin is acting erratic and she's trying to stop him from jumping while trying to explain to him that it's okay for him to move on.

What are the "colours"?
The colours are both happiness and life in general. This is more of an Edwin thing as he is a painter and loves colours. So he sees happiness in colours and colours in happiness.

You make Belleville seem like a "big city" in this book.
Because it is in this book. Fictional Belleville, Ontario is at least 3x bigger than real life Belleville in my mind.

What is the connection between Colby and Fiona?
What isn't, to be honest? Fiona is a much more reclusive character. She's quieter, more reserved in how she acts and speaks, I feel. I think of Fiona as the colours of pastels and greens and browns and blues. She loves nature and being alone. Colby is the opposite, whereas Fiona likes nature, Colby loves the city. Fiona likes quiet, and Colby loves the noise and business of life. Colby loves bright colours and neon lights and stark contrasts.

What's the importance of the ending of this book?
The importance is this: Move on. The ending is Edwin finally doing that. He's moving to a new city, he's written his story down in a journal—which was cathartic for him to move on—and he's ready to start a new life with Colby. He knows that she'll never replace Fiona. Edwin knows, however, that he loves Colby in a different but still an entirely valid and full way.

And finally, who is your favourite character?
That's easy. It's Colby. I just love her. I love that she's unabashed and carefree on the surface but she's also a lot softer than she might seem. She was the most fun I've had writing for a character thus far in my writing career (several books, dozens of characters).

A thank-you to Emily Yuill for giving me the passion to finish this book. Without her driving me to write more, I don't know if I could have ever even finished this novel. From the bottom of my heart, thank you.

And I'd like to *thank specially* Nicole, though she may never see this, her early support in my writing life has inspired me countless times to keep on writing whenever I felt like stopping. Our late-night conversations are ones I will never forget. Thank you. Wherever you may be, you're still a friend to me.

Alternate Epilogue

Epilogue (Alternate)

My voice is exhausted as I finish the story. I expect a reaction, but get nothing. "What?" I ask. Fiona stares back at me, unblinking and vacantly staring. I let out a sigh. "You don't have to say anything."
    Fiona sighs and rolls her head back before looking back at me. "Did you really *have* to kill me off, Edwin?"
    "Yes."
    "Why?"
    "I think it made the story better. Don't you?" I sigh. She must not enjoy hearing a story about her own death and then the subsequent love her boyfriend finds in another woman. "I can change it if you want?"
    "No. I loved the story," Fiona tells me. "I'm just salty that you killed me off."
    "Well, the alternative was you breaking my heart and me having to find love afterwards. So I thought maybe this was better."
    Fiona blows a raspberry and pouts, her perfectly shaped

lips forming a small O-shape as she nods. "Right. I suppose you are the writer, after all."

"Thank you."

"One question," Fiona says.

"What is it?"

"Why did you make yourself a painter? You've never painted once in your life." Fiona eyes me over. "Just curious."

"Because paintings are cool, and I wanted the character based on me to be cool."

"Aww," Fiona cups my cheek in her hand. "You're cool, babe."

"The coolest," Marshall states from the couch across the room

"Well, I liked it," Fiona says. "It's my new favourite book. And no, I'm not just saying that because I love you. I mean it."

"I liked it too," Derek chimes from the same couch that Marshall was on.

"You read it?" Fiona asks him, craning her head back.

He nods. "I proofread it for him."

Fiona turns back to me, seething with anger that I hadn't shown the finished manuscript to her first, but then she replaces that look with something else: a look of pride. Pride in me. "So are you gonna send it in?"

I nod. "As soon as I give it one more look-over."

"Good." She smiles. "I'm so proud of you, you little nerd."

"Thanks." I smile back at her, my heart vibrating with the happiness of this moment. Just the girl I love and the book I wrote and my two best friends sitting on a couch playing an NHL video game.

"Just promise to change one thing," Fiona tells me.

"What's that?" I ask her.

She grabs the manuscript from my hands and looks at the title page. "This," she says, "this title is ass. Change it to something good, something catchier."

"Like what?" I ask her, slightly offended at her remark, but not offended enough to stop her from changing the name, and not offended enough to take the manuscript back. Fiona is 100x smarter than I am, so whatever she thinks is best is probably best. I'm trying to get published, not get rejected. And names can sometimes really make it or break it.

Her eyes light up and she pulls a pen from her shirt's breast pocket. She had just gotten off work two hours ago (and was still in her work shirt) and I finished reading her my manuscript because we were all just hanging out, so why not. It seemed like a good time. I've spent the past week reading to her when we've had the time.

"So?" I ask.

"Here." She scratches out the original name for my book and replaces it with something that I had to agree was a lot better than what I had before: THE COLOURS BETWIXT

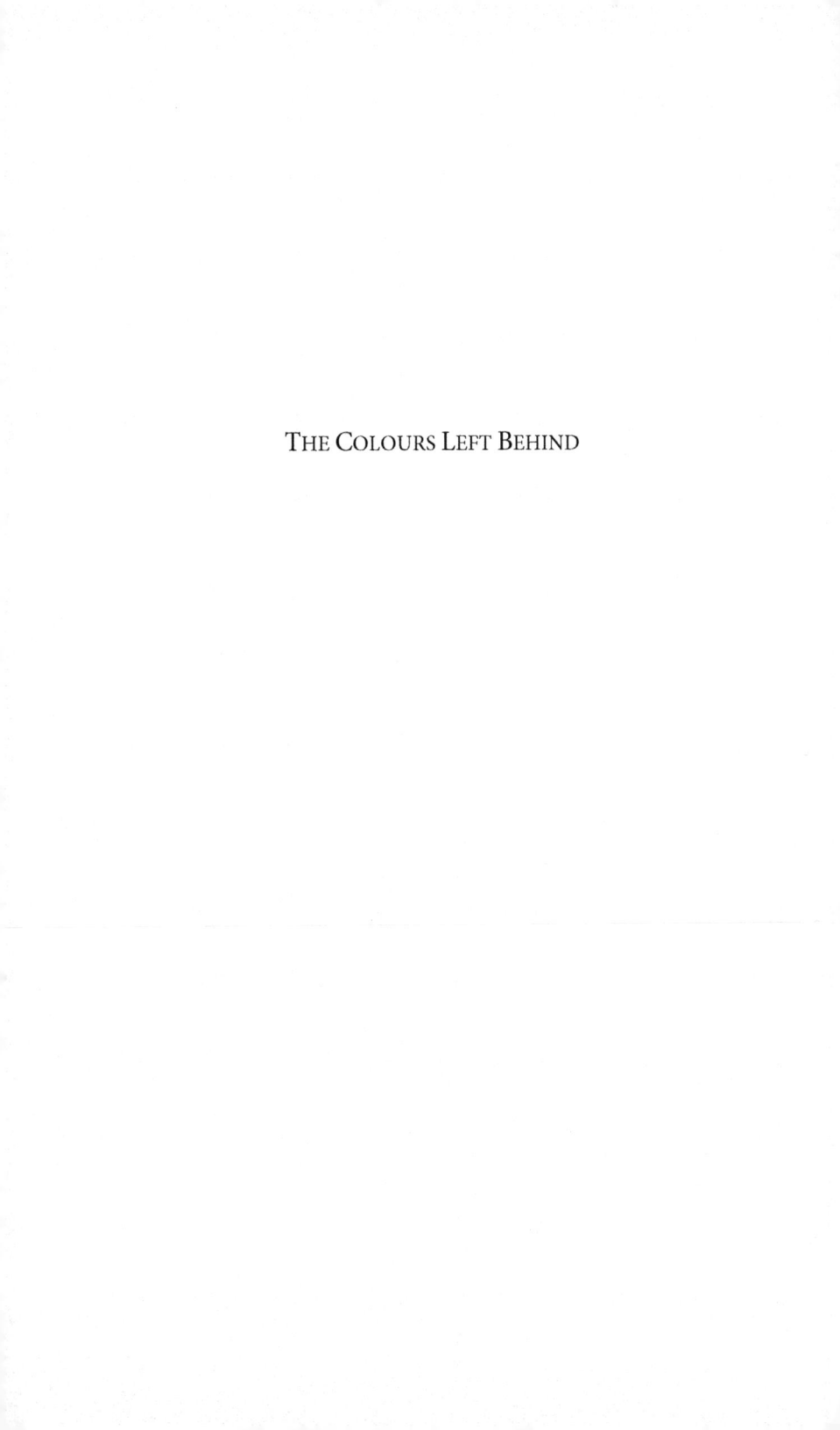

The Colours Left Behind

Fiona,

So here I am. Sitting in front of your grave. And I wonder where you are. I've spent the past nearly two years wondering. None of this is getting any easier for me or for Mom or Dad.
Edwin always spent so much time talking about how much people are like colours and how the world could be viewed on a spectrum of RGBs and CMYKs. But there's no colour here anymore, Fiona. You took all of that away. You were the palette we painted with. The light. The world stole that from us the day it stole you.
And it hurts every day in that house, Fee.
It hurts every day to see your empty room.
It hurts to see those bare walls that were once filled with posters of bands and actors and paintings.
It hurts to hear empty hallways in the middle of the night when I had grown used to hearing the dulcet tones of you and Edwin laughing softly or when he would read you bedtime stories to help you fall asleep.
It hurts so much because I can't wake you up when you've snoozed your alarm 4 times.
It hurts every day because we haven't had a family breakfast, lunch, or dinner together in nearly two years.
It hurts every day in that house, Fee, because you're not there. You're not there and we can't bring you back. *I* can't bring you back.
It hurts every day to live with the colours you left behind.
It will never stop hurting. Never.
I will always be your sister.
I will always miss you more than words can do justice.
Wherever you are now, Fiona… I hope it's beautiful and full of colour. I hope wherever you are is somewhere you can be truly happy and at peace.
I love you. Goodbye.

Love, Phoebe 💜

FIRST LOOK AT

a cabbage named FRED

a novel

d.i.richardson

CHAPTER ONE

I could start this off by saying I never had many friends in high school, or in elementary school for that matter. I was never a very outgoing kid, but that doesn't mean I'm a lost cause. I'm a great listener, an observer. I spent all my free time in class working and listening to the other kids talk about their adventures. I lived vicariously through those conversations never meant to be heard by me. And I didn't mind it. That was my life, it was who I was, and I liked it. Society might have you believe that you need to talk all the time, but that's not true. Only speak when you have something to say. Listen otherwise. And listen to hear what the other person is saying, not just until you can say something again.

So I listened. And learned. And I observed how people were. And that doesn't mean I was a total loner either. I had friends. Two close friends and a girlfriend (well, I had a girlfriend up until April and it's late June at this point in my story). But this isn't a story about my ex-girlfriend. I just needed it to be out there that I wasn't some horny 16-year-old virgin dying for one night of indelible passion. I had lost my virginity at 15 to a friend and quickly moved on to dating my first serious girlfriend. I was both of their first times. Not that it matters much to me, but it does to some people, and that's alright.

I wouldn't be where I ended up if not for each of those two girls shaping how I view love and relationships, I think. I'm only young still, so I've got a lot of shaping left to do. And again, I was an observer. I grew through eavesdropping on people. And I turned that into a hobby.

I had always found myself interested in writing. Whether it was song lyrics to songs with no music (poems, I guess) or short stories or even half-hearted attempts at novels. I loved writing. I wrote my first short story at 10 years old. It was a Halloween short story for my class. I wrote about a creepy mansion that had a murderer living inside of it, and the group of friends had to escape before they all died. It was titled *McMurder Mansion*. I know, it was truly riveting, but cut me some slack. I was ten.

Over time, my writing flourished though. The more I focused on other people, the more fascinated I got by the way people interacted. The subtleties in their voices and faces when they spoke and told stories. I even tried to focus on the emotions of people when they were crying on my shoulder. (I suppose part of the reason I ever got a girlfriend was because I *actually* paid attention to their emotions, and in my experience, girls are quite emotional.)

It took a long time for me to open up to people about my writing, actually. Writing and drawing seem to be the two art forms that get relegated to notebooks and computer folders and never shared with people. But I did eventually open up. I showed my friends and told people I wrote short stories and poems. I took a creative writing class the year prior to this year and it opened my eyes a lot. And though I had always thought about writing novels, I had never finished one (my record was 10 chapters in, or about 23,000 words, before I scrapped the whole thing). And then I just began writing a book and I kept writing it. And it got up to 50,000 words and my parents pressured me into submitting what I had to this writing camp in our area.

The writing camp—Lindrick Camp for Young Authors, Poets, and Writers—was located in the middle of the forest. It was only open to high school kids. Each summer, kids would go there and collaborate with other writers to become better writers and to network with each other so they could help each other out in the future. And it was good for brainstorming. And it was good for just being in a space where everybody understood you because they were *like* you.

I didn't really want to go though. I never had any interest in going to a summer camp. I liked the solitude of my room in the summer. The quiet, sleepy meadows behind my house. The distant sounds of the toll highway that had been built just a few years prior. I liked it at home. But my parents insisted I submit an application.

So I did.

And to nobody's surprise but my own, I actually got into the damn place. They offered me a spot and my parents refused to let me refuse the offer. The book I had entered was about two kids that get stuck in a mall during a blizzard. It's called {*23:59*}, if you cared.

My friends were excited, even though it meant I wouldn't get to see them for a long while. Our summer vacation starts June 27 and ends on September 5. That's 70 days. The camp starts on June 30, a Saturday, and ends on September 2, a Sunday, and that adds up to 65 days. Leaving just 5 days for me and my friends to hang out before school starts again.

The only benefits about this writing camp are these: 1) I get to write freely because that's literally all I'm there to do, and 2) the camp has mandatory writing classes and workshops and lectures and seminars through the summer and these things combined add up to one full English credit, meaning I get an extra free period next year instead of having to sit in a dull English class listening to an old man or woman drone on about Shakespeare or T. S. Eliot. And if I remember the packet correctly, it also grants us an elective credit, meaning we could take another free period if we so wished.

But anyway, that brings us to the day I packed...

My backpack was bulging. I had a several empty notebooks and my MacBook inside of it. I did all my novel writing on the MacBook, but I wrote poems, random thoughts, and drawings (correction: scribbly sketches) in the notebooks. I had another bag—strictly for clothing—sitting on my bed, full to the brim with clothes. Socks, jeans, underwear, and T-shirts. That's all I ever wore. My style was simple because simple never drew attention.

"Dalton!" my mom yelled up to me. "We have to leave soon. Are you gonna be ready or what?" I could tell by the tone in her voice that she was excited about this, more so than I was. It was just like going to school, except not at all like that. I guess I just didn't see how much writing camp would alter the course of my life. (But hindsight is 20/20 as they say.)

"Yeah!" I shouted back to her. "I'll be ready in a few." I sighed and shut my luggage bag, the one with my clothes. I took a look around my room. It was always weird seeing my room that one last time before leaving to go somewhere. Maybe I'm just a sap, or maybe I just always liked the nostalgic feeling it gave me. It's like saying goodbye to an friend knowing that you will, in fact, see each other again someday.

I zipped up my backpack. I did a mental double-check to make sure I didn't forget shampoo or deodorant. (There's a store on-camp, but I wanted to be prepared). I zipped up my luggage and dropped it to the ground.

I walked to the bathroom to go pee. It's a pretty far drive to this camp so I wanted to pee. I peed. I then washed my hands and looked at my face in the mirror. My defining quality had always (and will always be) my stark green eyes and my jet-black hair. Other than that, I'm pretty average. I don't have a striking jawline or a beautiful smile or a fancy haircut or anything like that. Just an average dude with dark hair and bright eyes that looks like he barely gets any sleep. *Aesthetic.*

I gave my teeth a quick brushing and rinsed my mouth with mouthwash before picking up my backpack, swinging it on my back, and then heading up the stairs with my luggage bag being dragged behind me. I bet my mom appreciated hearing every single *THUD* of the luggage bag on each step as I clamoured my way to the main floor.

"Lift," my stepdad teased as I made my way into the kitchen.

"But if I did that, how would everybody know that I disapproved of having to go to this stupid camp?" I asked. In the world of clichés, this was a popular one. The stroppy teenager going away to camp or a vacation thing. It's played out, but it's accurate. I didn't want to go to camp, and I didn't care how clichéd that made me.

"Come on, you'll have fun," my mom said, entering the kitchen from the living room. She smiled at me. "You will. Just give it a chance to be fun."

I scoffed. "You're right. My idea of fun is sitting around with a bunch of strangers, getting eaten alive by mosquitos, and taking turns doing dishes."

"That's not *all* camp is about," my sister, Liza, chimed in from her spot sitting on the stairs leading upstairs. I figured that she would come for the ride, but sometimes I would have believed that she had better things to do with her time.

"Because you've been to *this* camp?" I asked, rhetorically in theory.

"No, but my friend was at a band camp last year. She had a lot of fun." Liza's friend probably did have fun, and I would have fun too, if I were more like Liza's friend, but I am not, I am me, and that's who I had always been, and who I will always be. I'm not ashamed of me. I just didn't like to being around people all the time, with the exception of my friends and my girlfriend (when I have one). I decided not to answer Liza's comment. No point.

My stepdad took my luggage back and went outside to load it into the SUV. I heard the engine rumble to life. The time was nearing for me to say goodbye for the summer to my home. I had already said goodbye yesterday to my friends. I promised to message them (pending how good the service is at camp) and that I'd see them the first day I was back home.

And so it began.

Made in the USA
Middletown, DE
11 September 2020